OPEN-AIR
ADVENTURE STORIES
for Boys

Clell made up his mind, then turned to face death.

Open-Air
Adventure Stories
for Boys

Edited by ERIC DUTHIE

The writers are:

JAMES ALDRIDGE   CAPTAIN W. E. JOHNS
KENNETH ANDERSON   DON KNOWLTON
RICHARD ARMSTRONG   EDWARD LINDALL
JOSEPH E. CHIPPERFIELD   WALTER MACKEN
JACK FINNEY   JACK SCHAEFER
NEIL M. GUNN   SHOWELL STYLES
A. B. GUTHRIE   V. H. THOMAS
H. G. WELLS

ODHAMS BOOKS LIMITED

LONG ACRE LONDON

THE STORIES

IN THIS BOOK

No Medal for Matt

WALTER MACKEN

IT WAS a beautiful morning. The cliff top, at the western edge of the island, which lay some miles off the Irish coast, was a green carpet of closely cropped grass. Five hundred feet below, the water broke indolently over black jagged rocks. Its sinister sound was almost soothing. Westward, the Atlantic stretched calmly away to a limitless light-blue horizon.

Matt came toward the cliff from the village, walking on the enormous slabs of flat rock that covered the fields, which sloped steeply upward. The rocks were warm to the soles of his bare feet. Homespun trousers ending at the shin and a heavy knitted red jersey were making him sweat under the June sun. A canvas schoolbag flopped up and down on his hip as he journeyed, reminding him and bringing a frown between his brown eyes.

7

The climb up the slope was hard enough. He had to leap at times, and try to dodge the briars lurking in the crevices of the rocks. Sometimes the thorns scraped at the brown skin of his feet, leaving behind a scarlet scratch of blood. On both sides of him, small black-faced sheep, the kind that make such tender mutton, raised their heads to look at him and then moved cautiously away, following him with their eyes for a little, after he had passed, and then resuming the search for their meagre forage.

Matt was filled with a sense of guilt and injustice, and between the two of them his heart was very heavy. You are in school, see, just as he was yesterday. Near the end of the day, the sleepy part, the fellow beside him in the desk, young Pat Mullen, suddenly gives him a fierce puck in the ribs. Matt turns to clatter him, but before he can land even one blow on him, down the master comes and belts Matt. Matt protests that he is being belted in the wrong, and the master belts him again. Matt still protests, and the master, his face as red as the comb of a Christmas turkey, belts him once again and asks him does he want more. Matt says he doesn't want more. On his way home from school, burning with the injustice of it all, Matt tells himself that his father will right this wrong. His father is noted for his justice. "All right," says his father when Matt explains to him, "so the master was in the wrong. What do you want me to do, go up and hit the man? If every father did that, there would be not a school left in the universe." Couldn't he just tell him that he was in the wrong? Matt asks. No, he could not, his father says. Maybe the poor fellow was having trouble with his wife, or maybe he had an interior ailment that was persecuting him. Well, you will just have to tell him he was in the wrong, Matt says. His father gets angry then and shouts that he'll be damned if he will do anything of the sort, and even if this time Matt has been belted in the wrong, it will do him no harm, because there were times when he wasn't belted before and should have been. Matt denies this, and his father walks out of the house saying, "If I don't go, I'll belt you, and where will

8

you be then?" His father is upset, because he doesn't like to think of Matt's being belted, right or wrong, but, being civilized, he can't go and hammer the poor teacher.

So now Matt saw that the whole world was a place of great injustice for boys; that there was no equity in it at all when even your father refused to stand up for you. That was why he had walked past the schoolhouse door this morning, just as if it wasn't there, and had headed for the tall cliffs. He had never done this before, because he liked school, except on Mondays and the first day after holidays. And even though he knew that he was right—it is necessary for every man to make some protest against injustice—he felt that he was wrong, and it seemed to him that some of the beauty had gone out of the day, and that this freedom he had chosen had, in some odd way, a chain on it.

When he had cleared the last obstacles barring his way to the cliff top, he stood there and looked back. He could see the whole island sloping away from his feet. It was shaped, he thought, like the kidney of a pig. He could see the golden beaches, and the sea beyond them reaching toward the distant mainland, which was hidden in a blue haze. He couldn't see his own house, but he could see the schoolhouse, and was sorry he was out of it, because just about now they would be chanting the multiplication tables, and he liked that. He also liked going into the yard at lunchtime and wolfing his jam sandwiches, so that he would have more time to play *capaillini conemara*, a game in which small boys, mounted on the backs of larger boys, raced each other.

He sighed and his heart was heavy, but his stomach was empty, so he sat on the grass and, after removing the books from his schoolbag, took the sandwiches his mother had made for his lunch and proceeded to eat them, and it was miraculous how the seagulls knew that there was food around. They thronged about him, screaming, from the sky and from the cliffs, and he amused himself by throwing crusts into the void and watching the wonderful swerv-

9

ing and twisting, the grace and the beauty of the gulls as they caught the crusts in flight.

My father will kill me, Matt thought then, and he looked over the water, thinking he might see his father's lobster boat if his father was doing this side of the island today. No boat was in sight. His father wouldn't actually kill him, Matt thought. He never raised a hand to him. It was his mother who always held the threat of him over Matt's head. Someday your father will kill you, Matt, she'd say. All the same, Matt knew that his father would be hurt by what he had done, and this made him feel a bit sad. He rolled on his stomach with his face over the cliff and looked down at the waves breaking on the rocks far, far below.

It was some while before he saw the movement—a fluttering movement, about fifty feet below him, on a ledge. He thought at first it might be a young gull, but then, as he watched closely, he saw that what moved was a rabbit, a plump young rabbit. He raised himself to his knees in surprise. A rabbit

They swerved and twisted and caught the crusts in flight.

fifty feet down the face of the cliff! How could he have got there? Did a big bird claw him and lose him, or was he chased by a fox so that he fell and landed on that ledge below, or what?

Will I climb down and get the rabbit? was the next thought that came into his head. A terrible thought. His eyes narrowed as he looked over every inch of the cliff to the ledge. Suppose I fall, he wondered, looking farther, to the cruel black rocks waiting below. Who would miss me? Isn't everyone against me? Even so, his heart had begun to thump excitedly. It would be a famous climb. He stood up straight now, his hands on his hips, his eyes very bright. If the rabbit was left there, he would die and become a skeleton, or a bird would scoop him. If Matt saved his life, what a hero Matt would be! I climbed down cliffs when I was smaller, he thought, but never this cliff. This was the highest on the island.

He was still standing up when the boat came around a promontory behind him. He didn't see it, of course, and he didn't hear it. The chug-chug of its diesel engine was not loud, because the boat was going slowly as it negotiated a channel through some rocks toward a cluster of bobbing buoys that marked lobster pots.

The man at the tiller raised his eyes and saw the figure of the boy up there on the cliff top. He took his pipe out of his mouth, which remained open in amazement. "Here, Tom!" he called to the other man, who was coiling a rope in the waist. "For the love of God, is that my Matt up there?"

Tom came back to him, shaded his eyes with his hand, and said, "By all that's holy, it is!"

"What's he doing up there?" Matt's father asked. "He should be at school."

Then Matt's father opened his lungs to let a shout out of them, but it was never emitted, because Tom suddenly clapped a hard hand over his mouth and the shout died in a strangled gurgle. Tom took his hand away, and the two of them stood there, looking up, petrified with fear,

11

the hair rising on the back of their necks at the sight of the boy casually letting himself down over the cliff.

"Oh, my God!" groaned Matt's father.

"If you shouted, you would have startled him," Tom whispered.

"He'll fall! He's mad! What's come over him?" Matt's father asked in anguish, his eyes glued painfully to the small figure slowly descending the sheer face. In that red jersey of his, it was all too easy to see him.

"Birds' eggs or something," said Tom. "I never saw anybody climbing that bit. He'll be kilt!"

Matt's father swung the tiller to bring the boat in toward the foot of the cliff. Tom struggled with him, and forced the tiller so that the boat turned out again. He switched off the engine.

"Are you mad?" he asked. "You can't get within fifty yards of the place. The tide is low. Will you kill us as well?"

"He'll fall! He'll fall!" said Matt's father.

"Well, if he falls now," said Tom, annoyed at the boy, "you'll only get his body. The rocks are up."

"Oh, my God!" said Matt's father.

Matt's heart was thumping and his mouth was dry. Even so, there was a soaring in his breast. He was glad he was in his bare feet. His big toes were wonderful, the way they could feel, gauge, and grip a narrow crevice. The cliff face was almost solid granite, which, for all its height, had many times been washed by enormous waves. The sea water had sought every weakness, and here and there had scooped out the poor spots in the stone. So there were cracks for Matt's thin fingers and his hardened toes. All the same, you could be frightened, he thought, if you hadn't climbed down cliffs before. He knew where he was going, but he didn't want to look down to see. Clinging like a fly, he lowered himself bit by bit, until below him, out of the corner of his right eye, he could see the end of the ledge where the rabbit crouched.

Down in the boat, Matt's father, who was in the middle of a prayer, thought he could feel the hairs turning grey

"For the love of God, is that my Matt up there?"

on his head. He relaxed a little as he saw his son's feet feeling for a ledge and then resting there firmly.

Matt was happy to feel his feet on solid rock, though it was a very narrow ledge. The rabbit went to the far end of it, on the right, but he was still within reach of Matt's hand. Matt lowered his body slowly, gripping the surface of the cliff with the nails of his left hand and reaching for the rabbit with his right.

He grabbed the rabbit's fur. Don't struggle, don't struggle, Matt shouted at him in his heart, or you'll have the two of us over. He gripped him tightly. The animal stiffened. Slowly, Matt lifted him, and then carefully inserted him in the open schoolbag on his hip and strapped the flap shut.

Matt rested for a moment. He felt good now. Then he took a few deep breaths and started the climb up. The rabbit remained very still in the bag.

By now, Matt's father was kneeling, his hands covering his eyes. "What's he doing now, Tom?" he asked. "What in the name of God is he doing now?"

"He's on his way up," Tom said quietly. "He'll likely make it. What scoundrels boys are! What did he do it for? He got something. I wouldn't do that to rescue a king. That fellow will be a famous man or he'll end up hung."

"God bring him to the top," said Matt's father.

On the cliffside, Matt whispered to himself, "Going up is not as bad as going down." Because you can see. It looked fierce far just the same. The granite had torn his fingers. The middle ones were bleeding. And the sides of his toes were bleeding, too. He could feel them. Above, he could see a few slivers of green grass on the very top, beckoning to him. I'm coming, he silently called up to them, laughing. Wait'll you see. But it seemed a long time to him, before his hand rested on the coolness of the grass, and he paused, breathless, and then pulled himself over the top.

It seemed a lifetime to his father before he heard Tom's pent-up breath expelled and his voice saying, with a sigh,

"He is over. He is over now." Matt's father couldn't say anything.

Matt was now lying on the grass, feeling it with one cheek. His fist was beating the ground. "I did it! I did it!" he said out loud. What a tale to tell, he thought, but who will believe me? But what does it matter if nobody believes me? It was a great and famous climb, so it was.

Then, from the depths below, he heard a voice hailing and hailing, so he stood up and looked over the edge. Oh, it was his father and Tom. He hoped they hadn't seen him climbing down to the ledge. His father would murder him!

"What you doing? What the hell you think you're doing?" he faintly heard Tom saying.

So they *had* seen him! Then he remembered the rabbit. The rabbit would change things. Because of the rabbit, his father would be pleased with him. He'd be pleased, you'd see, and forget all about his dodging school. He opened the schoolbag and, reaching for the rabbit with his left hand, caught him by the hind legs and extracted him. Then he expertly hit him on the back of the neck with the edge of his right hand, so that the rabbit died, swiftly executed, in a second.

And Matt waved the body of the rabbit above his head, leaning out perilously over the cliff, and, with one hand curved around his mouth, shouted down, "Hey, Father! Father! You'll have rabbit stew tonight. You hear that? Rabbit stew tonight!"

He laughed as he waved the rabbit, because his father loved rabbit stew, he really did. Then Matt gathered up his schoolbooks and put them back in his bag, along with the rabbit, and hurried down the slope, over the long fields of great flat rocks, toward home.

And his father still sat, completely drained, completely exhausted, in the bottom of the lobster boat.

15

Indian Medicine

A. B. GUTHRIE

THE MIST along the creek shone in the morning sun, which was coming up lazy and half-hearted, as if of a mind to turn back and let the spring season wait. The cottonwoods and quaking aspens were still bare and the needles of the pines old and dark with winter, but beaver were prime and beaver were plenty. John Clell made a lift and took the drowned animal quietly from the trap and stretched it in the canoe with three others.

Bill Potter said, "If 'tweren't for the Injuns! Or if 'tweren't for you and your notions!" For all his bluster, he still spoke soft, as if on the chance that there were other ears to hear.

Clell didn't answer. He reset the trap and pulled from the mud the twig that slanted over it and unstoppered his goat-horn medicine bottle, dipped the twig in it and poked it back into the mud.

"Damn if I don't think sometimes you're scary," Potter went on, studying Clell out of eyes that were small and

16

set close. "What kind of medicine* is it makes you smell Injuns with nary one about?"

"Time you see as many of them as I have, you'll be scary too," Clell answered, slipping his paddle into the stream. He had a notion to get this greenhorn told off but he let it slide. What was the use? You couldn't put into a greenhorn's head what it was you felt. You couldn't give him the feel of distances and sky-high mountains and lonely winds and ideas spoken out of nowhwere, ideas spoken into the head by medicines a man couldn't put a name to. Like now. Like here. Like this idea that there was brown skin about, and Blackfoot skin at that.

"I seen Blackfeet enough for both of us," he added. His mind ran back to old comrades and a time that seemed long ago because so much had come between; to days and nights and seasons of watching out, with just himself and the long silence for company; to last year and a hole that lay across the mountains to the south, where the Blackfeet and the Crows had fought, and he had sided with the Crows and got a wound in the leg that hurt sometimes yet. He could still see some of the Blackfeet faces. He would know them, and they would know him, being long-remembering.

He knew Blackfeet all right, but he couldn't tell Bill Potter why he thought some of them were close by. There wasn't any sign he could point to; the creek sang along and the breeze played in the trees, and overhead a big eagle was gliding low, and nowhere was there a footprint or a movement or a whiff of smoke. It was just a feeling he had, and Potter wouldn't understand it, but would only look at him and maybe smile with one side of his mouth.

"Ain't anybody I knows of carries a two-shoot gun but you," Potter said, still talking as if Clell was scared over nothing.

Clell looked down at it, where he had it angled to his hand. It had two barrels, fixed on a swivel. When the top one was fired, you slipped a catch and turned the other up.

* "Indian Medicine"—his special knowledge, "know-how" and artfulness.

One barrel was rifled, the other bigger and smooth-bored, and sometimes he loaded the big one with shot, for birds, and sometimes with a heavy ball, for bear or buffalo, or maybe with ball and buck both, just for what-the-hell. There was shot in it this morning, for he had thought maybe to take ducks or geese, and so refresh his taste for buffalo meat. The rifle shone in the morning sun. It was a nice piece, with a patch box a man wouldn't know to open until someone showed him the place to press his thumb. For no reason at all, Clell called his rifle Mule Ear.

He said, "You're a fool, Potter, more ways than one. Injuns'll raise your hair for sure, if it don't so happen I do it myself. As for this here two-shooter, I like it, and that's that."

Bill Potter always took low when a man dared him like that. Now all he said was "It's heavy as all hell."

Slipping along the stream, with the banks rising steep on both sides, Clell thought about beaver and Indians and all the country he had seen—high country, pretty as paint, wild as any animal and lonesome as time, and rivers unseen but by him, and holes and creeks without a name, and one place where water spouted hot and steaming and sometimes stinking from the earth, and another where a big spring flowed with pure tar; and no one believed him when he told of them, but called him the biggest liar yet. It was all right, though. He knew what he knew, and kept it to himself now, being tired of queer looks and smiles and words that made out he was half crazy.

Sometimes, remembering things, he didn't see what people did or hear what they said or think to speak when spoken to. It was all right. It didn't matter what was said about his sayings or his doings or his ways of thinking. A man long alone where no other white foot ever had stepped got different. He came to know what the Indians meant by medicine. He got to feeling like one with the mountains and the great sky and the lonesome winds and the animals and Indians, too, and it was a little as if he knew what they knew, a little as if there couldn't be a secret but was whispered to him, like the secret he kept hearing now.

"Let's cache," he said to Potter. The mist was gone from the river and the sun well up and decided on its course. It was time, and past time, to slide back to their hidden camp.

"Just got one more trap to lift," Potter argued.

"All right, then."

Overhead the eagle still soared close. Clell heard its long, high cry.

He heard something else, too, a muffled pounding of feet on the banks above. "Injuns!" he said, and bent the canoe into the cover of an overhanging bush. "I told you."

Potter listened. "Buffalo is all. Buffalo trampin' around."

Clell couldn't be sure, except for the feeling in him. Down in this little canyon a man couldn't see to the banks above. It could be buffalo, all right, but something kept warning, "Injuns! Injuns!"

Potter said, "Let's git on. Can't be cachin' from every little noise. Even sparrers make noise."

"Wait a spell."

"Scary." Potter said just the one word, and he said it under his breath, but it was enough. Clell dipped his paddle. One day he would whip Potter, but right now he reckoned he had to go on.

It wasn't fear that came on him a shake later, but just the quick knowing he had been right all along, just the holding still, the waiting, the watching what to do, for the banks had broken out with Indians—Indians with feathers in their hair, and bows and war clubs and spears in their hands; Indians yelling and motioning and scrambling down to the shores on both sides and fitting arrows to their bow strings.

Potter's face had gone white and tight like rawhide drying. He grabbed at his rifle.

Clell said, "Steady!" and got the pipe that hung from around his neck and held it up, meaning he meant peace.

These were the Blackfeet sure enough. These were the meanest Indians living. He would know them from the Rees and Crows and Pierced Noses and any other. He

"Don't point that there rifle 'less you want a skinful of arrows."

would know them by their round heads and bent noses and their red-and-green leather shields and the moccasins mis-matched in colour, and their bows and robes not fancy, and no man naked in the bunch.

The Indians waved them in. Clell let go his pipe and stroked with his paddle. Potter's voice was shrill. "You fool! You gonna let 'em torment us to death?"

That was the way with a mouthy greenhorn—full of himself at first, and then wild and shaken. "Steady!" Clell said again. "I aim to pull to shore. Don't point that there rifle 'less you want a skinful of arrows."

There wasn't a gun among the Indians, not a decent gun, but only a few rusty trade muskets. They had battle axes, and bows taken from their cases, ready for business, and some had spears, and all looked itching for a white man's hair. They waited, their eyes bright as buttons, their faces and bare forearms and right shoulders shining brown in the sun. Only men were at the shore line, but Clell could see the faces of squaws and young ones looking down from the bank above.

An Indian splashed out and got hold of the prow of the canoe and pulled it in. Clell stepped ashore, holding up his pipe. He had to watch Potter. Potter stumbled out, his little eyes wide and his face white, and fear showing even for an Indian to see. When he stepped on the bank, one of the Indians grabbed his rifle and wrenched it from him, and Potter just stood like a scared rabbit, looking as if he might jump back in the canoe any minute.

Clell reached out and took a quick hold on the rifle and jerked it away and handed it back to Potter. There was a way to treat Indians. Act like a squaw and they treated you bad; act like a brave man and you might have a chance.

Potter snatched the gun and spun around and leaped. The force of the jump carried the canoe out. He made a splash with the paddle. An arrow whispered in the air and made a little thump when it hit. Clell saw the end of it, shaking from high in Potter's back.

Potter cried out, "I'm hit! I'm hit, Clell!"

"Come back! Easy! Can't get away!"

Instead, Potter swung around with the rifle. There were two sounds, the crack of the powder and the gunshot plunk of a ball. Clell caught a glimpse of an Indian going down, and then the air was full of the twang of bow-strings and the whispered flight of arrows, and Potter slumped slowly back in the canoe, his body stuck like a pincushion. An Indian splashed out to take the scalp. Two others carried the shot warrior up the bank. Already a squaw was beginning to keen.

Clell stood quiet as a stump, letting only his eyes move. It was so close now that his life was as good as gone. He could see it in the eyes around him, in the hungry faces, in the hands moving and the spears and the bows being raised. He stood straight, looking their eyes down, thinking the first arrow would come any time now, from any place,

21

and then he heard the eagle scream. Its shadow lazed along
the ground. His thumb slipped the barrel catch, his wrist
twisted under side up. He shot without knowing he aimed.
Two feathers puffed out of the bird. It went into a steep
climb and faltered and turned head down and spun to the
ground, making a thump when it hit.

The Indians' eyes switched back to him. Their mouths
fell open, and slowly their hands came over the mouth
holes in the sign of surprise. It was as he figured in that
flash between life and death. They thought all guns fired a
single ball. They thought he was big medicine as a marks-
man. One of them stepped out and laid his hand on Mule
Ear, as if to draw some of its greatness into himself. A
murmur started up, growing into an argument. They
ordered Clell up the bank. When he got there, he saw one
Indian high-tailing it for the eagle, and others following,
so's to have plumes for their war bonnets, maybe, or to
eat the raw flesh for the medicine it would give them.

There was a passel of Indians on the bank, three or four
hundred, and more coming across from the other side.
The man Clell took for the chief had mixed red earth with
spit and dabbed it on his face. He carried a bird-wing fan
in one hand and wore a half-sleeved hunting shirt made of
bighorn skin and decorated with coloured porcupine quills.
His hair was a wild bush over his eyes and ears. At the
back of it he had a tuft of owl feathers hanging. He yelled
something and motioned with his hands, and the others
began drifting back from the bank, except for a couple of
dozen that Clell figured were head men. Mostly, they wore
leggings and moccasins, and leather shirts or robes slung
over the left shoulder. A few had scarlet trade blankets,
which had come from God knew where. One didn't wear
anything under his robe.

The squaws and the little squaws in their leather sacks
of dresses, the naked boys with their potbellies and swollen
navels, and the untried and middling warriors were all
back now. The chief and the rest squatted down in a half
circle, with Clell standing in front of them. They passed a

He heard the eagle scream . . . and shot without knowing he aimed.

pipe around. After a while they began to talk. He had some of the hang of Blackfoot, and he knew, even without their words, they were arguing what to do with him. One of them got up and came over and brought his face close to Clell's. His eyes picked at Clell's head and eyes and nose and mouth. Clell could smell grease on him and wood smoke and old sweat, but what came to his mind above all was that here was a man he had fought last season while siding with the Crows. He looked steadily into the black eyes and saw the knowing come into them, too, and watched the man turn back and take his place in the half circle and heard him telling what he knew.

They grunted like hogs, the Blackfeet did, like hogs about to be fed, while the one talked and pointed, arguing that here was a friend of their old enemies, the Crows. The man rubbed one palm over the other, saying in sign that Clell had to be rubbed out. Let them stand him up and use him for a target, the man said. The others said yes to that, not nodding their heads as white men would, but bowing forward and back from the waist.

Clell had just one trick left. He stepped over and showed his gun and pointed to the patch box and, waving one hand to catch their eyes, he sprang the cover with the other thumb. He closed the cover and handed the gun to the chief.

The chief's hands were red with the paint he had smeared on his face. Clell watched the long thumbnail, hooked like a bird claw, digging at the cover, watched the red fingers feeling for a latch or spring. While the others stretched their necks to see, the chief turned Mule Ear over, prying at it with his eyes. It wasn't any use. Unless he knew the hidden spot to press, he couldn't spring the lid. Clell took the piece back, opened the patch box again, closed it and sat down.

He couldn't make more medicine. He didn't have a glass to bring the sun down, and so to light a pipe, or even a trader's paper-backed mirror for the chief to see how pretty he was. All he had was the shot at the eagle and the patch box on Mule Ear, and he had used them both and had to take what came.

Maybe it was the eagle that did it, or the hidden cover, or maybe it was just the crazy way of Indians. The chief got up, and with his hands and with his tongue asked if the white hunter was a good runner.

Clell took his time answering, as a man did when making high palaver. He lighted his pipe. He said, "The white hunter is a bad runner. The other Long Knives think he runs fast. Their legs are round from sitting on a horse. They cannot run."

The chief grunted, letting the sign talk and the slow words sink into him. "The Long Knife will run." He pointed to the south, away from the creek. "He will run for the trading house that the whiteface keeps among the Crows. He will go as far as three arrows will shoot, and then he will run. My brothers will run. If my brothers run faster—" The chief brought his hand to his scalp lock.

The other Indians had gathered around, even the squaws and the young ones. They were grunting with excitement. The chief took Mule Ear. Other hands stripped off Clell's hunting shirt, the red-checked woollen shirt underneath, his leggings, his moccasins, his small-clothes, until he stood white and naked in the sun, and the squaws and young ones came up close to see what white flesh looked like. The squaws made little noises in their throats. They poked at his bare hide. One of them grabbed the red-checked shirt from the hands of a man and ran off with it. The chief made the sign for "Go!"

Clell walked straight, quartering into the sun. He walked slow and solemn, like going to church. If he hurried, they would start the chase right off. If he lazed along, making out they could be damned for all he cared, they might give him more of a start.

He was two hundred yards away when the first whoop sounded, the first single whoop, and then all the voices yelling and making one great whoop. From the corner of his eye he saw their legs driving, saw the uncovered brown skins, the feathered hair, the bows and spears, and then he was running himself, seeing ahead of him the far tumble and roll of high plains and hills, with buffalo dotting the distances and a herd of prairie goats sliding like summer mist, and everywhere, so that not always could his feet miss them, the angry knobs of cactus. South and east, many a long camp away where the Bighorn River joined the Roche Jaune, lay Lisa's Fort, the trading house among the Crows.

He ran so as to save himself for running, striding long and loose through the new-sprouting buffalo grass, around the cactus, around the pieces of sandstone where snakes were likely to lie. He made himself breathe easy, breathe deep, breathe full in his belly. Far off in his feelings he felt the cactus sting him and the spines pull off to sting again. The sun looked him in the face. It lay long and warm on the world. At the sky line the heat sent up a little shimmer. There wasn't a noise anywhere except the thump of his feet and his heart working in his chest and his breath sucking in and out and, behind him, a cry now and then from the Indians, seeming not closer or farther away than at first. He couldn't slow himself with a look. He began to sweat.

A man could run a mile, or two or three, and then his breath wheezed in him. It grew into a hard snore in the throat. The air came in, weak and dry, and burned his pipes and went out in one spent rush while his lungs sucked for more. He felt as if he had been running on forever. He felt strange and out of the world, a man running in a dream, except that the ache in his throat was real and the fire of cactus in his feet. The earth spread away forever, and he was lost in it and friendless, and not a proper part of it any more; and it served him right. When a man didn't pay any mind to his medicine, but went ahead regardless, as he had done, his medicine played out on him.

Clell looked back. He had gained, fifty yards, seventy-five, half a musket shot; he had gained on all the Indians except one, and that one ran as swift and high-headed as

He was 200 yards away when the first whoop sounded.

a prairie goat. He was close and coming closer.

Clell had a quick notion to stop and fight. He had an idea he might dodge the spear the Indian carried and come to grips with him. But the rest would be on him before he finished. It took time to kill a man just with the hands alone. Now was the time for the running he had saved himself for. There was strength in his legs yet. He made them reach out, farther, faster, faster, farther. The pound of them came to be a sick jolting inside his skull. His whole chest fought for air through the hot, closed tunnel of his throat. His legs weren't a part of him; they were something to think about, but not to feel, something to watch and to wonder at. He saw them come out and go under him and come out again. He saw them weakening, the knees bending in a little as the weight came on them. He felt wetness on his face, and reached up and found his nose was streaming blood.

He looked over his shoulder again. The main body of Indians had fallen farther back, the the prairie goat had

27

gained. Through a fog he saw the man's face, the chin set high and hard, the black eyes gleaming. He heard the moccasins slapping in the grass.

Of a sudden, Clell made up his mind. Keep on running and he'd get a spear in the back. Let it come from the front. Let it come through the chest. Let him face up to death like a natural man and to hell with it. His feet jolted him to a halt. He swung around and threw up his hands as if to stop a brute.

The Indian wasn't ready for that. He tried to pull up quick. He made to lift his spear. And then he stumbled and fell ahead. The spear handle broke as the point dug in the ground. Clell grabbed at the shaft, wrenched the point from the earth and drove it through the man. The Indian bucked to his hands and knees and strained and sank back. It was as easy as that.

Bending over him, Clell let his chest drink, let his numb legs rest, until he heard the yells of the Indians and, looking up, saw them strung out in a long file, with the closest of them so close he could see the set of their faces. He turned and ran again, hearing a sudden, louder howling as the Indians came on the dead one, and then the howling dying again to single cries as they picked up the chase. They were too many for him, and too close. He didn't have a chance. He couldn't fort up and try to stand them off, not with his hands bare. There wasn't any place to hide. He should have listened to his medicine when it was talking to him back there on the creek.

Down the slope ahead of him a river ran—the Jefferson Fork of the Missouri, he thought, while he made his legs drive him through a screen of brush. A beaver swam in the river, its moving head making a quiet V in the still water above a dam. As he pounded closer, its flat tail slapped the water like a pistol shot, the point of the V sank from sight, and the ripples spread out and lost themselves. He could still see the beaver, though, swimming under water, its legs moving and the black tail plain, like something to follow. It was a big beaver, and it was making for a beaver

28

lodge at Clell's right.

Clell dived, came up gasping from the chill of mountain water, and started stroking for the other shore. Beaver lodge! Beaver lodge! It was as if something spoke to him, as if someone nudged him, as if the black tail pulled him around. It was a fool thing, swimming under water and feeling for the tunnel that led up into the lodge. A fool thing. A man got so winded and weak that he didn't know medicine from craziness. A fool thing. A man couldn't force his shoulders through a beaver hole. The point of his shoulder pushed into mud. A snag ripped his side. He clawed ahead, his lungs bursting. And then his head was out of water, in the dark, and his lungs pumped air.

He heard movement in the lodge and a soft churring, but his eyes couldn't see anything. He pulled himself up, still hearing the churring, expecting the quick slice of teeth in his flesh. There was a scramble. Something slid along his leg and made a splash in the water of the tunnel, and slid again and made another splash.

His hands felt sticks and smooth, dry mud and the softness of shed hair. He sat up. The roof of the lodge just cleared his head if he sat slouched. It was a big lodge, farther across than the span of his arms. And it was as dark, almost, as the inside of a plugged barrel. His hand crossing before his eyes was just a shapeless movement.

He sat still and listened. The voices of the Indians sounded far off. He heard their feet in the stream, heard the moccasins walking softly around the lodge, heard the crunch of dried grass under their steps. It was like something dreamed, this hiding and being able to listen and to move. It was like being a breath of air, and no one able to put a hand on it.

After a while the footsteps trailed off and the voices faded. Now Clell's eyes were used to blackness, the lodge was a dark dapple. From the shades he would know it was day, but that was all. He felt for the cactus spines in his feet. He had been cold and wet at first, but the wetness dried and the lodge warmed a little to his body. Shivering, he lay down, feeling the dried mud under his skin, and the soft fur. When he closed his eyes he could see the sweep of distances and the high climb of mountains, and himself all alone in all the world, and, closer up, he could see the beaver swimming under water and its flat tail beckoning. He could hear voices, the silent voices speaking to a lonesome man out of nowhere and out of everywhere, and the beaver speaking, too, the smack of its tail speaking.

He woke up later, quick with alarm, digging at his dream and the noise that had got mixed with it. It was night outside. Not even the dark dapple showed inside the lodge, but only such a blackness as made a man feel himself to make sure he was real. Then he heard a snuffling of the air, and the sound of little waves lapping in the tunnel, and he knew that a beaver had nosed up and smelled him and drawn back into the water.

When he figured it was day, he sat up slowly, easing his muscles into action. He knew, without seeing, that his feet were puffed with the poison of the cactus. He crawled to the tunnel and filled his lungs and squirmed into it. He came up easy, just letting his eyes and nose rise above the water. The sun had cleared the eastern sky line. Not a breath of air stirred; the earth lay still, flowing into spring. He could see where the Indians had flattened the grass and trampled an edging of rushes, but there were no Indians about, not on one side or the other, not from shore line to sky line. He struck out for the far shore.

Seven days later a hunter at Fort Lisa spotted a figure far off. He watched it for a long spell, until a mist came over his eyes, and then he called to the men inside the stockade. A half-dozen came through the big gate, their rifles in the crooks of their arms, and stood outside and studied the figure too.

"Man, all right. Somep'n ails him. Look how he goes."

"Injun, I say. A Crow, maybe, with a Blackfoot arrer in him."

30

"Git the glass."

One of them went inside and came back and put the glass to his eye. "Naked as a damn jay bird."

"Injun, ain't it?"

"Got a crop of whiskers. Never seed a Injun with whiskers yet."

"Skin's black."

"Ain't a Injun, though."

They waited.

"It ain't! Yes, I do believe it's John Clell! It's John Clell or I'm a Blackfoot!"

They brought him in and put his great, raw swellings of feet in hot water and gave him brandy and doled out roast liver, and bit by bit, that day and the next, he told them what had happened.

They knew why he wouldn't eat prairie turnips afterward, seeing as he lived on raw ones all that time, but what they didn't understand, because he didn't try to tell them, was why he never would hunt beaver again.

Secret Airstrip

EDWARD LINDALL

ED BARLOW's broad and sunburnt features were heavy with
a mixture of resentment and anger, a vast disquietude, as
he stumped down from the house and turned the corner of
his implement shed. His brown eyes, narrowed against the
late morning sunlight after the shadow of the house,
shafted a glare at Charlie Bigtoe and Tommy Tucker,
chanting a liquid-sounding native song as they worked
unhurriedly at putting a new rail into the stockyard fence.

"Hi, boss," Charlie Bigtoe called, grinning like piano
keys across his big black face.

"Good morning," Barlow grunted and didn't mean it,
either as a comment or a wish. It was a dark, emotional
thunderhead of a morning.

He turned abruptly into the big iron shed that sheltered
the machines he had so painstakingly acquired over the
years: a small secondhand bulldozer for dam building, a

harvester for summer feeding-crops, a couple of old trucks, and a battered but efficient jeep, the motor that supplied electricity for the house and outbuildings and pumped water when the windmill failed. He took a greasegun from a rack nailed to the wall-timbers and advanced on the jeep.

It didn't really need greasing; it was smooth with care, but it was the dirtiest job around the place. And he needed it. He needed a job that he could hate because that way he could work off steam. He would have preferred, of course, to have taken Collie, his wise old stockhorse, and gone riding in the scrub. But the plane had landed out past the hills the previous afternoon. Its purpose was unknown, its presence a mystery. He knew something illegal was going on; something he had either to report or to wink at. He wasn't sure which. So he didn't want to leave the homestead while the plane was down. He might learn too much. People might even think he was involved.

He cursed now, thinking of the plane, and swung his big strong-framed body on to the front seat of the jeep, one long leg swinging, the other anchored to the ground.

Blast the plane! he thought now. He had seen it first seven weeks ago, or rather read its tracks, and Mary, his wife, had been arguing quietly all that time, pushing her viewpoint with the awful inflexibility of someone who knows she is right and cannot appreciate any other rightness than her own. She was tall and rounded, dark-eyed and dark-haired, and with a will like a team of donkeys. She had flared into a new hostility the moment yesterday when she had seen the plane. And he knew she must have been watching for it, because in all the times it must have landed on the airstrip he had never spotted it, a speck against an immensity of sky. She had insisted, almost frantically, that he should tell the police.

Barlow wished again now, as he had wished so many times, that he had kept his mouth shut. But so few unusual things happened in the busily placid life of Brolga Downs, a thousand square miles of cattle country in the lonely northern territory of Australia, that it had been natural to come home and tell of his discovery.

He had been hunting strays with Charlie Bigtoe and Tommy Tucker in the thick scrub on the far side of the low hills fifteen miles north of the homestead, driving them into a rough V-fence preparatory to pushing them back, as a herd, into the main pasture lands. And they had ridden along the old abandoned airstrip, a secret wartime base for the American Liberator bombers that had operated against the Japanese in Timor and Indonesia, until the war rolled farther north.

Charlie Bigtoe, with his radar eyes, had seen them first . . . tyre tracks leading off the strip into one of the many old bays beneath the fringing trees. And the bay had been cleared of its new-grown curtain of bushes. A dozen drums of fuel stood along its edge, and there were the oil drip patches and the fat tyre tracks of a three-ton truck. Charlie Bigtoe and Tommy Tucker could read mechanized tracks as easily as they could identify the age and weight of honey ants, the dimensions of a kangaroo. The tracks were four weeks old. And there were men's tracks too, a few of them big and booted, the majority small and curiously muffled, without heels.

Barlow had filled it in from there. He had heard rumours on his infrequent trips to Darwin of the organized smuggling of Chinese refugees into Australia. And then, at the old airstrip, he knew he had stumbled on the feedline. These muffled tracks were from the sandals of Chinese refugees being smuggled in to work in the market gardens of the southern cities, in Chinese restaurants, in coastal ships. Poor homeless devils, Barlow thought, who should be entering Australia lawfully, given a home in their homeless world.

The plane, he deduced from the tyre tracks and the state of the strip, was some sort of four- or six-seater, doubtless one of those fast American lights. It would carry up to ten thin Chinese, and maybe more, on island-hops down through the back areas of Indonesia and Timor.

"You will radio Sergeant Lawson, of course," Mary had said when he told her, intensely serious across the white-clothed spotlessness of their dinnertable.

Barlow had raised his eyebrows, his big broad face bland, his brown eyes a little wider, and the crowsfeet wrinkles at the. corners deeper from the movement.

"Why?"

"These men are breaking the law."

"So what? It's a stupid, cruel law. The few Chinese they bring in don't do any harm and, anyway, the poor devils deserve a break."

Mary shook her head slowly and slightly, her lips touched with a small sadly-wise smile. After an adult lifetime in the territory, it was astonishing how little of the heat and grinding dust showed in her face.

"And you still hate Sergeant Lawson," she said. "You won't side with him on anything. Not even on the law."

Barlow had felt like shaking his head then, too, like a fighter who, having been hit, needs to shake himself back to clarity. This was an old and unresolved conflict. Sergeant Lawson, sitting big and square and pompous in his one-man post sixty miles to the south-west, by the stock route river crossing, was the type of man Barlow never could have liked, even if Lawson hadn't, on that blazing day five years before, arrested him on a baseless charge of cattle stealing.

The circuit judge had dismissed the case for want of evidence; Barlow was freed, but he had been deeply humiliated. He had spent five sweltering days in the police post's lock-up, had been treated like a criminal through sheer stupidity, and he knew that once mud was thrown, some stuck. So he had hated Lawson with a bitter, all-but-consuming hatred which, even though it mellowed with the years, had never really disappeared.

He had tried to convince Mary that it was all forgotten, and for long periods she believed, or pretended to believe him. Then, out of some careless remark, her suspicions would be renewed. She worried about it, the hate and its

35

They took spears and boomerangs and went roaming in the bush.

effects. It was something there, in the back of his mind.
But now, with the Chinese, it was out in the open again,
worrying Mary and exasperating him.

He had put on a patience he didn't feel, settling his
shoulders deliberately, building a cigarette with an unhurried precision of calloused fingers.

"I don't hate Lawson," he said quietly. "I don't like
him. That's all."

"Ed." She was suddenly tense, shredding his proffered
truce with urgent hands. "Don't play games with me.
You're still bitter, and you're letting it sway your judg-
ment."

"All right," he said suddenly, bitingly. "I still hate him.
But that doesn't mean I'm not right about the smuggling."

"Ed." Mary's voice became deeper. Beseeching.

"Don't you see? This hate is eating you up. You can't
think straight."

"Mary," he said quietly, drawing on the cigarette, looking down his nose at it. "You're reading things into this, the way you always do."

She had leaned across to touch him, then stopped, as though repulsed. She sat up stiffly. "It's your duty, as a citizen, to report this plane."

"I've got other duties," he said shortly. "I'm a man, too. I've got duties as a man, duties to mankind."

Then he had watched the worry deepen on her face and wondered about the expression of his feelings. It was true, but where the words had come from he did not know. They were not the sort of words he used; not cattleman's words. He felt sympathy for the Chinese, thought they were having a rough deal, and somehow those simple feelings had been translated into "duties to mankind".

The phrase could have come from some unremembered book. Duties to mankind. It was true enough, and the pity was that Mary couldn't see it. She could only see his hate for Lawson.

Barlow levered himself off the jeep seat with a sigh, swinging the greasegun easily in his big hand, hearing again the liquid song of Charlie Bigtoe and Tommy Tucker and wondering what they would think of duties to mankind. They had, he thought, with darting envy, a simple and philosophic attitude to life. They took it as it came and adapted to its contours. They were first-class stockmen—he could never run Brolga Downs without them—but whenever the mood came upon them, they shed their boots and jeans and coloured shirts, stripped down to loincloths, took spears and boomerangs, and went roaming in the bush.

They stayed out for days, even weeks, to come back rested, fit and happy, stockmen again, resuming their married lives in the whitewashed cottages where their women waited for them. And now, in the midst of all the white man turmoil, they were getting the urge for walkabout again. Barlow had noticed that they both had boomerangs thrust into their belts, which showed the way their thoughts were tending. No duties to mankind there, Barlow thought ruefully. They *were* mankind.

Then Barlow sensed that he was not alone in the shed. He didn't believe in miracles of sixth sense; skilled bushmen didn't. Everything came through observation and identification, from variations of the normal. Now he stood perfectly still, listening. And it came again, a jagged slur of breathing. He reversed the greasegun in his hand with a quick flip, waited for the sound again, placed it in the deep shadow behind the harvester, and crossed to the doorway on silent feet to sign-talk Charlie Bigtoe and Tommy Tucker. It always paid to stack the odds.

They advanced on padding feet, the three of them, stalking the breather without too much seriousness. Occasionally tramps tottered through, aimless and harmless for the most part, but sometimes with a nuisance value. The men split at the harvester, one going round the front and two round the back. And then they stopped, looking down at the dusty ground, at the scarecrow thing that sprawled there in exhausted sleep. Thin and frail. Shrivelled. Barlow put the greasegun on the sideboard of the harvester, vaguely ashamed to have it in his hand. Charlie Bigtoe and Tommy Tucker leaned far forward, peering with big eyes, their broad black faces sagging with pity and concern.

"Chinese," Barlow said, feeling the stirring of a vast uneasiness, a touch of fate, a sense of arriving at some crossroads of the mind.

"Bin come from dat plane, mine tinkit," Charlie Bigtoe said.

Tommy Tucker pointed at the bare feet, sticking bonily from the torn blue overalls the man wore, and they were black with dried blood.

"Bin walk longtime plenty fast," he said. "Bin someone after 'im, like dust come dis way now."

"What dust?" Barlow demanded sharply.

Tommy Tucker waved a hand towards the hills, the airstrip. "Dat way. Maybe five, maybe six mile out."

Barlow dropped to his knees and shook the Chinaman, softly at first, then more roughly when he did not come awake. But not too roughly. The man was a bag of bones that could easily be shaken into dry component parts. Then the eyes opened slowly, dark slits that grew almost round with fear, and he was trying to scramble away. But Barlow grabbed his right hand and began to shake it, smiling and nodding to make his friendship clear. It worked. The man sat up, was still, a young-old man with a sunken mask of suffering for a face. And then Barlow saw the long angry furrow of a bullet wound across his shaven head.

"What's this?" He pointed.

The Chinaman stared a moment, then used his fingers to make a gun, gesturing in the general direction of the hills. He put two fingertips on the ground, and made the fingers run, stumbling and falling as they went. Someone out there had tried to kill him and he had run away. And that some-one, Barlow guessed, was on the way now to settle the account. What more, what were the rights of the case, the

Barlow shook the Chinaman, whose eyes grew round with fear.

background, he could not guess as yet. The Chinaman could have started it, although from his condition it seemed unlikely. The man was ill, in addition to his exhaustion, and he had obviously been in a bad way before he set out on his desperate flight. Barlow rose abruptly to his feet and stood back, thinking, figuring quickly. He did not know how many men were coming from the plane, but he knew they would be tough. Traffickers in human cargo would not be gentle men.

"Charlie," he said. "Tommy. Take this man into the scrub and keep him hidden. Quickly. Don't leave tracks."

The stockmen didn't hesitate, but stripped off their boots. They moved so quickly it was certain they had anticipated him. They stooped together and hauled the Chinaman to his feet. But he collapsed, so they swung him between them and made for the wide back door. Barlow walked behind them, taut and watchful, saw them pad quickly round and behind the house, their big bare feet like cushions on the hard-baked ground, and disappear into the scrub.

From the front garden of her cottage, Maudie Bigtoe shaded her eyes to stare.

Barlow waved to her and went back to the shed, got a roll of fencing-wire, a pair of heavy pliers, and began unnecessarily strengthening the stockyard fence, working from the outside. He had thought at first to wait on the verandah of the house, but realized that would have brought Mary out to meet the callers—with imponderable results if she should identify them. It was safer at the stockyards, where he could play his cards in simulated innocence, test the men and determine his course of action, free of the sort of storm that Mary might provoke.

Ten minutes later the truck arrived, bursting from the scrub track into the cleared space round the homestead, pulling up in an unmannerly cloud of dust some few feet from the stockyard. Barlow straddled his pliers across the top rail and put down his fencing-wire, like a methodical man about to enjoy a break. His big face was calm but his mind was working swiftly. The truck, complete with canvas canopy, would be the one they used to transport fuel, he reasoned, and take off their Chinese.

The two men who swung down from the cabin were tough, dressed in grubby khaki shirts and slacks, hatless, and with pistols bulky at their hips. The driver was Australian, big, red-faced, and carrot-haired, with a reckless brutality about him. The other, and he had to be the pilot, was slight and dark, with a thin black moustache and a scruff of facial stubble, black eyes, and a hard, cruel mouth. Probably Portuguese, Barlow thought.

"Howdy," the Australian said, stumping to the fence, with the pilot catfooting just behind, darting black eyeshafts at the house and outbuildings.

"Good day," Barlow said.

"We're lookin' for a man," Red-face said curtly. "Thought you might've seen him. Chinese. Got a bullet wound on the scalp."

Barlow rubbed his hands on his trousers, wishing he had a rifle leaning against the fence, but knowing it would have ruined his act of innocence. "I'm Ed Barlow," he said. "This is my place: Brolga Downs."

Red-face nodded shortly. "We reckoned he'd head this way."

No names, Barlow thought. Aloud, he said, "How come the bullet wound?"

"Madman," the Portuguese said in soft but deadly tones. "We take him south to hospital in our truck here, but he grow sick . . . want to fight. We camp out there, past your hills, for tie him up, but he snatch gun . . . my gun." He slapped the pistol at his hip for emphasis. "Thees one. An' try kill himself."

Red-face nodded gravely, pulling his mouth in a grimace. "We tried to grab him, but he run."

The teamwork shrieked rehearsal, and if Barlow had needed anything further to tell him they were lying it was Red-face's spurious gravity. Not a word about the plane; that was to be expected. Smugglers didn't advertise. But

41

they were lying too about the Chinaman, who was very far from mad. And Barlow detected a callousness, almost of contempt, behind their plausibility. He felt a cold rage growing in him, more searing, more bitter than anything he had felt for Sergeant Lawson; for his anger was not about himself, but for others. For all the illegal migrants these men had carried and planned to carry in the future.

These men confirmed what his mind had already constructed without his bidding, a thought-picture of what had happened at the plane. They had tried to kill a sick man because he had been a burden, a risk of disclosure, the way slave-ship captains in the old days had thrown their cargoes overboard at the first sign of capture by a man-o'-war. Or perhaps when the other Chinese had been stowed aboard the truck, they had tried to force him back on to the plane, to be dropped into the smiling Timor Sea.

And Barlow knew then, as he had known instinctively since he had first seen the fugitive, what it was he had to do. Despite his sympathy for the Chinamen, he had to stop the trade. He had to take these men and give them to the police, to Sergeant Lawson of the rock-hard head, who was the sole residence of authority. And he wouldn't be doing it for Mary's reasons, the breaking of the law, but because of their brutality; because it was the only way to protect other men, other hopeless, homeless men who trusted them with their lives.

"And what makes you think he came this way?" he asked evenly.

"He's a town man," Red-face said, "an' this is the only house." He grinned, suddenly, brutally, without humour. "And we found some tracks back at the creek crossing. You know, the one just before you get here."

"Well, that narrows the field," Barlow said. He ran a square hand ruminatively across his jaw, thinking that it was probably the first true thing that they had said, but wanting to appear helpful. He needed to stall. It was one thing to resolve to take them; another to figure how.

"Give me a moment and I'll get my rifle," he said easily.

"I'll help you search."

"Why, thanks," Red-face said. "That's real nice."

"We got the guns," the Portuguese said harshly. "Why you want to bring one?"

"Forget it, Silva," Red-face snapped. "Sure he wants a gun."

Barlow went up to the house, fifty yards away, and took a light repeater from the gun-rack in the hall, moving quietly so as not to attract Mary's attention. He could hear her bumping away at housework somewhere about the kitchen. He loaded the rifle from a box above the rack, held steady for a moment, making sure he was under control, then turned towards the door. He was going to walk down there to the stockyard, bland-faced and pacing steadily, and put the rifle on them before they had time to think about getting out their pistols. But as he went out on to the verandah, eyes searching for their target, they were each side of the door. He was neatly caught between them.

"Well, let's go," he said steadily. "We'll try the out-buildings. See if he's crawled in somewhere."

They combed through the implement shed, the feed barn, and the fuel dump, with Barlow always in the middle. And they did it cleverly. Real professionals. If Barlow had not intended to get the drop on them he would never have noticed their suave positioning. As it was, it grated on him, drove him to anger and frustration. There seemed no way of carrying out his plan, and yet there had to be. They started on the stockmen's homes, those neat whitewashed cottages he had built for Bigtoe and Tucker and their workmates. And there he found his chance.

Maudie Bigtoe, Charlie's wife, was still in her patch of garden, dusting beans against red spider, keeping tabs, a big broad-shouldered woman with a smiling face and a quick intelligence. Barlow touched his throat casually, in the native finger-talk sign for enemies, and saw her black eyes gleam.

"Maudie, you see any strange man today?" He paused, letting her wait for his meaning, balancing on his nerve

He touched his throat casually—the native sign for enemies—and said: "Maudie, you see any strange man today?"

edges. "Like out in the scrub? Any man you see?"

She looked with interest at the men on either side of Barlow, at their watchfulness, at their loosely holstered pistols. "Yair, boss," she said at last. "Dat feller way." And she jerked her head towards the piece of scrub where Charlie, Tommy and the Chinaman were hiding. "Seen strange feller all right dat way."

Barlow took a grip on himself to stop his relief from showing. "Well, gentlemen," he said carefully. "Lead on."

Red-face grinned. Triumphantly. "My honour."

So Barlow followed Red-face with Silva close behind, walking between two guns that would not hesitate to leap out and fire, between two men who had been doing something he had once imagined to be humane, but discovered, face-to-face, to be inhuman, brutal, because these men were so.

He was going to take them into the scrub because he had two trusted helpers there, Charlie Bigtoe and Tommy

Tucker, who did not care a cuss about the issues, but would fight for him. He was taking them into the scrub because he could not handle them in the open. But once inside the trees, the advantage would be his despite all their manoeuvres. He would have as allies two of the finest bushmen in the world, two shadows. . . . Just the same, there was a tight band round his throat. His mouth was dry.

Inside the line of trees the brash light of the day was filtered, and the peopled silence of the homestead became murmurous with small noises. Red-face and Silva took out their pistols, and Barlow had the chilling feel of Silva's pointed right in the middle of his back. There was no sign of the stockmen, but Barlow was certain at least one of them, probably Charlie Bigtoe, was somewhere close. He couldn't know for sure; he could only guess. And it was on that guess that he was going to act. He had to show them he wanted help. And there was only one way to do it.

He eased back the bolt of his rifle. And Silva said quietly, hissingly, from behind, "You do not need that, mister. We have guns."

"Sure," Red-face said, turning and grinning evilly. "You might trip and shoot someone."

Then the dry, throaty rattle of a brush turkey sounded out to the right, fairly close, a little to the rear. And Barlow's senses leapt, for there were no turkeys so near the house. He stepped up close to Red-face.

"What's that?" Silva rasped, jerking his head round.

Barlow saw the head jerk and knew his chance had come. He cocked the rifle swiftly, jumping round in front of Red-face and thrusting the rifle into his belly. "Hold it," he snapped at Silva, watching the boil of fury in the dark face, the trembling brink of violence in the pistol hand.

"So you know," Red-face said flatly, his blue eyes cold and hard. "You crazy fool. We have to kill you now."

"You first," Barlow said. "Tell your pal to drop his gun."

"So you know. You crazy fool! We have to kill you now."

"Like hell," Red-face said. "You won't shoot." He grinned. "You haven't got that sort of guts."

"Maybe I don't need it," Barlow said, and then he was sure of it because the shadow had moved again, not far from Silva. He waited a breath-held moment. Then he heard the whistle of swift flight, saw a dark flash in the air . . . and a boomerang crashed into Silva's head. The man dropped down without a sound, without a kick or flutter, just dropped softly to the ground.

"Turn round," he said to Red-face harshly. "You've got a job to do."

They made a slow procession, Red-face carrying Silva, and the two stockmen cradling the sick Chinaman. And while Bigtoe and Tucker sat on guard with rifle and captured pistols, Barlow went racing into the house.

"Mary," he called. "Mary." She came from the kitchen and met him at the hall door, a rapt, tense expression on her face. "Get on the radio," he said. "Call Lawson and tell him we've got some prisoners."

"I have," she said. "I saw you coming."

"You knew?" He stared at her, seeing her expression for the first time. "You knew what was happening?"

She nodded jerkily. She was under the after-stress of excitement. "I saw the boys carry off that Chinaman, then the two men came—they looked so horrible, I guessed who they were." Then she smiled, a little tremulously, betraying the tension she was trying so hard to hide. "I watched you. I feared you were helping them."

Barlow stared again. He opened his mouth to speak, but she slid her arms round his neck and buried her face in his shoulder.

"Oh, Ed," she whispered. "I prayed you'd see it my way and call the police. And now you have."

"The law's the law," he said. "You were right." He'd even speak nicely to Lawson when he came. Shake his hand. . . . And hope this time the façade of forgotten bitterness would remain intact.

Contents of the
Dead Man's Pocket

JACK FINNEY

AT THE LITTLE living-room desk Tom Benecke rolled two sheets of flimsy and a heavier top sheet, carbon paper sandwiched between them, into his portable. *Inter-office Memo*, the top sheet was headed, and he typed tomorrow's date just below this; then he glanced at a creased yellow sheet, covered with his own handwriting, beside the typewriter. "Hot in here," he muttered to himself. Then from the short hallway at his back, he heard the muffled clang of wire coat hangers in the bedroom closet, and at this reminder of what his wife was doing he thought: Hot, hell —guilty conscience.

He got up, shoving his hands into the back pockets of his grey wash slacks, stepped to the living-room window beside the desk and stood breathing on the glass, watching the expanding circlet of mist, staring down through the autumn night at Lexington Avenue, eleven storeys below. He was a tall, lean, dark-haired young man in a pullover sweater, who looked as though he had played not football, probably, but basketball in college. Now he placed the heels of his hands against the top edge of the lower window frame and shoved upward. But as usual the window didn't budge, and he had to lower his hands and then shoot them hard upwards to jolt the window open a few inches. He dusted his hands, muttering.

But still he didn't begin his work. He crossed the room to the hallway entrance and, leaning against the doorjamb, hands shoved into his back pockets again, he called, "Clare?" When his wife answered, he said, "Sure you don't mind going alone?"

"No." Her voice was muffled, and he knew her head and shoulders were in the bedroom closet. Then the tap of her high heels sounded on the wood floor and she appeared at the end of the little hallway, wearing a slip, both hands raised to one ear, clipping on an earring. She smiled at him—a slender, very pretty girl with light brown, almost blonde, hair—her prettiness emphasized by the pleasant nature that showed in her face. "It's just that I hate you to miss this movie; you wanted to see it too."

"Yeah, I know." He ran his fingers through his hair. "Got to get this done, though."

She nodded, accepting this. Then, glancing at the desk across the living-room, she said, "You work too much, though, Tom—and too hard."

He smiled. "You won't mind, though, will you, when the money comes rolling in and I'm known as the Boy Wizard of Wholesale Groceries?"

"I guess not." She smiled and turned back towards the bedroom.

At his desk again, Tom lighted a cigarette; then a few moments later as Clare appeared, dressed and ready to leave, he set it on the rim of the ash tray. "Just after seven," she said. "I can make the beginning of the first feature."

49

She was dressed and all set for the movies.

He walked to the front-door closet to help her on with her coat. For an instant he was tempted to go with her; it was not actually true that he had to work tonight, though he very much wanted to. This was his own project, unannounced as yet in his office, and it could be postponed. But then they won't see it till Monday, he thought once again, and if I give it to the boss tomorrow he might read it over the week-end. . . . "Have a good time," he said aloud. He gave his wife a little swat and opened the door for her, feeling the air from the building hallway, smelling faintly of floor wax, stream gently past his face.

He watched her walk down the hall, flicked a hand in response as she waved, and then he started to close the door, but it resisted for a moment. As the door opening narrowed, the current of warm air from the hallway, channelled through this smaller opening now, suddenly rushed past him with accelerated force. Behind him he heard the slap of the window curtains against the wall and the sound of paper fluttering from his desk, and he had to push to close the door.

Turning, he saw a sheet of white paper drifting to the floor in a series of arcs, and another sheet, yellow, moving towards the window, caught in the dying current flowing through the narrow opening. As he watched, the paper struck the bottom edge of the window and hung there for an instant, plastered against the glass and wood. Then as the moving air stilled completely the curtains swinging back from the wall to hang free again, he saw the yellow sheet drop to the window ledge and slide over out of sight.

He ran across the room, grasped the bottom of the window and tugged, staring through the glass. He saw the yellow sheet, dimly now in the darkness outside, lying on the ornamental ledge a yard below the window. Even as he watched, it was moving, scraping slowly along the ledge, pushed by the breeze that pressed steadily against the building wall. He heaved on the window with all his strength and it shot open with a bang, the window weight rattling in the casing. But the paper was past his reach and, leaning out into the night, he watched it scud steadily along the ledge to the south, half plastered against the building wall. Above the muffled sound of the street traffic far below, he could hear the dry scrape of its movement, like a leaf on the pavement.

The living-room of the next apartment to the south projected a yard or more farther out towards the street than this one; because of this the Beneckes paid seven and a half dollars less rent than their neighbours. And now the yellow sheet, sliding along the stone ledge, nearly invisible in the night, was stopped by the projecting blank wall of the next apartment. It lay motionless, then, in the corner formed by the two walls—a good five yards away, pressed firmly against the ornate corner ornament of the ledge, by the breeze that moved past Tom Benecke's face.

He knelt at the window and stared at the yellow paper for a full minute or more, waiting for it to move, to slide off the ledge and fall, hoping he could follow its course to the street, and then hurry down in the elevator and retrieve it. But it didn't move, and then he saw that the paper was caught firmly between a projection of the con-voluted corner ornament and the ledge. He thought about the poker from the fireplace, then the broom, then the mop—discarding each thought as it occurred to him. There was nothing in the apartment long enough to reach that paper.

It was hard for him to understand that he actually had to abandon it—it was ridiculous—and he began to curse. Of all the papers on his desk, why did it have to be this one in particular! On four long Saturday afternoons he had stood in super-markets, counting the people who passed certain displays, and the results were scribbled on that yellow sheet. From stacks of trade publications, gone over page by page in snatched half-hours at work and during evenings at home, he had copied facts, quotations and figures on to that sheet. And he had carried it with him to the Public Library on Fifth Avenue, where he'd spent a dozen lunch hours and early evenings adding more. All were needed to support and lend authority to his idea for a new grocery-store display method; without them his idea was a mere opinion. And there they all lay, in his own improvised shorthand—countless hours of work—out there on the ledge.

For many seconds he believed he was going to abandon the yellow sheet, that there was nothing else to do. The work could be duplicated. But it would take two months, and the time to present this idea, damn it, was *now*, for use in the spring displays. He struck his fist on the window ledge. Then he shrugged. Even though his plan were adopted, he told himself, it wouldn't bring him a raise in pay—not immediately, anyway, or as a direct result. It won't bring me a promotion either, he argued—not of itself. . . .

But just the same, and he couldn't escape the thought, this and other independent projects, some already done and others planned for the future, would gradually mark him out from the score of other young men in his com-pany. They were the way to change from a name on the payroll to a name in the minds of the company officials. They were the beginning of the long, long climb to where he was determined to be, at the very top. And he knew he was going out there in the darkness, after the yellow sheet fifteen feet beyond his reach.

By a kind of instinct, he instantly began making his intention acceptable to himself by laughing at it. The mental picture of himself sidling along the ledge outside was absurd—it was actually comical—and he smiled. He imagined himself describing it; it would make a good story at the office and, it occurred to him, would add a special interest and importance to his memorandum, which would do it no harm at all.

To simply go out and get his paper was an easy task—he could be back here with it in less than two minutes—and he knew he wasn't deceiving himself. The ledge, he saw, measuring it with his eye, was about as wide as the length of his shoe, and perfectly flat. And every fifth row of brick in the face of the building, he remembered—leaning out, he verified this—was indented half an inch, enough for the tips of his fingers, enough to maintain balance easily. It occurred to him that if this ledge and wall were only a yard above ground—as he knelt at the window staring out, this thought was the final confirmation of his intention—he could move along the ledge indefinitely.

On a sudden impulse, he got to his feet, walked to the front closet and took out an old tweed jacket; it would be cold outside. He put it on and buttoned it as he crossed the room rapidly towards the open window. In the back of his mind he knew he'd better hurry and get this over with before he thought too much, and at the window he didn't allow himself to hesitate. . . .

He swung a leg over the sill, then felt for and found the ledge a yard below the window with his foot. Gripping the bottom of the window frame very tightly and carefully, he slowly ducked his head under it, feeling on his face the sudden change from the warm air of the room to the chill outside. With infinite care he brought out his other leg, his mind concentrating on what he was doing. Then he slowly stood erect. Most of the putty, dried out and brittle, had dropped off the bottom edging of the window frame, he found, and the flat wooden edging provided a good gripping surface, a half inch or more deep, for the tips of his fingers.

Now, balanced easily and firmly, he stood on the ledge outside in the slight, chill breeze, eleven storeys above the street, staring into his own lighted apartment, odd and different-seeming now.

First his right hand, then his left, he carefully shifted his finger-tip grip from the puttyless window edging to an indented row of bricks directly to his right. It was hard to take the first shuffling sideways step then—to make himself move—and the fear stirred in his stomach, but he did it, again by not allowing himself time to think. And now—with his chest, stomach, and the left side of his face pressed against the rough cold brick—his lighted apartment was suddenly gone, and it was much darker out here than he had thought.

Without pause he continued—right foot, left foot, right foot, left—his shoe soles shuffling and scraping along the rough stone, never lifting from it, fingers sliding along the exposed edging of brick. He moved on the balls of his feet, heels lifted slightly; the ledge was not quite as wide as he'd expected. But leaning slightly inward towards the face of the building and pressed against it, he could feel his balance firm and secure, and moving along the ledge was quite as easy as he had thought it would be. He could hear the buttons of his jacket scraping steadily along the rough bricks and feel them catch momentarily, tugging a little, at each mortared crack. He simply did not permit himself to look down, though the compulsion to do so never left him; nor did he allow himself actually to think. Mechanically—right foot, left foot, over and again—he shuffled along crabwise, watching the projecting wall ahead loom steadily closer. . . .

Then he reached it and, at the corner—he'd decided how

With infinite care he brought out his other leg.

he was going to pick up the paper—he lifted his right foot and placed it carefully on the ledge that ran along the projecting wall at a right angle to the ledge on which his other foot rested. And now, facing the building, he stood in the corner formed by the two walls, one foot on the ledging of each, a hand on the shoulder-high indentation of each wall. His forehead was pressed directly into the corner against the cold bricks, and now he carefully lowered first one hand, then the other, perhaps a foot farther down, to the next indentation in the rows of bricks.

Very slowly, sliding his forehead down the trough of the brick corner and bending his knees, he lowered his body towards the paper lying between his outstretched feet. Again he lowered his fingerholds another foot and bent his knees still more, thigh muscles taut, his forehead sliding and bumping down the brick V. Half squatting now, he dropped his left hand to the next indentation and then slowly reached with his right hand towards the paper between his feet.

He couldn't quite touch it, and his knees now were

pressed against the wall; he could bend them no farther. But by ducking his head another inch lower, the top of his head now pressed against the bricks, he lowered his right shoulder and his fingers had the paper by a corner, pulling it loose. At the same instant he saw, between his legs and far below, Lexington Avenue stretched out for miles ahead.

He saw, in that instant, the Loew's theatre sign, blocks ahead past Fiftieth Street; the miles of traffic signals, all green now; the lights of cars and street lamps; countless neon signs; and the moving black dots of people. And a violent, instantaneous explosion of absolute terror roared through him. For a motionless instant he saw himself externally—bent practically double, balanced on this narrow ledge, nearly half his body projecting out above the street far below—and he began to tremble violently, panic flaring through his mind and muscles, and he felt the blood rush from the surface of his skin.

In the fractional moment before horror paralysed him, as he stared between his legs at that terrible length of street far beneath him, a fragment of his mind raised his body in a spasmodic jerk to an upright position again, but so violently that his head scraped hard against the wall, bouncing off it, and his body swayed outwards to the knife edge of balance, and he very nearly plunged backwards and fell. Then he was leaning far into the corner again, squeezing and pushing into it, not only his face but his chest and stomach, his back arching; and his finger-tips clung with all the pressure of his pulling arms to the shoulder-high half-inch indentation in the bricks.

He was more than trembling now; his whole body was racked with a violent shuddering beyond control, his eyes squeezed so tightly shut it was painful, though he was past awareness of that. His teeth were exposed in a frozen grimace, the strength draining like water from his knees and calves. It was extremely likely, he knew, that he would faint, slump down along the wall, his face scraping, and then drop backwards, a limp weight, out into nothing. And to save his life he concentrated on holding on to con-

He looked down—an explosion of terror roared through him.

sciousness, drawing deliberate deep breaths of cold air into his lungs, fighting to keep his senses aware.

Then he knew that he would not faint, but he could not stop shaking nor open his eyes. He stood where he was, breathing deeply, trying to hold back the terror of the glimpse he had had of what lay below him; and he knew he had made a mistake in not making himself stare down at the street, getting used to it and accepting it, when he had first stepped out on to the ledge.

It was impossible to walk back. He simply could not do it. He couldn't bring himself to make the slightest movement. The strength was gone from his legs; his shivering hands—numb, cold and desperately rigid—had lost all deftness; his easy ability to move and balance was gone. Within a step or two, if he tried to move, he knew that he would stumble clumsily and fall.

Seconds passed, with the chill faint wind pressing the side of his face, and he could hear the toned-down volume of the street traffic far beneath him. Again and again it slowed and then stopped, almost to silence; then presently, even this high, he would hear the click of the traffic signals and the subdued roar of the cars starting up again. During a lull in the street sounds, he called out. Then he was shouting "*Help!*" so loudly it rasped his throat. But he felt the steady pressure of the wind, moving between his face and the blank wall, snatch up his cries as he uttered them, and he knew they must sound directionless and distant. And he remembered how habitually, here in New York, he himself heard and ignored shouts in the night. If anyone heard him, there was no sign of it, and presently Tom Benecke knew he had to try moving; there was nothing else he could do.

Eyes squeezed shut, he watched scenes in his mind like scraps of motion-picture film—he could not stop them. He saw himself stumbling suddenly sideways as he crept along the ledge and saw his upper body arc outwards, arms flailing. He saw a dangling shoe-string caught between the ledge and the sole of his other shoe, saw a foot start to move, to be stopped with a jerk, and felt his balance leaving him. He saw himself falling with a terrible speed as his body revolved in the air, knees clutched tight to his chest, eyes squeezed shut, moaning softly.

Out of utter necessity, knowing that any of these thoughts might be reality in the very next seconds, he was slowly able to shut his mind against every thought but what he now began to do. With fear-soaked slowness, he slid his left foot an inch or two towards his own impossibly distant window. Then he slid the fingers of his shivering left hand a corresponding distance. For a moment he could not bring himself to lift his right foot from one ledge to the other; then he did it, and became aware of the harsh exhalation of air from his throat and realized that he was panting. As his right hand, then, began to slide along the brick edging, he was astonished to feel the yellow paper pressed to the bricks underneath his stiff fingers, and he uttered a terrible, abrupt bark that might have been a laugh or a moan. He opened his mouth and took the paper in his teeth, pulling it out from under his fingers.

By a kind of trick—by concentrating his entire mind on first his left foot, then his left hand, then the other foot, then the other hand—he was able to move, almost imperceptibly, trembling steadily, very nearly without thought. But he could feel the terrible strength of the pent-up horror on just the other side of the flimsy barrier he had erected in his mind; and he knew that if it broke through he would lose this thin, artificial control of his body.

During one slow step he tried keeping his eyes closed; it made him feel safer, shutting him off a little from the fearful reality of where he was. Then a sudden rush of giddiness swept over him and he had to open his eyes wide, staring sideways at the cold rough brick and angled lines of mortar, his cheek tight against the building. He kept his eyes open then, knowing that if he once let them flick outwards, to stare for an instant at the lighted windows across the street, he would be past help.

He didn't know how many dozens of tiny sidling steps

he had taken, his chest, belly and face pressed to the wall; but he knew the slender hold he was keeping on his mind and body was going to break. He had a sudden mental picture of his apartment on just the other side of this wall —warm, cheerful, incredibly spacious. And he saw himself striding through it, lying down on the floor on his back, arms spread wide, revelling in its unbelievable security. The impossible remoteness of this utter safety, the contrast between it and where he now stood, was more than he could bear. And the barrier broke then, and the fear of the awful height he stood on coursed through his nerves and muscles. . . .

A fraction of his mind knew he was going to fall, and he began taking rapid blind steps with no feeling of what he was doing, sidling with a clumsy, desperate swiftness, fingers scrabbling along the brick, almost hopelessly resigned to the sudden backward pull and swift motion outward and down. Then his moving hand slid on to not brick but sheer emptiness, an impossible gap in the face of the wall, and he stumbled.

His right foot smashed into his left ankle-bone; he staggered sideways, began falling, and the claw of his hand cracked against glass and wood, slid down it, and his finger-tips were pressed hard on the puttyless edging of his window. His right hand smacked gropingly beside it as he fell to his knees; and, under the full weight and direct downward pull of his sagging body, the open window dropped shudderingly in its frame till it closed and his wrists struck the sill and were jarred off.

For a single moment he knelt, knee bones against stone on the very edge of the ledge, body swaying and touching nowhere else, fighting for balance. Then he lost it, his shoulders plunging backwards, and he flung his arms forward, his hands smashing against the window casing on either side; and—his body moving backwards—his fingers clutched the narrow wood stripping of the upper pane.

For an instant he hung suspended between balance and falling, his finger-tips pressed on to the quarter-inch wood strips. Then, with utmost delicacy, with a focused concentration of all his senses, he increased even further the strain on his finger-tips hooked to these slim edgings of wood. Elbows slowly bending, he began to draw the full weight of his upper body forward, knowing that the instant his fingers slipped off these quarter-inch strips he'd plunge backwards and be falling. Elbows imperceptibly bending, body shaking with the strain, the sweat starting from his forehead in great sudden drops, he pulled, his entire being and thought concentrated in his finger-tips. Then suddenly, the strain slackened and ended, his chest touching the window-sill, and he was kneeling on the ledge, his forehead pressed to the glass of the closed window.

Dropping his palms to the sill, he stared into his living-room—at the red-brown davenport across the room, and a magazine he had left there; at the pictures on the walls and the grey rug; the entrance to the hallway; and at his papers, typewriter and desk, not two feet from his nose.

At that moment the window slammed shut and his body swayed outwards, fighting for balance.

A movement from his desk caught his eye, and he saw that it was a thin curl of blue smoke; his cigarette, the ash long, was still burning in the ash-tray where he'd left it—this was past all belief—only a few minutes before.

His head moved, and in faint reflection from the glass before him, he saw the yellow paper clenched in his front teeth. Lifting a hand from the sill he took it from his mouth; the moistened corner parted from the paper, and he spat it out. . . .

For a moment, in the light from the living-room, he stared wonderingly at the yellow sheet in his hand and then crushed it into the side pocket of his jacket.

He couldn't open the window. It had been pulled not completely closed, but its lower edge was below the level of the outside sill; there was no room to get his fingers underneath it. Between the upper sash and the lower was a gap not wide enough—reaching up, he tried—to get his fingers into; he couldn't push it open. The upper window panel, he knew from long experience, was impossible to move, frozen tight with dried paint.

Very carefully observing his balance, the finger tips of his left hand again hooked to the narrow stripping of the window casing, he drew his right hand, palm facing the glass, and then struck the glass with the heel of his hand.

His arm rebounded from the pane, his body tottering, and he knew he didn't dare strike a harder blow.

But in the security and relief of his new position, he simply smiled; with only a sheet of glass between him and the room just before him, it was not possible that there wasn't a way past it. Eyes narrowing, he thought for a few moments about what to do. Then his eyes widened, for nothing occurred to him. But still he felt calm: the trembling, he realized, had stopped. At the back of his mind there still lay the thought that once he was again in his home, he could give release to his feelings. He actually *would* lie on the floor, rolling, clenching tufts of the rug in his hands. He would literally run across the room, free to move as he liked, jumping on the floor, testing and revelling in its absolute security, letting the relief flood through him, draining the fear from his mind and body. His yearning for this was astonishingly intense, and somehow he understood that he had better keep this feeling at bay.

He took a half-dollar from his pocket and struck it against the pane, but without any hope that the glass would break and with very little disappointment when it did not. After a few moments of thought he drew his leg up on to the ledge and picked loose the knot of his shoelace. He slipped off his shoe and, holding it across the instep, drew back his arm as far as he dared and struck the leather heel against the glass. The pane rattled, but he knew he'd been a long way from breaking it. His foot was cold and he slipped the shoe back on. He shouted again, experimentally, and then once more, but there was no answer.

The realization suddenly struck him that he might have to wait here till Clare came home, and for a moment the thought was funny. He could see Clare opening the front door, withdrawing her key from the lock, closing the door behind her and then glancing up to see him crouched on the other side of the window. He could see her rush across the room, face astounded and frightened, and hear himself shouting instructions: "Never mind how I got here! Just open the wind—" She couldn't open it, he remembered, she'd never be able to; she'd always had to call him. She'd have to get the building superintendent or a neighbour, and he pictured himself smiling and answering their questions as he climbed in. "I just wanted to get a breath of fresh air, so—"

He couldn't possibly wait here till Clare came home. It was the second feature she'd wanted to see, and she'd left in time to see the first. She'd be another three hours or— He glanced at his watch; Clare had been gone eight minutes. It wasn't possible, but only eight minutes ago he had kissed his wife good-bye. She wasn't even in the theatre yet!

It would be four hours before she could possibly be

home, and he tried to picture himself kneeling out here, finger-tips hooked to these narrow strippings, while first one movie, preceded by a slow listing of credits, began, developed, reached its climax and then finally ended. There'd be a newsreel next, maybe, and then an animated cartoon, and then interminable scenes from coming pictures. And then, once more, the beginning of a full-length picture—while all the time he hung out here in the night.

He might possibly get to his feet, but he was afraid to try. Already his legs were cramped, his thigh muscles tired; his knees hurt, his feet felt numb and his hands were stiff. He couldn't possibly stay out here for four hours, or anywhere near it. Long before that his legs and arms would give out; he would be forced to try changing his position often—stiffly, clumsily, his co-ordination and strength gone —and he would fall. Quite realistically, he knew that he would fall; no one could stay out here on this ledge for four hours.

A dozen windows in the apartment building across the street were lighted. Looking over his shoulder, he could see the top of a man's head behind the newspaper he was reading; in another window he saw the blue-grey flicker of a television screen. No more than twenty-odd yards from his back were scores of people, and if just one of them would walk idly to his window and glance out. . . . For some moments he stared over his shoulder at the lighted rectangles, waiting. But no one appeared. The man reading his paper turned a page and then continued his reading. A figure passed another of the windows and was immediately gone.

In the inside pocket of his jacket he found a little sheaf of papers, and he pulled one out and looked at it in the light from the living-room. It was an old letter, an advertisement of some sort; his name and address, in purple ink, were on a label pasted to the envelope. Gripping one end of the envelope in his teeth, he twisted it into a tight curl. From his shirt pocket he brought out a book of matches. He didn't dare let go the casing with both hands but, with

The blazing fragment fell.

the twist of paper in his teeth, he opened the match-book with his free hand; then he bent one of the matches in two without tearing it from the folder, its red-tipped end now touching the striking surface. With his thumb, he rubbed the red tip across the striking area.

He did it again, then again, and still again, pressing harder each time, and the match suddenly flared, burning his thumb. But he kept it alight, cupping the match-book in his hand and shielding it with his body. He held the flame to the paper in his mouth till it caught. Then he snuffed out the match flame with his thumb and forefinger, careless of the burn, and replaced the book in his pocket. Taking the paper twist in his hand, he held it flame down, watching the flame crawl up the paper, till it flared bright. Then he held it behind him over the street, moving it from side to side, watching it over his shoulder, the flame flickering and guttering in the wind.

There were three letters in his pocket and he lighted each of them, holding each till the flame touched his hand and

65

then dropping it to the street below. At one point, watching over his shoulder while the last of the letters burned, he saw the man across the street put down his paper and stand—even seeming, to Tom, to glance towards his window. But when he moved, it was only to walk across the room and disappear from sight. . . .

There were a dozen coins in Tom Benecke's pocket and he dropped them, three or four at a time. But if they struck anyone, or if anyone noticed their falling, no one connected them with their source, and no one glanced upwards.

His arms had begun to tremble from the steady strain of clinging to this narrow perch, and he did not know what to do now and was terribly frightened. Clinging to the window stripping with one hand, he again searched his pockets. But now—he had left his wallet on his dresser when he'd changed clothes—there was nothing left but the yellow sheet. It occurred to him irrelevantly that his death on the sidewalk below would be an eternal mystery; the window closed—why, how, and from where could he have fallen? No one would be able to identify his body for a time, either—the thought was somehow unbearable and increased his fear. All they'd find in his pockets would be the yellow sheet. *Contents of the dead man's pockets,* he thought, *one sheet of paper bearing pencilled notations— incomprehensible.*

He understood fully that he might actually be going to die; his arms, maintaining his balance on the ledge, were trembling steadily now. And it occurred to him then with all the force of a revelation that, if he fell, all he was ever going to have out of life he would then, abruptly, have had. Nothing, then, could ever be changed; and nothing more— no least experience or pleasure—could ever be added to his life. He wished, then, that he had not allowed his wife to go off by herself tonight—and on similar nights. He thought of all the evenings he had spent away from her, working; and he regretted them. He thought wonderingly of his fierce ambition and of the direction his life had taken; he thought of the hours he'd spent by himself, filling the yellow sheet that had brought him out here. *Contents of the dead man's pockets*, he thought with sudden fierce anger, *a wasted life.*

He was simply not going to cling here till he slipped and fell; he told himself that now. There was one last thing he could try; he had been aware of it for some moments, refusing to think about it, but now he faced it. Kneeling here on the ledge, the finger-tips of one hand pressed to the narrow strip of wood, he could, he knew, draw his other hand back a yard perhaps, fist clenched tight, doing it very slowly till he sensed the outer limit of balance, then, as hard as he was able from the distance, he could drive his fist forward against the glass. If it broke, his fist smashing through, he was safe; he might cut himself badly, and probably would, but with his arm inside the room, he would be secure. But if the glass did not break, the rebound, flinging his arm back, would topple him off the ledge. He was certain of that.

He tested his plan. The fingers of his left hand claw-like on the little stripping, he drew back his other fist until his body began teetering backwards. But he had no leverage now—he could feel that there would be no force to his swing—and he moved his fist slowly forward till he rocked forward on his knees again and could sense that his swing would carry its greatest force. Glancing down, however, measuring the distance from his fist to the glass, he saw that it was less than two feet.

It occurred to him that he could raise his arm over his head, to bring it down against the glass. But, experimenting in slow motion, he knew it would be an awkward girl-like blow without the force of a driving punch, and not nearly enough to break the glass. . . .

Facing the window, he had to drive a blow from the shoulder, he knew now, at a distance of less than two feet; and he did not know whether it would break through the heavy glass. It might; he could picture it happening, he could feel it in the nerves of his arm. And it might not;

he could feel that too—feel his fist striking this glass and being instantaneously flung back by the unbreaking pane, feel the fingers of his other hand breaking loose, nails scraping along the casing as he fell.

He waited, arm drawn back, fist balled, but in no hurry to strike; this pause, he knew, might be an extension of his life. And to live even a few seconds longer, he felt, even

With every last scrap of strength he struck.

out here on this ledge in the night, was infinitely better than to die a moment earlier than he had to. His arm grew tired, and he brought it down and rested it.

Then he knew that it was time to make the attempt. He could not kneel here hesitating indefinitely till he lost all courage to act, waiting till he slipped off the ledge. Again he drew back his arm, knowing this time that he would not bring it down till he struck. His elbow protruding over Lexington Avenue far below, the fingers of his other hand pressed down bloodlessly tight against the narrow stripping, he waited, feeling the sick tenseness and terrible excitement building. It grew and swelled towards the moment of action, his nerves tautening. He thought of Clare —just a wordless, yearning thought—and then drew his arm back just a bit more, fist so tight his fingers pained him, and knowing he was going to do it. Then with full power, with every last scrap of strength he could bring to bear, he shot his arm forward towards the glass, and he said, *"Clare!"*

He heard the sound, felt the blow, felt himself falling forward, and his hand closed on the living-room curtains, the shards and fragments of glass showering on to the floor. And then, kneeling there on the ledge, an arm thrust into the room up to the shoulder, he began picking away the protruding slivers and great wedges of glass from the window frame, tossing them in on to the rug. And, as he grasped the edges of the empty frame and climbed into his home, he was grinning in triumph.

He did not lie down on the floor or run through the apartment, as he had promised himself; even in the first few moments it seemed to him natural and normal that he should be where he was. He simply turned to his desk, pulled the crumpled yellow sheet from his pocket and laid it down where it had been, smoothing it out; then he absently laid a pencil across it to weight it down. He shook his head, wonderingly, and turned to walk towards the closet.

There he got out his topcoat and hat and, without waiting to put them on, opened the front door and stepped out, to go find his wife. He turned to pull the door closed and the warm air from the hall rushed through the narrow opening again. As he saw the yellow paper, the pencil flying, scooped off the desk and, unimpeded by the glassless window, sail out into the night and out of his life, Tom Benecke burst into laughter and then closed the door behind him.

The Rockslide

DON KNOWLTON

THE BOY stood in the doorway of the shack on the side of the mountain, looking down, away down, across the valley. He held a cup of coffee. He had come up early that Saturday morning in the old jeep and cooked breakfast. He wanted to get in another weekend on the mountain before school started again.

It was his mountain. Oh, he didn't own it. The range, most of it, was inside the national park boundaries. The shack was right on the line. But just the same, the mountain belonged to him; or rather, he belonged to the mountain.

They said in Pinedale, down below, where his father taught in the college, that Kit Sherry was a strange lad. Bright enough, but shy. Solitary sort of an individual. He knew what they said, and he did not care. He was in love with the mountain.

Kit knew that mountain as a city boy knows his back-yard. He knew it in rain and in sunshine, in moonlight, in mist, in driving snow.

There was the long slope that purple flowers covered in July. There were the reaches of open pines, with grass underfoot. There were the brooks, two on his side of the mountain, that came tearing down in a rush through tangles of brush. There was the high, placid pond, where the beavers worked. There was the clearing with the dead, blackened stumps where the fire had gone through four years before; berries and fireweed grew there now. There was the little wood, tucked away in a fold, where there still stood tall spruces that the timbermen had spared. There was the meadow, up above, scattered with larches, where the anemones put on their white beards after they blossomed.

There was the clear spring in a little pocket right on the timber line where columbine bloomed in August. And, above and beyond all else, the rocks.

There were ways to get up and over, to twist in and round, those rocks. There were bypasses to sheer cliffs, curious ways along knife edges, ladderlike steps to spots that looked inaccessible—if you knew them. And Kit did.

It was the end of August. There had been the nightly nip of cold—at daybreak there had probably been a film of ice on the water bucket that hung by the spring—but as yet no hard frost to turn the aspens yellow.

Kit finished his coffee and began washing his breakfast dishes. As he did so he turned on his portable radio. The music suddenly broke off. The announcer said, "We interrupt this programme again to repeat a special news bulletin. This morning Barney Zucco, the notorious Chicago gangster, held up the Pinedale Bank. He shot down the cashier and a clerk in cold blood, scooped up some eleven thousand dollars, and made his getaway in a green Cadillac. Both men are dead.

"Zucco, known as the Muscle, contrived two days ago to escape from an FBI squad who thought they had him cornered in Chicago. He is wanted on charges of dope smuggling and extortion, and is presumed to have been the man behind a series of killings in South Chicago.

"Zucco is reported to have headed south on Route 168. Police throughout the state have been alerted. Zucco is over six feet tall, broad-shouldered, and powerfully built. He has black hair, black eyes, and regular, handsome features. He was wearing a brown checked suit, brown tie, brown shoes, and no hat. He carries a gun in his right-hand coat pocket. We return you now to the regular programme."

By that time the few dishes were done, and Kit turned off the radio. As he did so, he heard the whine of a high-powered car coming up the road.

That's strange, he thought. He stepped to the door—and as he did so there pulled up, beside his parked jeep, a green Cadillac convertible.

The man who got out was over six feet tall, broad-shouldered, and powerfully built. He had black hair, black eyes, and regular, handsome features. He wore a brown checked suit, brown tie, brown shoes, and no hat. His right hand was thrust into his right coat pocket—and in that pocket there was a bulge.

The man looked at the tall, skinny youngster in blue jeans and open shirt who stood in the doorway.

"Say, kid," he said, "where does this road go?"

"It doesn't go anywhere," answered Kit. "It just goes to here. This is where it ends."

The regular, handsome features of the man in the brown suit contorted in a sort of spasm.

"Well, how do I get out of here?"

"Only back the way you came."

"But I can't—hell, there must be some way to get from here to some place else—"

"Not by road," said Kit.

"What do you mean, not by road?"

There was a long pause, while they stared at each other. Finally Kit took a deep breath.

72

"You'd better come inside, Mr. Zucco," he said. "Somebody might come along and see you."

In a flash the man's gun was out of his pocket. He held it before him, motioning Kit to step back into the shack, following him in, and closing the door. Kit sat down at the table, and Zucco sat opposite him, holding the gun.

"Kid," said Zucco, "I've *got* to get out. I've got to get away. You understand that, don't you?"

Kit nodded.

"Those damn fools at that bank—I *had* to do it. I didn't have time in Chicago to get money. A man has to have money, doesn't he?"

Kit said nothing.

"You know how to get me out of here. All right—do it, see? Either you get me out or—"

He gestured with the gun. "Get the idea?"

"I get it," said Kit. "But there's only one way. Up over the mountain."

"What do you mean, up over—on *foot*?"

Kit nodded. "Look, Mr. Zucco," he said, "you've got to understand just where you are and what you're up against. Here, have some coffee, and I'll explain to you."

"There's no time—"

"You don't want to get caught, do you?"

Moving slowly, while Zucco fiddled with the gun, Kit poured him a cup of coffee. Then he got from the wood-box an old piece of wrapping paper, and from a shelf a stubby pencil. He sat down next to Zucco, spreading the paper on the table.

"I'll draw you a map. Here's Pinedale. Now, south-west of Pinedale runs the Pinion Mountain range. We're on the side of it, here. It runs for miles. It's high.

"Now you took Route 168 out of Pinedale. It runs up through a narrow valley and turns a bit right, like this— and crosses the Pinion range at Harper's Pass, about fifty miles from Pinedale. You see, it heads right into the range. There are mountain spurs on both sides. None of these sideroads go anywhere. They just lead up to places like

"Kid, I've got to get out—I've got to get away."

this one, and then come to a dead end. When you don't show up at the pass, the police will know you turned up one of these sideroads. They'll search them, one by one, until they find your car. Sooner or later—"

"O.K., O.K.," said Zucco. "So what do we do?"

"Like I said. We go up over the mountain."

Kit drew another line on the map. "On the other side of the range," he said, "there's a main highway running from south-west to north-east. Nobody would ever dream of looking for you over there. And there are through buses on that road. There's a bus stop by an old mine. We go up over the top and down to that bus stop."

"But—"

"There are some old clothes of Dad's in the cupboard that will fit you well enough," Kit said. "Of course, you can't wear his shoes, but you'd better get into some slacks and a shirt of his. You'd look funny at that old mine getting into a bus with those city clothes of yours, especially after the broadcast this morning. If I were you, I'd burn them up in the stove."

"But—"

"Think it over."

"You sit right where you are," commanded Zucco. Taking his gun with him, he rummaged in the cupboard. He swore as he rammed his brown checked suit into the stove. He swore some more as he put on an old pair of khaki slacks, a dirty flannel shirt, and a torn hat.

"That's better," Kit said. "Now, drive your car on past my jeep and right into that thicket of young pines. They might hunt for a week before they'd find it there."

"You drive it. I'll sit in the back seat."

Kit did. Behind him was Zucco, with the gun.

When they got back to the shack, Zucco was carrying a canvas bag labelled PINEDALE BANK. Kit did not have to ask what was in it.

Kit put a big hunk of cheese, a loaf of bread, and a canteen of water in a light knapsack.

"What's that for?" asked Zucco.

"Grub. It's all I've got, and it's all we'll get to eat for the rest of the day. We'll be lucky if we get down to that other road by dark. You'd better put that moneybag in my pack and let me carry it. It'll get in your way."

Zucco laughed nastily.

"Fat chance! The dough and the gun stay with me—*you* go ahead."

"Naturally I'll go ahead," Kit said politely, "because you don't know where to go."

They started along a faintly traced zigzag path at the back of the shack. Suddenly Kit stopped. "There's one thing that worries me, Mr. Zucco," he said. "Tell me—have you ever climbed a big mountain?"

"No, why?"

"I'm just wondering whether you can make it."

"What do you mean!"

"Well, it's a long way up and it isn't like walking on a trail. There *isn't* any trail. We've got to crash through the brush, and we've got to do some rough climbing on the rocks. If you're not used to mountains—"

"So what's a mountain?" Zucco gestured his contempt for mountains. "Listen, kid," he said, "I could break you in two with one hand. You think they call me the Muscle just for fun? Now get going."

He was indeed a big brute of a man, thought Kit: thick-shouldered, deep-chested, with the arms of a prize fighter and the legs of a wrestler. Big—heavy. He would weigh, Kit guessed, at least fourteen stone.

"O.K.," agreed Kit. "Here we go."

And he turned uphill, off the path, and struck straight up the mountainside.

It was a thicket of brambles and scrub, that first stretch. Branches snagged them. Stumps scratched them. Loose stones tripped them up on the steep slope. Kit squeezed up and through. Zucco, gun in one hand and moneybag in the other, kept getting caught like a fly in a web.

"Hey, wait for me!" he yelled.

The gun, Kit noticed, had gone into his pocket. Zucco

now had one free hand to grab with. Even so, he kept slipping and sliding.

"Don't go so fast!" he called.

At the end of an hour, Zucco was panting hard. Sweat was running down his face.

"We'll take a rest," he said.

"We just can't, Mr. Zucco, if we're going to make it."

Then they entered the old burn. Fire had gone through there years before and killed the timber. The dead trees had fallen—and a new crop of pines had sprouted up. They were now about twenty-five feet tall, standing very thick, with interlaced branches extending at shoulder height. The ground was covered with tall ferns—and concealed beneath them, lying like jackstraws in all directions, were the still-undecayed trunks of the fallen trees.

The place was a succession of booby traps. Zucco kept falling down. He fell forwards, backwards, and sideways. His face was a mass of scratches. Sometimes, when he fell, the moneybag would go flying off into the ferns, and he would have to make a frantic search for it.

"Why don't you tie that bag round your neck?" suggested Kit. Zucco did.

Up, always up, and rather steeply they went, until finally they came upon a brook that leapt down over mossy rocks. Zucco drank deeply and washed his hot face.

"How much farther?" he asked.

"Mr. Zucco, you don't seem to realize that this is a big mountain. We'd better keep going."

And Kit started right up the bed of the roaring brook.

"That way?"

"Yes," Kit explained, "we have to go up the brook, because that's the only way up this part of the mountain. To the right there's an impassable cliff, and to the left there's an overhang."

Zucco groaned and followed.

It became obvious at once that Zucco had never balanced himself upon the irregular stones of a creek bed. He teetered, fell, and was soon splashed from head to foot.

"Can't you push on a little faster, Mr. Zucco?" asked Kit.

Then they came to a stretch that was really steep. The creek slid down a shale slope, slippery with slime, with nothing to hold on to except the tips of willow branches. Kit scrambled up, and from the top called down impatiently.

Three times Zucco almost made it to the top—and three times he and his moneybag cascaded to the bottom.

"We're losing precious minutes, Mr. Zucco," Kit complained. On the fourth try Zucco reached the top of the shale. He lay flat on his belly in the bed of the brook and tried to get back his breath.

"Let's be on our way," insisted Kit. "It's getting late."

A few moments later they emerged upon a vast slope of broken rock. They were above the timber line. Looking out from the side of the mountain, towards the valley, Pinedale was just a blob on a plain of yellow and blue.

"Up there," said Kit, "is where we're going."

Zucco looked up—and up and up. The green gave way to the grey, and there were cliffs and great outcropping masses of rocks, and here and there little pockets of snow. They were at the foot of a broken rock slope beneath a vertical rampart.

"We go up to the base of the cliff," Kit said.

Rocks with sharp, uneven edges. Rocks that were loose and turned when one stepped on them. And steeper than a gangway. Slip, tumble, scrabble on all fours. Zucco's breath came in great gasps. His windpipe was getting raw. The sun burnt fiercely.

"Can't you step on it a little?" asked Kit. "I'm really getting worried."

They reached the foot of the cliff. There was a tiny shady patch of almost level land—and Zucco flung himself upon it.

"Well," Kit said cheerfully, "let's rest here a bit and have lunch. We'll need to stoke up. We've got a hard climb just ahead of us."

78

He opened the knapsack and took out the bread, cheese, and canteen. He handed the canteen to Zucco. "Drink plenty of water," he advised him. Zucco did.

"Nothing like cheese to keep you going on a climb," Kit observed.

"I'm not hungry," Zucco said.

"Hungry or not, you'd better eat. You'll need it. Plenty of bread too."

"It's awful dry."

"Wash it down with water. Get some food into you!"

With urging, Zucco took in a considerable load of cheese, bread, and water.

"O.K.," Kit said. "Now let's go."

They skirted the base of the cliff, to the left, until they came to a fissure that was little less than vertical.

"Here's where we go up," Kit announced. "There are good handholds and footholds, but you have to watch your step."

"It's the only way up this part of the mountain," said Kit.

It was as steep as a ladder. One look told Zucco that it could not be climbed. But there was the boy, above him.

They began working their way up. The moneybag flapping from Zucco's neck caught on the rocks and got in the way of his hands.

"Hey!" he yelled. "Put this damn thing in your pack!" And he handed it up to Kit.

It was work, gruelling work, that rock climb. Zucco could hardly make his muscles obey. There was, too, inside him, a feeling that something was very wrong indeed.

"I've got to stop for a while!" he called to Kit.

He stopped—and looked down. Looked down, and screamed. For he was falling off the mountain! He pressed himself against it. He held on to the rocks with an iron grip.

"Help!" he yelled. "I can't hang on!"

Kit came back down to him.

"You're all right," he said. "Just don't look down. Now, put your left foot here—"

"No, no!"

"And your right hand here—"

"No, I can't!"

It took five minutes to persuade Zucco to loosen one hand. Kit literally put Zucco's hands and feet in the right places. Zucco was trembling. He babbled incessantly that he couldn't, he couldn't, he couldn't.

"Just one more tricky place, and we will be on a ridge," Kit said. They managed it—and came out on the top of a broken-rock hogback, not more than five feet wide. On both sides it dropped off, off, off.

Zucco looked down to the right, he looked down to the left, and with a groan he lay down and threw up cheese, bread, and water for a long time.

"That's too bad," said Kit.

After a while Zucco sat up. "I'm not going any farther," he said.

Kit looked out over the vast panoramas that unfolded on both sides of the ridge—wave after wave of spurs from the main range, which topped them to the north-east.

"It gets awfully cold up here at night," he remarked.

No response.

"After the fourth day you'll get pretty hungry—"

"Shut up!"

After a moment Kit started up the narrow hogback.

"Hey, don't leave me!" There was panic in that voice.

"Mr. Zucco," Kit said, "if you want to stay up here and die slowly all by yourself, that's your business. But I want to get down off this mountain before it gets dark." And again he headed up the hogback.

"Stop right where you are!"

Kit turned. Zucco had his gun out.

"Now, Mr. Zucco!" Kit protested. "Does that make any sense? If you shoot me you can never find your way down."

Zucco put the gun back into his pocket.

He could not walk; he crawled, mumbling, gasping, swearing. Thus, after a long time they came to the spot where the hogback joined the main divide. Here all was rock, bare rock.

"Climbing's about over," Kit called out cheerfully. "Come up here and take a look down the other side."

Zucco wriggled his way up the final slope and looked over the edge. He looked down, straight down, two thousand feet. The drop-off was as vertical as the side of a building.

And, for Zucco, the earth began to turn. It whirled slowly round and round, oscillating meanwhile up and down. Valleys rose, peaks sank, in rotation. And Zucco sprawled grotesquely, in the grip of wave after wave of the most horrible nausea.

"We walk along the edge of this drop-off for a way," Kit began.

"Oh no!"

"It's easy. Almost level. Then we cross the rockslide. Beyond it one short push up, and then we're over the hump and down we go to the other road."

But Zucco did not move. He was muttering. "Mary,

81

As Kit showed him how, Zucco gazed and trembled.

Mother of God, save me," Kit heard. And incoherent mumbling about people and places. "I *had* to shoot them." Spasms of tears and retching.

Kit saw the gun sticking half out of Zucco's pocket. He slipped it out and put it in his own. He helped Zucco to his feet. "Hang on to me," he said.

The path was almost like a city pavement, about four feet wide, between the drop-off on the left and a towering straight-up cliff on the right. The sun was getting low in the west when they rounded a corner of a high buttress and came to a steep smooth slope surmounted by walls of rock that rose high towards the sky.

"That's the top of the main peak up there," Kit explained. "We have to go round it. To do that we have to cross this rockslide. Do you know about rockslides?"

But Zucco was sitting down, eyes closed. Kit shook him and slapped his face. "Come on!" he said, and there was a most peculiar expression on his face as he said it. "You've got to listen to me. This rockslide is formed by the stones that fall off the big cliffs above it. It goes all the way down the side of the mountain. See?"

He pointed. As far down as the eye would carry, the slide extended, down, down, past side escarpments, down and through the timber, down to where its bottom was lost in mistiness.

"The minute anything lands on that rockslide it starts to move. If you just stand in it, it moves and you move with it—and that starts a rock avalanche and you get caught in it. Understand?"

Zucco nodded in an idiotic sort of way.

"So to cross a rockslide, you have to run—and you have to lift your knees way up high. You can't stand still. Get the idea?"

Zucco said nothing.

"All right; now watch me, and do what I do. It's only about a hundred feet across, this high up. It's easy, if you do it right."

And Kit headed across the slide. He ran, bringing his

knees up high. With each step the stones and gravel started to slide—but with each step, running, he got his foot out again before the slide could gain momentum. In no time at all he was across.

"Now *you* do it."

Zucco braced himself, tested the edge of the slide with a trembling foot and stepped out into it.

"Run!" yelled Kit. "Bring your knees up high!"

But Zucco did not run. The movement of the gravel, every time he put his foot in it, seemed to paralyse him. With each step he took, he sank deeper.

About a third of the way across he tried in vain to free a leg—and he stood still. He began to move downhill. The whole hillside began to tremble; the whole slide began to move.

Deeper and deeper Zucco sank; faster and faster down he went. The growing rumble turned into a roar. There was one last scream from Zucco—and then the avalanche, gathering momentum and picking up rocks half as big as a house, thundered on down into the valley far below.

Kit dusted his hands, as if to rid them of dirt. He hurried on a bit, turned sharply down a short, steep slope and came to the well-beaten trail that led to the shack. He went down it at a dogtrot. When he got near the shack, in the dusk, he slowed and began to whistle a loud tune. He kept his eyes on the alert.

Sure enough, when he was still just round the corner from the shack, a loud voice yelled, "Come out with your hands up!"

Kit did—and at the clearing was confronted by three state policemen with levelled guns. So they had found Zucco's car.

"Oh, it's you," one said. "We thought so, but we weren't taking any chances. Where's Zucco?"

"He's up on the mountain under about a thousand tons of rock," answered Kit. "What I need is some coffee."

Until he had started the fire and boiled a pot, he would not say a word. Then, with steaming cups before them,

"Here's his gun and here's the 11,000 dollars."

the four sat round the table in the shack.

In detail, and interrupted by many questions, Kit recounted everything that had happened that day. . . .

"Well I'll be damned," finally said the big policeman with the black moustache. "But how did you come to think of it?"

"Chicago," answered Kit. "I reckoned anybody who'd lived at lake level all his life would be likely to get the mountain sickness. I got out of him that he'd never been on a big mountain. I felt sure that if I could just get him up high enough—"

"The idea of taking him up through the old burn and the creek bed and the chimney climb, and the hogback!" exclaimed the little policeman with the blue eyes. "When all the time there was a trail—"

"Well," explained Kit, "I reckoned I'd better condition him. I had to get him sick and all tired out, or he *might* have got across the rockslide."

"What gets me," said the big one, "is the way you dreamed up that cock-and-bull story about a road on the other side and a bus stop at an old mine. What if he *knew* there wasn't any such road? What if he knew there was nothing in that direction but wilderness, for miles and miles?"

"It was a chance I had to take. There wasn't much time, and I had to think of something that would get him *up* there."

"Up the rockslide?"

Kit nodded.

"That's what you were aiming for, from the start?"

Kit said nothing.

"Well, let's go," said the big officer. "We'd better get down to a phone and turn in a report. Coming down with us, Kit?"

Kit shook his head.

"O.K. We'll be back in the morning."

The police got into their car.

"Wait a minute!" called Kit from the shack doorway. "Here's his gun—and here's the eleven thousand dollars." He tossed them out.

"Well I'll be double damned," said the big officer. He got out of the car and came back to Kit. "Boy," he said, "you ought to be mighty proud of this day's work." And he put his arm round Kit's shoulders.

"Somehow," Kit said, and his voice almost broke, "somehow I can't feel that way."

"He would have killed you."

"I know."

The big policeman shrugged—and then off they all went, down the road.

Kit stood in the doorway of the shack, looking down, way down, across the valley. And then he looked at the mountain—his mountain. The moon was just rising over the pines.

I ought to cook supper, he thought. But somehow he was not hungry. He sat down, with his head in his hands.

"I warned him," he said finally, aloud. "I told him to run, and to lift his knees up high."

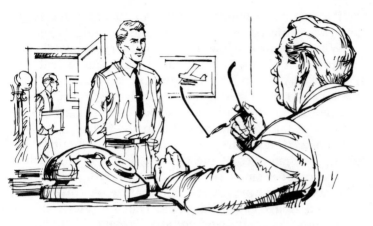

The Case of the
Submerged Aircraft

CAPTAIN W. E. JOHNS

BIGGLES TOOK a second glance at the expression on the face of his chief, Air Commodore Raymond of the Special Air Police at Scotland Yard, as, in response to an order, he walked into the headquarters office.

"Why are you looking at me like that?" inquired the Air Commodore.

Biggles smiled. "I was wondering why *you* were looking like that."

"Sit down and I'll tell you. What would you say if I told you there is reason to believe that an aeroplane is standing on the bottom of a Highland loch?"

"I hope the pilot finds it comfortable," returned Biggles evenly. "What is this? Has some crank designed an aircraft for underwater aviation?"

"It may not turn out to be funny," said the Air Commodore, seriously. "I want you to fly up to confirm the report."

"Who told you about this, sir?"

"I've just had a phone call from an official of the Highland Hydro-Electric Board. He thought we'd like to know."

"What type of machine is this—military or civil?"

"He doesn't know. That's what I want you to find out. If it's an R.A.F. type the Air Ministry can take over. This is what I'm told. There is, in the north-west corner of the Cairngorms, a sheet of water called Lochnaglash. As a matter of detail, and this should help you to find it, it is the lowest of a string of three lochs deep in the mountains, each taking the spill-over of the one above it. Lochnaglash is the source of a small river called the Glash, which is a tributary of the Spey, twelve miles away. A rough track leads to a village called Balashlin. That's fourteen miles."

"Sounds like pretty wild country," remarked Biggles.

"It is. For some months of the year snow makes the place inaccessible. The land was once a deer forest. But deer-stalking is now out of fashion, and with the death of the laird the place came into the market. It was bought by the Forestry Commission who have made some experimental plantings but are no longer working there. Apparently the hydro-electric people have had an eye on the water. The lochs are fed by snow melting on the high tops. Anyway, they sent a man up to check the height of the water at summer level. As a result of the recent drought he found the water exceptionally low. Showing above the surface is an object that looks like the top of an aeroplane rudder. There's no question of it being a tree because there are no trees near except the small stuff planted by the Forestry people and they're some distance away."

"If it is a machine it must have been there for some time," stated Biggles. "It must be years since we had a record of an aircraft disappearing without trace."

The Air Commodore nodded. "It could be a relic of the war. But the easiest way to settle the matter is for you to fly up and have a look. I suggest you take the Otter and land on the loch; otherwise you'd have to get a boat from somewhere to reach the object. There isn't one on the spot, which is why the hydro-electric man could do nothing there."

"Okay, sir." Biggles looked at his watch. "I'll get off right away while the weather's fine. The Cairngorms, with cloud about, are no place for low flying. It shouldn't take us long to get this sorted out."

Biggles returned to his own office, where his police pilots were waiting.

"What's the drill?" asked Ginger.

Biggles grinned. "The Loch Ness monster, sick of being ridiculed, has popped up in a place called Lochnaglash. It looks like an aircraft. We're flying up in the Otter to catch it by the tail. We shall need the large-scale map of Banff-shire and, I suppose, our bathing costumes. And Ginger, you might bring along the file on post-war machines that have disappeared, for possible identification."

"How long is this job going to take?" asked Algy.

"It shouldn't take long—why?"

"Hadn't we better take something to eat in case we get stuck there for the night?"

"Yes," agreed Biggles. "There's nothing to be had on the spot. Let's get mobile. I'll tell you what I know about this business on the way up."

Four hours later, in clear weather, the Otter, an amphibious aircraft on the establishment of the Air Police, was losing height as it circled over the objective, which had not been difficult to find. But it was not such an easy matter to get down, on account of the towering hills which held the three lochs in a long narrow valley, with the result that while Lochnaglash had plenty of length it hadn't much width. In fact, it was only after three attempts to get down had failed that Biggles succeeded by flying through the only break, a narrow funnel through which the overflow of the lochs escaped during the spring thaw, to form a minor tributary of the Spey.

Even before the keel had kissed the water, dark and sinister even under a summer sky, Ginger could see the object that had brought them to the spot. It was the only mark to break the unruffled surface, on which the surrounding hills were reflected with the faithfulness of a

Their objective was easy to find,

mirror. Only a few inches of the object showed, some fifty yards or so from a strip of detritus, the only feature that bore any resemblance to a beach. For the rest, the heather-clad slopes of the hills, with forbidding outcrops of rock, fell sheer into the water. A white streak showed where a sunless corrie still held its snow. There was not a soul, or a living creature, in sight, except an eagle, high overhead. Nor was there a tree, although a small clump of shrubby birch had managed to gain a foothold at one end of the beach. In a word, it was a typically remote Highland scene.

"A dismal sort of place to finish up," remarked Bertie.

"About as wild a spot as you'd find," returned Biggles, taxi-ing on slowly towards the mark which Ginger had pointed out. "If it's like this in summer think what it must be like in the winter, with snow everywhere and the loch a sheet of ice."

"That's an aircraft rudder all right," asserted Algy, as they approached the object. "Who on earth could have

90

ot such an easy matter to get down.

tried to get down here?"

"We should soon know," answered Biggles as, with the Otter edging towards the mark, he switched off. "Stand by with the anchor, Ginger, as we come alongside. The water can't be deep or nothing would show above the surface."

"I'd say that rudder belongs to a Gipsy Moth," said Algy.

"Then it has probably been here for a long time," replied Biggles. "De Havillands must have made hundreds of Gipsys, but you don't see so many about nowadays."

The Otter drifted nearer and came silently to rest. When it was so close to the rudder that Ginger could have touched it he lowered the anchor, slowly, so as not to disturb the water.

They all leaned over the side to wait for the ripples to settle down, but even before this occurred the shape of an aircraft could be seen clearly through the crystal water. It appeared to be on even keel but slightly down by the nose, for which reason the tail unit was the only part to break the surface. The upper side of the top plane was about six feet down. The machine stood in a position parallel with the beach on a slightly shelving bottom of broken rock.

"It's a Gipsy," said Biggles definitely. "I fancy this is an old story."

There was silence for a minute as they continued to stare down. "There's no one in it," said Ginger. "I'm pretty sure both seats are empty."

"Thank goodness for that," muttered Bertie. "Corpses give me the willies."

"Can anyone make out the identification letters?" inquired Biggles. Not even when the water was dead still could the letters be seen, this being due, apparently, to a slight coating of silt, or weed.

"The pilot, whoever he was, must have been out of his mind to try to get down here," declared Bertie.

"Not necessarily," returned Biggles.

"You think it was an accident?"

"One would assume that, but I'm by no means sure."

"What do you mean?" queried Ginger.

"Let's look at it like this," suggested Biggles. "Had that machine gone in out of control surely it would have broken up when it hit the water. In such cases the wings are buckled, if not actually torn off at the roots; yet as you can see for yourselves, this aircraft is not only intact but is on even keel. Again, had the machine crashed there would have been a body in at least one of the seats. There seems to be something unnatural about this."

"The pilot, with engine trouble, might have been making for that bit of a beach and undershot," offered Ginger.

"In which case the nose would be pointing to the beach. I doubt if he'd see that beach from up topsides, anyway. Put yourself in the pilot's position. You're in trouble. Which would you choose, to ditch yourself miles from anywhere or take a chance on dry land, even if that meant a crack-up?"

"I'd go for the heather."

"So would I," asserted Biggles. "Remember the job I had to get down even with a machine in good order. The way I came was the only way in, but I wouldn't care to try it with a groggy engine."

"But half a mo', old boy," protested Bertie. "The alternative to what you're saying is, the pilot put the machine here *deliberately*. Does that make sense?"

"No," admitted Biggles. "But neither do a lot of things that happen. I can't believe this machine crashed, by which I mean hit the water hard. The pilot could of course have done a belly-flop. But why here, knowing he'd have to swim for it? I have a feeling this machine came here for a definite purpose, although what that could be I haven't a clue. I can see only one possible alternative. This might have happened in the winter, when the loch was ice-bound. When the ice melted the machine would go down quietly in the position in which we now see it. There are two arguments against that. The pilot would have to know the loch was frozen over, and secondly, having got down, would he just walk away and abandon the machine without reporting it?"

"In winter conditions it wouldn't be possible to get a rescue party here," put in Algy. "He might have died from exposure trying to reach help."

"In which case the body should have been found when the snow went. The Forestry people have been working about here, don't forget, testing the soil."

"He might have been drowned," put in Ginger.

"Even so the body would come to the surface. He wasn't trapped in the cockpit. But why are we wasting time guessing? How many Gipsy Moths have you in that file of missing machines, Ginger? I saw you going through it on the way up."

"I can only recall three," answered Ginger, producing the file. "One went west on a flight to the Cape. Another, belonging to a planter flying back to Malaya, either went down in the Channel or disappeared somewhere in Europe."

"Neither of those would come this way. Carry on."

"The other was the case of that man whom the police wanted to interview in connexion with a murder. A fellow named Alva Murray, an ex-commando, was thought to have shot his wife. He took off in a Gipsy and was never seen again. We helped in the search for him. You decided he'd found a hideout on the Continent."

Biggles frowned. "I remember that business. It must have been seven or eight years ago. It was in June, so we can forget the ice theory should this turn out to be the machine. If ever there was a deliberately planned job that was it. Murray joined a flying club to get his 'A' licence—as he said. Even then he must have known what he was going to do because while he was under instruction he drew all his money from the bank, about four thousand pounds, a few hundreds at a time. Then he shot his wife, took off in a club machine and vanished. It turned out he was a jealous type and thought she'd been playing him up. At least, that was what it looked like. What were the registration letters?"

"GB-XKL."

Biggles got up. "This could be it. If it is, it's no wonder we never found it. But we'll soon settle that. A man planning to disappear could hardly find a better place, or devise a more cunning method. I'll go down. The sides of the fuselage, being vertical, should be clear of muck."

He got into his bathing costume, lowered himself gently into the water and swam down. For half a minute the others could see him working his way along the side of the fuselage; then he shot to the surface.

"Brr. That water's cold!" he exclaimed, as he climbed back on board. "No matter. At last we know where GB-XKL ended its career. But that's still a long way from knowing where Murray finished up. While I'm getting my togs on run the machine up on the beach. We'll stretch our legs and eat a sandwich while we think about this."

In a few minutes they were sitting on dry stones, in warm sunshine. "Are we going to try to haul the Gipsy ashore?"

asked Ginger.

"Not for the moment," decided Biggles. "It's better where it is."

"Why?"

"I'm assuming Murray is still alive. If this story gets out he'll hear about it and take fright. After all this time he must think he's sitting pretty. If he learns that the machine has been found he'll be more difficult to find than he may be at present. By thunder! He must have brains, and nerve, to work out a scheme like this."

"Then you think he ditched the machine here deliberately?" questioned Bertie.

"If you remember, I suspected someone had done just that before we knew who it was," returned Biggles. "Everything pointed to that. But one or two things still puzzle me. Murray must have known exactly what he was going to do, in which case he would have made the necessary prepara-

First, he had to identify the sunken plane.

tions. That implies that he knew all about this place—the beach, the depth of the water, and so on. Obviously, he had been here before. His name tells us he was a Scot so he may have come from these parts. The ambition of every Highlander who leaves home is to get back to his beloved heather. It's in the blood. Murray may have come home."

"These preparations you talk about," put in Ginger. "I don't see that he would have to make any. Having ditched the machine all he had to do was swim ashore."

"He had to get other things ashore beside himself. If he intended to lie low for a while he'd need food. He'd want to dry his clothes. He also had a little matter of four thousand pounds with him. He'd have more sense than to go straight to the village, knowing that in these parts the arrival of a stranger is a subject for conversation and conjecture." Biggles got up and walked towards the clump of birch.

"What are you going to do?" asked Algy.

"I'm going to see if Murray left behind any signs of his arrival here. He wouldn't leave anything on the beach and there aren't many hiding places."

They all walked to the bushes.

Almost at once they came upon a spot where, long ago, a fire had been lighted.

"I'd say that's where he dried his clothes," remarked Biggles. "Hello! What's this?" Stooping, he lifted from the tangle of encroaching heather a length of window cord. As he pulled on it more and more came to light until there must have been fifty yards of it. At the end was an object so strange that it produced ejaculations of astonishment from all except Biggles. It was the deflated remains of a pair of water-wings, sometimes used for swimming instruction.

"So he couldn't swim," said Ginger.

"As a commando he'd have to be able to swim," reminded Biggles. "But he had other things to get ashore beside himself. A kit-bag, for instance. I've never tried swimming with one but I imagine it would be awkward.

Don't forget he had four thousand in notes. He wouldn't want to get them soaking wet. I'd say these wings kept his luggage afloat while he hauled it ashore with the cord. I told you this chap had his scheme cut and dried. If he put the machine down carefully it wouldn't sink at once. He'd have time to take off some of his clothes and put them in a bag brought for the purpose. All he had to do then was inflate the wings, tie them on, swim ashore with the cord and pull his luggage after him. Well, this answers one question. All we have to do now is follow his trail, but after all this time that won't be easy. Let's go back."

Biggles thrust the cord into the heather where he had found it and led the way back to the machine.

"You'll never catch up with him now," asserted Algy. "This chap was too smart to leave a trail."

"Don't you believe it," argued Biggles. "Even the smartest murderers usually make one slip. This chap has already made one by leaving that cord there. No doubt he was in a hurry to get away."

"It was thousands to one against anyone finding it," said Ginger.

"That may be what he thought, but as you see, a thousand to one chance can come off. The trouble with these rural jobs is, there's no one on the spot to question," concluded Biggles, as, seated on the stones, they finished their meal with biscuits and cheese and coffee from the thermos.

"There's someone coming now," observed Ginger.

They all looked up. Striding down a deer track from the hill behind them came a powerfully built man, black-bearded, wearing a kilt of Lovat tweed, carrying in his hand a Highland *cromach*—a long, strong, ash stick with a crook at the end, an instrument that serves many useful purposes in such country. On his head he wore a Laggan bonnet, sometimes called a deer-stalker. With the handle of a *skean-dhu*, the Highland name for a dagger, showing above the top of his stocking, where it is usually carried, he fitted into the scene perfectly.

97

"I wonder what he's doing here," said Biggles. "He doesn't look like a Forestry worker. Might be a shepherd looking for lost sheep—no, if he was a shepherd he'd have a dog. So he would if he was a gamekeeper."

The man came up. Biggles spoke. "Good morning, Mr.—"

"Macrae's the name. I saw the plane circling and came to see what ye were at."

"What did you think we might be doing?"

"I thought ye might be after the eagles' eggs."

Biggles smiled faintly. "I'd never have thought of that. Do people come after eagles' eggs?"

"Aye, they do that, with yon devils of collectors in London paying five pounds a time, and up to fifty pound for a clutch."

"So you take care of the eagles," prompted Biggles.

"Aye. For the Scottish Bird Protection Society."

"An interesting job. How long have you been doing that?"

"Five years."

"Do you live here all the year round?"

"Aye."

"How do you manage in the winter?"

"I manage fine."

"Then you have a house here?"

Macrae pointed with his stick. "I have a wee place doon the glen. In the old days it was the stalker's hoose."

"It must be the only house this side of Balashlin."

"Aye. It is."

"What about the big place I noticed over there, standing in some trees, as I flew over?" Biggles pointed.

"Och, ye mean the old lodge. It's a ruin. The laird didna do a thing about it, tho' they say he should have done."

"Why, if there's no more deer-stalking?"

"He had money from the Government to put it right. They took it over in the war."

"For what purpose?"

"They put some troops in, and they knocked the place

98

"I thought ye might be after the eagles' eggs."

to pieces like they always do."

"What troops did they put in?"

"I couldna tell ye that. But you're free with your questions, mon. What might ye be doing here?"

"As you see, having a picnic. I imagine it's the first time a plane has landed on the loch."

"Aye. I'd think that. Ah weel. I'll awa' an' look to me nests. Good dee to ye."

"Good morning, Mr. Macrae. We shan't touch your eagles."

"I'll be after ye if you do. They're protected by law, ye ken." The man strode off at the long, ground-covering gait of a man born in the hills.

"Well, old boy, there's one man not likely to die in a road accident," remarked Bertie. Biggles lit a cigarette.

"What do we do next—go home?" queried Ginger.

"No."

"But there's nothing else we can do here."

"There's one thing I'm going to do. I want to cast an

99

eye over this empty lodge."

"Then let's get on with it."

"Not yet."

"Why?"

"Because that chap on the hill will be watching us. I don't want word to get around that we're poking about here."

"You think Murray might still be in the district?"

"He might."

Algy stepped in. "But what are you expecting to find at the lodge?"

"According to Macrae the Government requisitioned it during the war. They put troops in it. I want to know what troops they were."

"What troops have you in mind?" inquired Ginger.

"The place might have been a Commando Training School," returned Biggles. "I don't say it was, but there were some in the Highlands in the war. If I'm right it would give us a line on how Murray knew about the loch. He was a commando. We'll wander round presently. There's no point in going home only to come back again tomorrow. Fetch the torch from the machine, Ginger. We may need it."

They waited until the sun sank behind the hills, throwing the valley into gloom, and then set off at a brisk pace.

It was a long walk over hard going, and Ginger was thankful when the stand of Scots pines that hid the lodge loomed darkly against the sky.

The once smart lodge, now silent and dilapidated, with rotting hutments accompanying it to ruin, presented a depressing spectacle in an atmosphere of melancholy which the interior, when Biggles opened the door and went in, did nothing to dispel. All furniture had been removed. Some foolscap sheets of type-written matter hung from the wall in the empty hall.

Biggles walked over. "Number Seven Commando Training unit. Daily Routine Orders," he read aloud. Turning to face the others he went on. "So now we know. Murray

100

was stationed here during the war. That's how he knew of the place. What a hide-out! I'd say he came back here."

Followed by the others Biggles went down a corridor to the kitchen. A cheap frying pan and kettle were rusting on the stove. An enamel plate, with a knife and fork on it, were in the sink. He opened the back door and went out. In a corner was a heap of brown, long-dead heather. He kicked away some of it to expose a pile of empty cans. "These weren't army rations," he said, picking up a sardine tin. "Yes," he went on. "This was Murray's objective when he ditched his aircraft."

"Is there any reason why he shouldn't still be here?" asked Ginger, looking slightly alarmed.

"Plenty of reasons, one of which being the Forestry Commission people have been here." He pointed to a row of long-handled brushes: "There is some of their fire-fighting equipment. No. Murray only came here while the hue and cry was on, long enough perhaps for him to change his appearance. He couldn't bring a lot of food. Enough to last him a week or two at the outside. Then he'd have to go where some was available, to lay in a fresh stock."

"So it's a question of where did he go from here," said Ginger.

"Exactly."

"There might still be fingerprints on the handle of that frying pan," observed Algy.

"Even if they turned out to be his they wouldn't help us to find him. We needn't bother with that at this juncture."

"What are you going to do?"

"We'll go back to the machine and spend the night in the cabin. In the morning we'll have a look round. Murray might not be far away."

The walk back to the loch, in the dark, was tiring work, and would have been dangerous had they not had the advantage of a moon, nearly full. As they trudged along the stony beach towards the machine suddenly Ginger stopped, gazing out across the star-reflecting water.

"Can you see what I can't see?" he exclaimed, in a

puzzled voice.

"What can't you see?" asked Algy.

"The rudder."

"Well, blow me down!" muttered Bertie. "The water must be rising."

"Either that or Biggles caused the machine to move when he went down to it," opined Algy, casually.

"That could have happened," agreed Biggles. He walked on towards the bushes.

"Where are you going?" asked Ginger.

"I want to have another look at that cord," replied Biggles. "Give me the torch." He went on alone, but was soon back.

"That's enough for today," he said. "Let's turn in."

The next day dawned with the weather still clear and fine.

"Where do we start looking for Murray?" asked Ginger.

Biggles, who had been somewhat preoccupied, answered: "For a start I'm going down the glen to have another word with Macrae. His cottage will be by the river so it shouldn't be hard to find."

Presently they set off, taking an old deer track that skirted the loch. This soon brought them to a rock shelf over which a trickle of water spilled to form the little river Glash. Following the stream, sparkling in the sunshine, a walk of twenty minutes revealed, a little way ahead, a stone cottage nestling in a stand of wind-warped pine and silver birch. Beyond it ran a cart track, following the river. Macrae, apparently having seen them coming, was waiting, hands on hips.

"What can I do for ye?" he greeted.

"You can answer some questions," returned Biggles. "You say your name is Macrae?"

"That's richt."

"We are police officers," stated Biggles. "I have reason to believe you are the Alva Murray who we have been anxious to interview in connexion with the murder of his wife seven years ago. I must warn you that anything you say—"

Biggles got no farther. Never did a man move faster than the one who called himself Macrae. In a flash he had whipped up his *skean-dhu*. With this in his hand he backed towards the house. "Don't come near me," he growled. "Ye'll no tak me alive."

"Don't be a fool, Murray," said Biggles curtly. "That sort of talk won't help you."

Murray dashed into the house and slammed the door.

"Watch out!" cried Ginger urgently, as a window was opened and the barrels of a twelve-bore appeared.

They dashed to the nearest cover, a dilapidated venison larder. The gun blazed, shot spattering against the wall of the building.

"If we try to get to that house someone will be killed," said Biggles calmly. "I should have taken into account that we're dealing with a man who has had commando training. He can't get away and he must know it; but being guilty of murder he won't care who else he kills. I was prepared for trouble, but not a twelve-bore."

"What are we going to do?" asked Algy, anxiously. "It would be suicide to face that gun."

"He's armed and resisting arrest," Bertie pointed out. "We should be justified in using our guns."

"I'd rather not," said Biggles. "There's only one thing to do. We shall have to fetch help. Algy, go back to the machine. Fly south until you can contact the Yard on the high-frequency. Tell the chief what's happened and ask him to notify the county police. Make it snappy."

Algy ran off. The others settled down to wait, and watch.

The day wore on. The sun climbed over its zenith. High overhead an eagle soared on rigid wings. From time to time a cock grouse croaked a warning to his kind.

Late in the afternoon the gun crashed again, showing that Murray was still within.

"Who's he shooting at?" queried Bertie.

"Just letting us know he's still about, I imagine."

"I can hear a vehicle coming up the track," said Ginger.

Presently it appeared. From a jeep stepped four police officers, one an inspector.

"Watch your step," called Biggles.

The inspector ignored the warning. He walked straight to the door of the house. "Come out of that, Murray," he shouted. "Let's have no nonsense."

Finding the door locked he walked round the house and looked in a window. Then, turning, he beckoned.

Biggles and his party joined him at the window. Inside, on the floor, in a crumpled heap lay Murray, the gun beside him.

Biggles' eyes opened wide. "We didn't do that," he told the inspector. "He must have shot himself. We heard a shot."

"Aye, I'd think that," said the inspector, without emotion. "It's the sort of thing I'd expect him to do when he realized he hadn't a chance. He'd choose to die in the heather rather than be hanged in a city gaol."

Biggles, rather pale, shook his head. "Well, there it is. I'll leave this to you, now, Inspector, if you don't mind," he said, glancing up as the Otter roared past on the way to the loch. "You'll find an aeroplane in Lochnaglash, near the beach, the one Murray used to get here. It's hardly worth salvaging but you may need it for evidence. We'll get along. Thanks for your help."

Biggles turned away, and followed by the others walked back to the loch to find the Otter on the beach.

"Thanks," Biggles told Algy. "It's all over. He shot himself. For him, probably, it was the best way out. We'll get along home. I'm afraid I didn't handle that too well."

"What beats me is how you knew Macrae was Murray," said Ginger.

"You saw what I saw, and heard what I heard," stated Biggles. "I told you it needs a very smart murderer never to make a mistake. Murray made several. The first was coming near us, otherwise we might never have known he was there. He couldn't keep away. He saw us coming down

The gun blazed as they dashed to the nearest cover.

and a guilty conscience and anxiety to know what we were doing brought him along. Then he made the fatal blunder of lying. He said his was the only house between here and Balashlin. He only admitted the lodge was there when I said I'd seen it. Then he said he didn't know what troops had been there. A regiment always leaves its mark, so that was asking me to believe that in the years he had lived here he had never been to the place. I was already suspicious when I noticed the black handle of the commando knife which he carried as a *skean-dhu*. That was silly. Maybe he had grown careless over the years."

"And I didn't notice a thing," said Bertie, sadly.

"There was more to it than that," went on Biggles. "I don't think he had realized that the water had dropped so low. Did he hope we hadn't noticed the rudder? He must have seen it as we stood here talking. Any man with nothing to fear would have called attention to it. During the hours we were away at the lodge I fancy he swam out to it and either pushed it under or cut it off. I knew he'd been here."

"How?"

"He was worried about us, and in his natural anxiety wondered if he had left anything about. He remembered that cord and the water-wings. When I went along there last night on our return from the lodge it was to see if they were still there. I wasn't surprised to find they'd gone. Only Murray could have known they were there. That was all I needed to know to confirm my suspicions. Maybe I was silly to confront him as I did but I hoped the shock would cause him to give himself away, as in fact it did. I should have guessed that having been a commando he'd show fight. But let's get home. We can just do it before dark."

Subsequent inquiries revealed that Murray had served at Lochnaglash Lodge during the war. He must have lived there for some time, in hiding, for it was not until some months after his arrival that he had bought the cottage from the owner, paying for it in cash. In the interval he had grown a beard and taken to wearing Highland dress. Then, feeling safe from recognition, he had made periodical visits to the village for stores, making his excuse for living far up the glen that he was an eagle-watcher for the Bird Protection Society, as in fact he was, having offered his services in a voluntary capacity—presumably as a cover.

It was a clever scheme that might never have come to light had it not been for the drought which exposed the tail of the Gipsy. Weather conditions were outside the murderer's calculations, but, as Biggles remarked, on this occasion they proved the old saying that "Murder will out."

The Ghost Tent

SHOWELL STYLES

"GETTING late, Mike!" muttered Colin.

"Pipe down, can't you?" hissed Mike impatiently.

The two boys were crouched uncomfortably in the rushes at the edge of a moorland pool. For miles all round them the wild bleak upland of Thirlby Moss stretched away in bog and heather and shaly ridge, invisible now in a grey mist that was already darkening with the early twilight of a March evening. Mike had the binoculars glued to his eyes, watching the reeds fifty feet away along the curving edge of the pool. Fifty feet was about as far as he could see, for the mist hid everything beyond that.

Something soft and wet and cold floated down through the mist and landed on Colin's nose. A snowflake. He glanced at the intent Mike and decided to say nothing; a keen bird-watcher doesn't like chatter when he's hoping for an identification. And Mike, who had Irish blood in him, was apt to be snappy when disturbed. All the same, they were a long way from their tent and night was coming on—to say nothing of the threat of snow. Colin shifted his cramped position very slightly, causing the camera that was slung round his neck to bump against his chest. Useless to hang on here, he thought. The light's far too bad now for a photo, even if it *does* turn out to be a Red-necked Phalarope. A photo was essential to prove their identification, because a Red-necked Phalarope had never been positively identified in this area. Both boys were members of the British Trust for Ornithology, and it was the rumour that someone had seen a bird resembling the Phalarope on the moor a few days ago that had brought them here, to camp for a wintry weekend in early March and confirm the rumour. If they succeeded—put the identification beyond all doubt—they would have added one more bit to the knowledge of birds and their movements. Almost like making history, thought Colin, shivering as two more large snowflakes settled on his face.

There was a slight movement in the reeds twenty feet away. Mike stiffened, motionless, the binoculars steady in his gloved hands. A small brown-grey bird waded perkily out into the shallow water at the edge of the pool, made a quaint bobbing bow, and waded back out of sight— exactly as though it had come out to receive their applause.

It got no applause from Mike.

"A blighted, ordinary Common Sandpiper!" he exclaimed wrathfully, not bothering to whisper. "Greenish legs, wing-bar, underparts white. Come on—we'll turn it in now."

Colin was glad to agree. They got up stiffly from their "hide" in the rushes and edged their way to more solid ground. The grey mist hemmed them in on every side, revealing only a narrow circle of uneven heather.

"Snow!" Mike said, turning his face upward. "Lucky we've got anoraks." He laced the hood of his windproof round his chin. "We can't be in for much of a snowstorm this time of year, though."

"I won't be sorry to get back to the tent and brew up

some hot soup," said Colin. "We must've come three miles. Think you can find it?"

Mike snorted. "Easy. That first tarn we tried was due east from the tent. This pool was south from the other, with a bit of west in it. We've only got to reverse the bearings."

As he spoke he was putting the binoculars into his rucksack and getting out a compass. He held the compass for a moment for the needle to stop swinging, got his direction— a little east of north—and started off across the heather into the mist, with Colin plodding close behind him. As if it had been waiting for them to move, the snow began to float down more thickly out of the greyness.

"Be nice to snug-up in the old Ant tonight," Mike said over his shoulder.

"The Ant" was their name for the Antarctic Junior tent which they owned jointly, a type of tent extremely popular with people who liked camping in the remoter places of Britain. Colin thought of their little green shelter with its sewn-in groundsheet and the two warm sleeping-bags and felt he would be very glad to get there. For as the minutes of their plodding progress through the mist lengthened to fifteen and twenty and then to half an hour the falling snow became gradually thicker and thicker. Down by the marshy pool—one of many on Thirlby Moss—there had been little wind, but Mike was heading up slightly rising ground and the mist began to blow about them, with the snow swirling out of it in spirals of big soft flakes. The short springy heather they were treading began to whiten, seeming to lighten the growing darkness. Only when Colin noticed that Mike's red anorak looked black against the mottled grey of mist and snow did he realize that night was close upon them now.

"Sort of weather to bring out the Grey Man," he shouted, trying to sound more cheerful than he felt.

He had to shout to overcome the increasing *whoo-oosh* of wind and snow. Mike only grunted in reply, and Colin remembered his Irish superstition. The Grey Man of

Thirlby Moss was an age-old ghost who was supposed to haunt the moorland at twilight. The old folk in Thirlby village still believed in it. Colin wished he hadn't mentioned the Grey Man.

He almost blundered into Mike, who had halted to peer at the compass, and then they were moving on again with a slight downhill slope beneath their feet. Ten paces was the utmost limit of visibility now, and the snow whirling in their faces made it worse. Their anoraks and woollen gloves were plastered with snow. Colin felt the cold seeping into his very bones. They had been out all day in a cold mist, crouching motionless for hours at a time to watch for the Red-necked Phalarope, and hadn't taken much food with them. Unwillingly he remembered stories of walkers who had died from exposure on this very moor. But that wouldn't happen to them, of course—they'd be safe in the tent in another twenty minutes or so.

Mike, who had been walking more and more slowly, suddenly halted again.

"We ought to have struck that other tarn by now," he said, "but the ground's starting to rise again."

"We've got a bit too high," Colin suggested. "If we head downhill to the left—"

"All right."

Both of them spoke casually, but each could hear the apprehension in the other's voice. To be off course in a snowstorm on Thirlby Moss, with night creeping fast through the drifting mist, was to be in grave danger, and they knew it. Down over the whitening heather they plodded. Though the snow now drove at them from the right flank instead of in their faces, so that it was easier to look ahead, the circle of darkness was closing in. It was like being blind. The wind was rising, too, numbing their cheeks and fingers. Colin felt very cold and tired—and a bit frightened.

Once again Mike came to a sudden halt, and this time Colin cannoned into him heavily. He felt Mike's fingers shaking as they clutched his arm.

111

SHOWELL STYLES

"A m-man," Mike chattered. "Over there—t-to the
left."

The tall shape that had loomed up a few paces away
through the snowstorm could have been the Grey Man
waiting for them. But Colin knew better.

"We're all right!" he cried joyfully. "It's that rock
spike—remember? Only two or three minutes from the
tent."

Mike recovered himself. "That's it! The little stream's on
the other side of this low rise. Come on!"

Going as fast as they could, they passed the rock pin-
nacle protruding from its pile of boulders. Uphill for a
few paces over the snowy heather, then more steeply
down.

"By gum!" Colin shouted, a bit shakily. "I'll be glad to
see that tent!"

They came to the little stream gurgling in its narrow bed
and turned down it. A pool, black in the white carpet that
now covered everything, showed just ahead.

"There's our washing-place!" exclaimed Mike. "But—"
He stopped. "We must have passed the tent—it was just
above that pool."

"Can't have done. The Ant was right by the stream."

The wind howled derisively, hurling the snow at them
as they turned and went slowly back beside the stream.
There was a flat place at the burnside, whitened now but
obviously a good camp-site. Both of them recognized it as
the place where they had camped the previous night, where
they had left the little tent to go searching the misty moorland for the Red-necked Phalarope.

But the tent was gone.

Mike was the first to find his voice, and it was a very
shaky voice.

"It can't be the place—it's the wrong stream."

Colin left him and hurried back to the little pool. When
he returned he was clutching something in his hand.

"It *is* the place, Mike," he said, trying to stop his teeth

112

Their tent was gone, and with it their hope of shelter.

from chattering. "Look—my toothbrush. I left it by the pool this morning."

There was a short silence, while the driving snow fled past them into the darkness.

"The tent blew down," Mike said suddenly. "That's what happened—we'll find it a few yards downstream."

He started down along the bank of the burn. Colin followed without a word. He knew how strongly those pegs had been put in; and the wind, fierce though it was, wasn't nearly violent enough to carry the Ant away. A little below the camp-site the stream curved sharply between its low banks of heather. There were rocks, snow-whitened, here. If the tent had indeed broken from its moorings it would have been caught up on those rocks.

"It's—it's uncanny!" muttered Mike, stopping by the rocks; and Colin knew he was thinking of the Grey Man of Thirlby Moss. "Who'd move the tent? And—what are we going to do? The snowstorm's blowing straight down this watercourse. We can't stay here. If we don't find some kind of shelter—"

He left the sentence unfinished. Colin had a sudden mental picture of the two of them wandering the moor in the snowstorm until they fell exhausted, to be found days later stiff and dead. He made himself speak firmly.

"Cross the moor and get on the track to Thirlby village. It's our only chance."

"It's a good eight miles," Mike said slowly. "And remember the track, Colin? We could hardly spot it in the mist yesterday, when there was no snow. We'd never find it now—even if we'd got the strength to get that far. And I'm pretty well done."

"So am I," Colin confessed miserably; and suddenly saw a ray of hope. "Peat-hags! I've read about people finding shelter under a peat-hag in a winter storm, and coming through safely. D'you remember when we were looking for a camp-site yesterday—"

"That's it!" Mike shouted. "Half a mile from camp, wasn't it—that peat bog we walked round? Good man.

114

Must be almost due south from here."

He got the compass out of his pocket. It was too dark to read the dial now, but there was a small torch in the rucksack. Mike got his direction and they climbed wearily up the side of the watercourse and set off once more across the storm-swept moorland into the night.

It should have been easier going with the snow driving from behind them, but both boys were rapidly becoming exhausted and stumbled frequently as they toiled across the snow-laden heather. Only half a mile, only half a mile —Colin found the comforting words going through and through his mind. Not long ago the snug little "Ant" had been his goal; now all his hopes were centred on the black, damp undercurve of a peat-hag where they might huddle shivering for the long hours of night. And he knew well that it meant the difference between life and death for both of them.

Mike had kept the torch in his hand so that he could consult the compass at intervals. The circle of light, when it flashed on, lit a dark-grey wall of mist with the whirl of white flakes racing past to vanish in it. When the torch went out again the night seemed utterly black for a few minutes until their eyes got accustomed to the dark once more and could see the same ceaseless turmoil of snow in front. Colin, numbed and leg-weary, forced himself to stagger on behind Mike's dark figure. He began to feel as if he was dreaming, and somehow the Red-necked Phalarope kept coming into his dream. "*Very small . . . bill black, longer and finer than grey phalarope's . . . rare inland in Britain . . . very tame . . .*"—phrases from the Bird Recognition book repeated themselves in his mind. Vaguely he knew that they should have reached the peat-bog by now—that they were going downhill, not up as they ought to do; but he was too weary to call out to Mike and tell him. Too weary to do anything beyond going on until he dropped. . . .

From just in front came a splash and a startled exclamation. Next moment Colin, too, had stumbled into the shallow water at the edge of a reedy pool. As he followed Mike's faltering steps to drier ground a gust of wind and snow smote him in the face. He reeled and nearly fell. He was at the end of his tether, and there was no shelter here.

And then Mike gave a shout. His torch shone on the snow-powdered pebbles at the pool's edge and on the level ground a pace or two above. Beyond the veil of snow a triangular shape hovered ghostlike, showing a familiar green through the white. It was the tent.

Comparing notes with Mike afterwards, Colin found that his friend had experienced the same feelings as himself. Utter astonishment at finding the "Ant" safely pitched by a pool far from where they had left it; then a most eerie sensation—partly fright at the uncanny business, partly a sudden memory of the Grey Man of Thirlby Moss; and lastly the realization that here, by a miracle, was shelter and safety. Whether the tent had got there by witchcraft, or whether this was the ghost of their vanished "Ant", didn't matter to a pair of half-frozen bird-watchers who had come very near to deadly peril. They reeled up to the tent, managed to undo the door-lacings with nerveless fingers, and fairly fell inside. Colin had a dim recollection of fumbling at boot-laces and stripping off wet socks and stockings. The sleeping-bag he struggled into didn't feel like his; probably it was Mike's, but it wasn't important. His friend was fastening the tent door and muttering something or other. Good old Mike! Colin felt warmth creeping back into his body. Outside, the snow whirled on and the wind pushed at the tent fabric. Inside it was snug— and safe. A wave of weariness and relief swept over him, and before Mike had crawled into the sleeping-bag beside him Colin was asleep.

According to Mike, they slept for eleven hours that night on Thirlby Moss. At any rate, when Colin woke and stretched stiff and aching limbs the sun had come over the low horizon and the tent was glowing with morning light. Mike had just woken up and was talking excitedly.

"Wh-what?" mumbled Colin sleepily.

"I said the mystery's partly explained," Mike repeated forcibly. "Look!" He pointed to some objects in a corner of the tent. "Tinned sausage—we didn't bring any. And these sleeping-bags. Blue covers, and ours are brown. *This isn't our tent!*"

"Great Godfrey!" Colin sat up and stared round him. "And you're right, too. It's an Antarctic Junior, same as ours, but it *isn't* ours. Whose is it, then? And where's our tent?"

"Don't ask me," said Mike. "Maybe it's a ghost tent. It was a snowstorm when we got into it—now the sun's shining. What's the betting we've been spirited away to a tropical island or somewhere? Let's have a look."

He said it lightly, but his fingers shook with excitement as he unfastened the tent door and pulled the fabric aside. The Irish in him was uppermost at that moment. Even Colin stared eagerly, wondering what he would see.

The opened door revealed a morning sky from which the sun was already clearing the slight haze, and a little moorland tarn with new-fallen snow sparkling on its shores. Wind and snowstorm had passed and left a wonderful morning of early spring. The pebbly beach of the tarn was a stride or two from the tent doorway, with brown rushes fringing the shining blue water. And just emerging from the rushes were five very small wading-birds with long, slim, black bills.

Mike froze motionless with his hand holding the tent curtain.

"Camera! Exposure-meter! *Quick*, man!"

He spoke under his breath and out of one corner of his mouth. Colin groped for the camera, hardly daring to breathe. The light-meter was in his anorak pocket. It'd have to be a hundredth of a second—f. 1·9 would just do it. As he raised the little camera he looked almost incredulously at the five small waders who were now pottering about and probing busily with their long beaks as if there was no tent twenty feet away from them. "*Very*

117

tame," said the bird book. That fitted right enough—and there was the dark-grey back with whitish streaks, the prominent wing-bar, and—yes! One of the waders, starting his summer plumage early, had the faintest hint of an orange band on his neck and upper breast. They were Red-necked Phalaropes!

The camera clicked. A swift wind-on and a second exposure to make sure. The colour-film would clinch this miraculous identification. A moment later Mike, who had been screwing his face into horrible contortions, let out a resounding sneeze and the five phalaropes instantly took wing. "*Whit-whit-whit!*" they piped as they vanished, con-

tinuing their long journey northward to the breeding-grounds in the Polar Sea.

Three hours later Colin and Mike were striding down in the March sunshine to Thirlby village in the valley below them. The "ghost tent" was strapped on Mike's rucksack and Colin was carrying the sleeping-bags and stores. A tough-looking lad who was plodding up the steep lane, which led to Thirlby Moss, halted and stared at the two as they approached.

"Good morning," he said hesitantly. "I—er—I suppose you don't happen to have my tent?"

"Camera! Exposure meter! Quick man!"

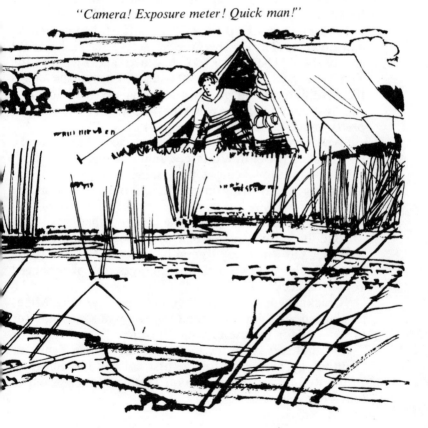

Mike glanced quickly at Colin and then grinned.

"I shouldn't wonder," he replied. "I suppose you don't happen to have ours?"

After that, it took only a moment for the other boy to identify "the ghost tent" as his. And two sets of explanations were exchanged.

"I'm dead keen on bird-watching," said their new acquaintance, "and I got hold of that chap who thought he'd seen a Red-necked Phalarope on the Moss a few days ago. He agreed to go up and camp with me, by the pool where he'd seen it. Well, it was very misty yesterday, as you know, and this chap woke up feeling ill. I could see he was really bad—malaria, it turned out to be—and I had to get him down to a doctor. It was a fearful game getting him down to Thirlby, because he got so feeble he could hardly stand. The doctor took him over and I went to the Thirlby Hostel, where I'm staying. Some of the chaps there volunteered to go up and bring my tent down—I was just about all in, you see—and I gave them some pretty vague directions—"

"And they brought down the wrong tent," Mike broke in. "That comes of the Antarctic Junior being so popular."

"Yes—and you being a pair, same as we were. I was just going up to bring in my tent. Yours is safe at the Hostel, by the way."

The three boys went down the lane together.

"Bad luck for you," Colin said thoughtfully as they walked, "but—in a way—good luck for us. Because we've not not only eaten your tinned sausages, but also bagged your Red-necked Phalarope."

"Cracking good sausages they were, too," grinned Mike; he glanced at Colin. "I reckon we owe you something for them—*and* for the use of your ghost tent."

And that is why, in the records of the British Trust for Ornithology, the credit for the first positive identification of the Red-necked Phalarope on Thirlby Moss is given to four people instead of two.

The Boy and the Salmon

NEIL M. GUNN

KENN MUMBLED and grumbled and kept his eyes shut, for being rudely wakened out of sleep was a thing that often happened to him. He had been up late last night because everyone had been busy over the departure of the boats in the morning for the distant fishing. There had been such comings and goings and preparations that the excitement had kept sleep away much longer than usual. In this little Highland community young boys were not sent to bed early, and though he might be shouted at to take himself off at ten o'clock, Kenn would often hang out until eleven. Last night it had been nearly midnight before sleep had curled him up in a corner of the kitchen, and his father had had to carry him to bed.

It was only when his mother's voice said something about the boats going away that he knew he must get up, so he muttered, "What are you wanting?" His mother told him that she wanted fresh water from the well. What an excuse for wakening a fellow! He could almost have cried. And when he did stagger out of bed and found from the greyness of the light that it could not be much more than six o'clock, his vexation became bitter. He stood in his shirt, whimpered moodily as he scratched himself, then slowly pulled on his trousers and his blue fisherman's gansey.

In the kitchen his father and mother were talking. He paid no attention to them, but picked up the bright tin pail and made it clatter against the jamb of the door as he went out.

The dawn air was cold and the touch of frost in the ground was such a shock to his bare feet that he nearly cried out. He should have put on his boots, holed as they were. He hoped his parents were watching him through the window and seeing what he had to endure.

In this mood he arrived at the well, which was at the foot of a steep bank by the side of the river. Carelessly he bumped the pail down on the flat stone, and at the sound, as at a signal in a weird fairy tale, the whole world changed. His moodiness leapt right out of him and fear had him by the throat.

For from his very feet a great fish had started ploughing its way across the river, the king of fish, the living salmon.

Kenn had never seen a living salmon before, and of those he had seen dead this was beyond all doubt the all-father.

When the waves faded out on the far side of the stream, where the bed was three feet deep, Kenn felt the great silence that lay upon the world and stood in the midst of it trembling like a hunted hare.

His eyes shot hither and thither, along horizons, down braes, across fields and wooded river-flats. No life moved; no face was watching.

Out of that noiseless world in the grey of the morning, all his ancestors came at him. They tapped his breast until the bird inside it fluttered madly; they drew a hand along his hair until the scalp crinkled; they made the blood within him tingle to a dance that had him leaping from boulder to boulder before he rightly knew to what desperate venture he was committed.

For it was all in a way a sort of madness. The fear was fear of the fish itself, of its monstrous reality, primal fear; but it was also infinitely complicated by fear of gamekeepers, of the horror and violence of law courts, of our modern social fear. Not only did his hunting ancestors of the Caledonian Forest come at him, but his grown-up brothers and his brothers' friends, with their wild forays and epic stories, a constant running the gauntlet against enemy forces, for the glory of fun and laughter and daring —and the silver gift of the salmon. A thousand influences had his young body taut as a bow, when at last, bending over a boulder of the old red sandstone, he saw again the salmon.

Fear rose at him afresh, for there was a greyness in its great dark-blue back that was menacing and ghostly. . . . He could see the eyes on each side of the shapely head and knew the eyes must see him. Still as a rock and in some mysterious way as unheeding, the salmon lay beneath him. Slowly he drew his head back until at last the boulder shut off sight of the salmon and released his breath.

As before, he looked all around him, but now with a more conscious cunning. Tiptoeing away from the boulder, he went searching downstream until he found a large flattish stone, and returned with it pressed against his stomach.

When he had got the best grip, he raised it above his head, and, staggering to the upper edge of the sandstone boulder, poised it in aim. Then he did not let it drop so much as contrive, with the last grain of his strength, to hurl it down on the fish.

Though untouched, the salmon was very clearly astonished and, before the stone had right come to rest, had the pool in a splendid tumult. For it was not one of those well defined pools of gradual depths. There were gravel banks in it and occasional boulders forming little rest

123

With all his might he hurled it down on the fish.

pools behind them. The tail was wide and shallow.

It was a sea-trout rather than a salmon pool, as became apparent in that first blind rush, when the fish thrashed the water to froth in a terrific boil on top of the gravel bank, cleared the bank, and, with back fin showing, shot across the calm water towards the well where he had been resting. So headlong was his speed that he beached himself not two yards from Kenn's pail. Curving from nose to tail, the great body walloped the stones with resounding whacks. So hypnotized was Kenn by this extraordinary spectacle, that he remained stiff and powerless, but inwardly a madness was already rising in him, an urgency to rush, to hit, to kill. The salmon was back in the shallow water, lashing it, and in a moment, released, was coming straight for him. Right at his feet there was a swirl, a spitting of drops into his face. The fish saw him and, as if possessed by a thousand otters, flashed up the deep water and launched himself, flailing wildly, in the rushing shallows of the neck.

And then Kenn went into action, caution and fear forgotten. It was in truth a madness not unlike the salmon's. In his blind panic, the fish had no regard for bodily stress; in his blind exaltation, neither had Kenn.

Less than a hundred yards beyond the shallows of the neck was a long dark pool, and in it lay escape. If the brute had been calm, been travelling by night, it could have made the passage with ease. But now, having lost its head, it defeated itself by its own strength and added to its panic by bashing its nose against boulders.

Kenn approached the scene with such speed that before one toe could slip on slime the other was forward to thrust him on. Landing knee-deep in the final jump, he tore a stone from the bed of the stream and, blinded by the salmon's splashings, let drive.

He missed by over a foot and there followed a jumble in which, in his excitement, he lunged fiercely and recklessly, to be left grovelling on his back as the salmon shot downward.

In his leap for the bank Kenn stumbled and was thrown

severely. But he had no consciousness of pain; only of loss of time, of awful fear lest the salmon should escape.

And running down the bank it seemed to him as if the salmon had escaped. No trace of "way" on the pool. Nothing. . . . Was that a swirl—far down? Making his way out of the pool!

On his toes again, Kenn sped downward, came in below the fish, and picking up a stone half the size of his head, went straight to the attack.

The water was now growing narrower and deeper, but it was tortured by boulders and sloping flagstones. Twice the salmon flashed past him, and now Kenn was not merely wading into the water, but falling and crawling and choking in it, yet ever with his dark head rising indomitably.

If the salmon had possessed an instinct for an enemy at all, it must have been for some animal like the otter, swift and sure in attack and deathly in grip. This rushing, sprawling, stone-throwing inhabitant of another world had fingers that slid off the back like caressing fingers of seaweed. Unable to bite yet pursuing relentlessly. Shake him off! A rush and a heave and the salmon bared his girth on a sloping flagstone. From the bottom, Kenn had raked a stone barely the size of his small fist, but he threw it with all his vigour and it scored a first direct hit. . . .

Back off the flagstone came the salmon with his nose pointing upstream, and he followed his nose. At the best of times it is awkward for a salmon to go downstream, but upstream, given depth and shoulder room, speed becomes a frenzy. This fish turned it into a debauch and reached the Well Pool like a demented torpedo.

Kenn had chosen his battleground and laid down the conditions of the fight.

And it was a saga of a fight. For Kenn had no weapons of attack other than his fists and what they could grab from the river bottom; no rod, hook, net, or implement of constraint or explosion. It was a war between an immature human body on the one side, and a superbly matured body

*He beached himself, walloped the stones and was
back in the river.*

of incredible swiftness and strength on the other. In physical length, laid out side by side, there would have been little difference between them.

But neither of them was laid out yet! Indeed so far there had been little more than the courteous slap on the cheek as gage of battle, and it had been delivered by Kenn.

The initial strategy, however, for such warfare could be summed up in the words "keep him on the run". All his tactics brought this about as their natural result, whether he was careering wildly up and down the bank, pausing to hurl a stone, or dashing into shallows to get at close quarters. The frenzy of both had first to be worn down, before the cunning brain could stalk the tired body.

A curious mood of fatalism comes upon a salmon that has committed its life to a pool. Up and down it will go, round this boulder, by the side of that, turning here, turning back again there, but never making any attempt to leave the known ground. No barrage of stones will drive it forth, however successfully timed. The dangers of the shallows are the dangers of the unknown, of death. If the pool be just deep enough a salmon will pass between swimming human legs rather than be driven forth, and in this restless fashion will ultimately tire out its enemies.

But if the Well Pool had not sufficient depth over a wide enough area to permit of this endless swimming, it had on the other hand its own suggestions for escape. The water was amber-coloured, for it was the tail-end of a mighty spate, and drained from peat-banks in distant moors; being for the most part shallow, it had a considerable flow; and the scattered pieces of rock against the ground inequalities offered a tired fish many a natural hiding place.

Indeed several times Kenn had his heart in his mouth when it seemed that the salmon had altogether vanished. In the dark shadow of a leaning stone where the amber water gurgled past, a dark-blue back was but a darker shadow. Then Kenn would spot the tail or the curve of the nose or the pallor of a fin; would be overcome with an emotion keener in its thrust than ever; would back away and hunt his stone. Splash! and the salmon was on its journey once more, betrayed by its great size.

This phase of the battle went on for a long time, until Kenn knew all the resting places and there began to grow in him a terrible feeling of power, terrible in its excitement, in its realization that he might be successful, and even more terrible in its longing.

There came a time when Kenn, having got the fish resting where he wanted him, went downstream to choose his stone, but no longer in blind urgency. He handled two or three before lifting one against his breast.

The salmon lay by the outer edge of a greenish underwater slab. By approaching it on a slant towards its tail, he could keep its head out of sight. Warily he did this until he came to the edge of the stream. But now he knew that however he stooped while wading in, the eyes would be disclosed. He did not hesitate; he let himself down into the water and, the stone against his stomach, slithered over the gravelly bottom on his stern. It was an autumn morning, after a night of hoar-frost, but when the water got fully about his body he felt it warm. Foot by foot he thrust himself on, until at last he could have put out a hand and touched the tail; and the tail was deep as his face and as taut.

Slowly he reared up on his knees, fighting down the sinking sensation that beset him, his hands fiercely gripping the stone. Anxiety now started shouting in him to heave the stone and be done, but, though trembling, he rose with infinite care, little by little, disclosing the back fin, the nape of the neck where the otter bites, and at last the near eye. The fish did not move. Inch by inch the stone went up. Then in one thrust he launched stone and body at the fish.

The thud of the stone on the great back was a sound of such potency that even in that wild drenching moment it sang above all else. For the stone had landed; the stone had got him! Spewing the river water forth, stumbling and falling, he reached the bank. Then both of them went berserk.

This great fish had not the slippery cunning, the evasiveness, of a small salmon or grilse. It tore around like a bull in a ring. Kenn began to score direct hits more often. He was learning the way. He could throw a stone ahead; he could madden; he could stalk warily and hear ever more exultingly the singing thud.

The fatal part for a salmon is the nape of the neck. The time came when Kenn landed there heavily with the narrow stone edge; the salmon circled and thrashed as if half paralysed or blinded; Kenn with no more stones at hand launched a body attack and received one wallop from the tail that sent him flat on his back; the salmon was off again.

The end came near the neck of the pool on the side opposite the well. Here the low bank of the river widened out into a grassy field. The tired fish, with pale mouth

In the grip of human hands the salmon went berserk.

gaping every now and then, went nosing into shallow water, where some upended flagstones might provide a new and dark retreat. But there was no hidden retreat there and Kenn, well down the pool, waited with wild hope. If it lay anywhere thereabouts until he got up, it would be finished! And it lay.

It actually lay in full view between two stone edges, its back fin barely covered. Kenn hit it as it moved and then fell on it. His hands went straight for the gills; one found a grip under a cheek, the other, slipping, tried for a hold on the body, and there and then began the oddest tussle that surely that river could ever have seen.

Under the burning grip of human hands, the salmon went frantic and threw Kenn about as if he were a streamer tied to its neck; the upended stones bashed his arms, his legs, the back of his head; the bony cheek dug into his wrist; but nothing could now dim the relentless instinct in him to roll both bodies from the shallow water on to dry land.

And this in time he accomplished. When his hand was shot from behind the cheek it drew gills with it.

The salmon flailed the dry stones with desperate violence, but Kenn was now in his own element, and ever he brought his body behind the body of the fish and shored it upwards, thrusting at the gills until his hands were lacerated and bleeding.

He dragged that fish over fifty yards into the grass park before he laid it down. And when it heaved in a last convulsive shudder, he at once fell upon it as if the river of escape still lapped its tail.

And now on this busy morning, angered against him for not returning with the well water, his mother suddenly saw him rounding the corner of the house towards the door of the back porch, face down, hands knotted behind his head, dripping wet and staggering. The salmon's nose was under his right ear, its tail was sweeping the ground behind. She gave way to him as he lurched in. Releasing his crooked fingers and heaving with a shoulder, he set the great fish with a mighty thump on the smooth blue flagstone at her feet.

She looked at the frightening size of the fish on the floor; she looked at her son and whispered, "Where did you get that?"

"In the river."

"Yourself?"

"Who else?"

His dark hair was flattened to rat tails. His brown eyes were black against the excited pallor of his face. There was a fighting spirit in him that suddenly pulled at her heart: "You're all wet. Every stitch of you."

At that moment his father came round the house.

"Come here, Davy," said the woman to him quietly.

The father came up. He looked at the fish; he looked at the boy. "God bless me!" he whispered. "Where did you get him?"

"In the Well Pool."

"God bless me, boy!" His features softened in a slow winning smile, touched to the breath of wonder. His son felt it without looking at it, felt it in the breath of his voice, and a weakening warmth ran about his heart.

"Did anyone see you?" asked his mother.

"No," he muttered.

"How did you land him?" asked his father.

"With my hands."

His father looked at the hands. Kenn, seeing for the first time that they had been bloodily combed by the gills, put them behind his back.

"And he's wet to the skin besides," nodded his mother in a rising tone that implied that all this was none of her doing. "You'll go in and change every stitch on you this minute."

Kenn paid no attention to her.

"Was there no one there at all?" his father asked in his quiet voice, still hushed in wonder.

"No."

He staggered home with his load, exultation in his heart.

The man looked at the fish. They all stared at it. It beat everything!

"Do you think," said the mother thoughtfully, "that Sans would like a bit?"

"What's the weight of him, do you think?" said Sans, the merchant.

"He's maybe twenty pounds," said Kenn's father tentatively.

"Twenty! If he's not over twenty-five I'll eat my bonnet!"

On the wooden scales used for weighing bags of meal, the merchant laid the fish. "Twenty, did you say? Very well." He put on twenty pounds—and pressed the beam—and chuckled. He added the seven weight. Nothing happened. Two more to make twenty-nine. Then, gently, one for thirty and the beam trembled.

"Bless me," said Davy softly.

"Thirty good," said Sans. He laughed and brought down his hand on Kenn's shoulder: "Good for you, my little hero!"

133

Something Lost

JACK SCHAEFER

June

THIS WAS far up in the mountains and still the great peaks climbed, thrusting up and thinning to the bare bones of rock above the timber-line. The high upland valley was lost among them, an irregular pocket caught in the soaring immensity, rimmed by the timeless rock, its glints of meadow green shading into the darker green of forest where it broke into the downward slopes. The figure of the man by the stream near the upper end of the valley, where the water slowed from its rush down the rocks, was un-

believably small in the vastness. He stood stooped by a sandbar where the riffles swung and died in a pool and the slant sunlight flashed on the worn tin in his hands and his shoulders rocked as his arms moved in a circular motion.

The motion stopped and the man bent his head farther to peer into the pan in his hands and the dull gleaming of the flakes there was reflected in the pale hazel irises of his eyes. He straightened and nodded his head in slow satisfaction. He studied the sandbar and the pool where the water slipped into apparent

134

stillness and the silt of years had settled to the bottom. He
raised his head and looked at the untouched wilderness
about him. The valley lay open around him, a half-mile
wide and a mile long, its level floor cut by the swinging
course of the stream. At its head the mountain wall rose
steeply in huge broken steps that the stream took in rushes
and falls as it drove down from the endless snow in the far
upper reaches of rock. Along the valley sides the slopes
climbed, tree-dotted and thicket-entangled, to stop against
the enduring stone, on the near side against a high sharp
ridge, on the opposite side against a vast rock buttress
towering out to a tremendous cliff edge. Between the ridge
and the buttress the valley entrance swept out to open
parkland that dropped abruptly into jack pine forest
covering the downward slopes and divided by the deepening gorge of the stream as it sought the lower levels. And
beyond the ground rose again, rising in ridge upon ridge
to the high eastward mountain barrier.

The man nodded his head again in slow satisfaction and
the sun shone warm on the broad flat planes of his face
beneath the wide squared brim of his hat. He took a
leather pouch from a pocket and eased the flakes into it.
He strode across the carpet of wild flowers bordering the
stream and bent to pick up the trailing lead rope of the
grazing burro. By the slope of the near valleyside, where a
thickening stand of spruce and juniper fringed the valley
floor, he stopped and pulled the rifle and axe and short
shovel from under the tie ropes and unfastened the pack
and picketed the burro on a twenty-foot rope length. He
selected a fallen tree, angling up, the upper end wedged in
a crotch of another tree. Using this as his ridgepole, he
began building his shelter. He shed his jacket and sweat
darkened his shirt as his short broad body swung in steady
rhythm and the axe blade bit into the springy wood.

Across the meadow green, across the wild-flower carpet
and the stream, half a mile across the stretching expanse of
valley floor and two hundred yards up the opposite slope

where bare rock jutted over a flat ledge, the great bear lay and watched the man. It lay limp on the ledge in the warm slant sun, hind legs sprawled back, front legs stretched forward with the big head, broad and dished to the muzzle, resting on the rock between them. A light breeze ruffled through the short brown fur made ragged by the remaining long still unshed hairs touched with silver on the tips. Its small far-sighted eyes followed the man's every move among the distant trees.

Eighty-odd miles away, over the mountain barrier to the east, where a ragged collection of rude log cabins and tents straggled along the side of an almost dry stream bed, men worked at their wooden cradles and sluice boxes and grumbled to themselves and each other. The showings of colour that had drawn them there to stake their claims

136

It watched his every move.

were dwindling. In the oblong tarpaulin-roofed shack that served as store and bar other men spoke of the one who had left, quietly, speaking to no one, abandoning his slow half-worked claim to disappear with his burro into the high distances to the west. Their talk was tainted with envious wondering. They argued with each other in edged monotones. Unrest and disappointment crawled through the mining camp.

Far up in his valley, as the midnight stars wheeled in their slow course, the man stirred on his bed of spruce boughs and sat up, suddenly alert. The embers of the fire outside the open end of his shelter had faded to a dull glow that meant nothing to the moonless dark under the trees. He heard the burro moving restlessly on its shortened

137

His eyes searched the pan for hint of gold.

picket rope. In the following silence he felt a familiar
prickling on the back of his neck as the short hairs there
stiffened in response to some instinct beyond reach of the
mind. His right hand moved and took the rifle and he was
leaning forward to rise when he heard the burro scream
and lunge to the end of the rope. He leaped to his feet and
stood in the open end of the shelter, baffled by the un-
relenting blackness of the night. Gradually he could make
out the darker shapes of the trees. He went cautiously
toward the burro and found it half choked by the taut
rope. He spoke softly and it pushed against him and
together they stood in a silence that lived and breathed
around them. There was not a single separate discernible
sound, yet the prickling persisted on his neck and the
flesh of the burro quivered against him. The prickling died
and the burro quieted and they stood in an empty silence.
The man returned to the fire and piled wood on it and
kneeled to blow until flames sprang and a circle of firelight
fought back the dark. He shifted the burro closer to the
circle before he lay again on his spruce bed.

In the morning the man found the tracks. Those of the forefeet were nearly seven inches wide and nine long, those of the hind feet eight inches wide and fourteen long. The claw marks of all five toes on each were plain. Apprehension crept along the man's spine. His hands tightened on the rifle. The tracks led in a circle around his camp and close in by the shelter and again by the place where the burro had first been picketed. He crawled inside his shelter to the low diminishing end where his meagre supplies, depleted by weeks of wandering, were cached behind a barrier of short logs. He took a handful of cartridges and dropped them into a jacket pocket. Outside again, he strode off, steady and unhurried, following the tracks away.

They led him across the stream below the pool and across the level of the valley. He lost them on the edge of a field of slide rock near the lower end of the valley. He skirted the field and could find no further trace. He turned back and began a thorough circuit of the valley.

He found signs in many places, old tracks caked where the ground had dried and fresher tracks in soft ground. He found three rubbing trees with bark worn thin and high up, higher than he could reach, gashes where the bark had been torn open crosswise by gripping jaws. He found the trail angling up the far slope to the ledge. Approaching the ledge, he saw the wide and narrowing crevice behind it leading back to blackness under the overhanging rock. No light could penetrate the inner dark depth. He dropped silently back down the trail fifty yards and crouched behind a big stone and shouted and there was no response except the jeering call of a jay. He shouted again and waited. At last he strode down the trail and across the valley. In a few moments he was stooped by the pool, his arms moving in circular motion as the sun glinted on the pan in his hands. But now he looked up at regular intervals and scanned the expanse all around him and the rifle lay within quick reach not more than a yard from his steady hands.

139

Out of the valley, eight miles around the jagged sweep of the vast rock buttress that towered above the opposite slope, out where the forest of jack pine below the edging parkland flowed unbroken down to the shore of a small lake, the great bear lay in a patch of sunlight on the soft needle carpet. Already it had forgotten the man and the burro. They were new sights, new scents, never before known, tucked away now in the reservoir of experience and would remain untouched until a fresh encounter summoned remembrance into being. They had been seen and smelled and investigated in the caution of the night and dismissed. There was no challenge in them for the bear to understand.

A marten drifted down the trunk of a nearby tree, stretching its small pointed head outward to stare intently at the bear. The scratch of the small claws in the bark was barely audible a few feet away, yet the bear's head rose. The marten scurried back up the tree. The big head dropped and the bear, full-fed and lazy, drowsed in the sunlight. The tree shadows moved slowly and crept to engulf the bear and it rose and padded softly on through the forest.

July

The man strode up the stretch of parkland that edged the forest and led to the valley entrance. The late afternoon sun was full in his face. Behind him the burro trotted obediently, weighted by the big pack, whose new canvas covering gleamed white in the sunlight. Where the parkland levelled to enter the valley he stopped and turned to look back the way he had come, down the long rolling forested slope sliced by the stream gorge and up and over the first high ridge beyond. Satisfied at last that no one followed, he turned again and led the burro up the valley and across the green carpet to his camp in the spruce and juniper fringe. Everything there was as he had left it eight days before. But in the soft ground by the pool he found

Envious rumours declared he had made a rich strike.

the big five-toed tracks crossing the stream toward his camp and going back again. He looked across the valley and up. The steep sideslope curving to the high rock buttress was splendid in the late sunlight and the overhanging rock and the ledge two hundred yards above the valley floor shone rust-red and grey against the green around them. A hawk floated in the air above the scattered clinging trees. There was no other sign of life. He strode back to his camp and began unpacking the burro.

Far to the eastward, over the mountain barrier, where the rude cabins and tents marred the bank of the stream bed, men talked to the keeper of the tarpaulined store and bar, worrying again the worn questions of four days about the one who had returned with his burro and bought supplies and shaken bright flakes out of a leather pouch in payment and disappeared again into the western heights. Already the legend was growing. He had made a rich strike. He was scooping dust out of rich silt pockets by the handful. He had unlimited wealth in dust and nuggets cached in his mountain hideout. The voice of a lean man

141

with narrow hatchet face gashed by a thin-lipped mouth was tinged with bitterness as he told of his failure in following the boot and hoofmark traces into the mountains. A trail that well hidden must have been deliberately cloaked to cover its destination. The talk warmed and eyes glittered and the storekeeper did good business.

Twice in the night the man awoke, alert and rising to sitting position on his bed of boughs. There was no sound beyond the barrier of logs with which he had closed the open end of his shelter except an occasional soft movement of the burro in the narrow high-poled enclosure he had built for it. In the morning there were no new tracks. It was the same the next night and the next and early during the night after that thunder echoed through the mountains and lightning laced down through the peaks and enough rain fell in the valley to dampen the ground and renew it for fresh writings by any living thing that walked it. In the morning the man took the rifle and made another thorough circuit of the valley. He found no fresh signs, no five-toed tracks except what remained of the old after the erasing action of the rain. But in the moist sand by the stream where it eddied around rolled rocks well below the pool, he found other tracks, split-hooved, deeply indented. He studied these a long moment. He followed them along the stream and when they faded into the firm sod he kept on down the valley. His stride, long for the length of his legs, gnawed steadily into distance.

Half an hour later he was skirting the vast rock buttress, pausing often to scan the sweep of slope opening below him. He was well around, out of sight of the valley entrance, when he saw the elk, three of them, more than a mile away, on the edge of the parkland that slipped abruptly into the jack pine forest. Patient and steady, he began the long approach, angling down the slope to put the light wind directly in his face.

Far ahead where the forest dipped into a deep ravine, a thin column of smoke floated upward from the inside hollow of the shattered stump of a long dead pine. The slow fire, legacy of the lightning, glowed faintly as it ate into the punklike wood. It edged through a split in the old bark and little flames began to flicker along the side of the stump. It worked down and began to creep through the carpet of brown needles. It crept to the tiny outstretched dried twigs of the branch ends of a fallen tree and moved hungrily along them, reaching for the more solid wood.

The man was on his hands and knees, lifting the rifle care-fully and setting it down gently with each forward movement of his right hand. He crawled to the top of a slight rise and lay flat to peer over. He was within rifle-shot of the elk. He eased the gun forward and let the sights sink down on the closest of the three. It stood quartering away from him and he aimed a bit behind and below the high foreshoulder and squeezed the trigger. He saw his elk leap a fraction of a second before the others and the three of them swirl and melt like sud-den swift shifting shadows into the forest. He rose and went forward and followed. He was well in among the trees when he found the first blood drops, spattered and dark from in-ternal bleeding. He lengthened his stride to follow the trace deeper into the forest. Forty minutes later, winded from climbing over and around down timber, he jumped the wounded elk out of a bushed hollow and his bullet, fired almost without aiming in the instant reflex of long experience, broke the animal's neck as it strove with flagging strength to leap away.

Down the slope, farther into the thick of the forest, the great bear prowled, sniffing for rotted logs among a tangle of fallen trees. It heard the second shot, faint yet distinct, a sound foreign and unknown. The big body stopped moving and the big head, unacquainted with fear in any form, rose and turned toward the sound. The bear waited, listening, then the head lowered and the long straight fore-claws sank into the outer shell of a log and, seeming without effort, ripped it open. The tongue, surprisingly small in the big mouth, licked quickly at the scurrying insects and slowed to take the sluggish wriggling white grubs.

The man worked steadily with his knife, quartering the elk carcass. He had already bled and dressed it. The small of his back ached from bending over and he straightened to rest it, and as his head came up he caught the first faint tang in the air. His body stiffened and the tiny premonitions running through him tightened into awareness. Smoke.

Smoke drifting over the forest ceiling and filtering down fine tendrils that could elude the eye but not the nose.

The man stood motionless, testing the breeze. It stirred gently, barely whispering through the branches above him. He started at a right angle to the direction of the breeze, straight up the slope, the shortest path to the edge of the forest and the open parkland. Steadily he hammered on and the breeze freshened and talked in the branches and smoke began weaving among the tree trunks from the left. He angled toward the right, and the

144

smoke thickened, and at last he stopped, listening between the laboured rush of his own breathing. The breeze strengthened and was a wind sighing high overhead, and faint and far he could hear, not so much heard as sensed, the sullen roar of the racing fire. Around him he could fairly feel the hurrying of panic, the small life of the forest moving, unseen but known, past him down the slope. A deer bounded out of the smoke and saw him and swerved and was gone. Without hesitation he turned and struck down the slope.

The smoke thickened and the light dimmed strangely and the roar rose until it was clearly audible and a high crackling breaking over it, and in a short while he was running, using his free hand to help him vault fallen logs, stumbling often and driving downward. The ground levelled and the trees ended and he broke through bushes and tripped full length into the shallow shore waters of a lake. The rifle leaped from his hand and disappeared beneath the surface and he scrambled after it. But the water deepened suddenly a few feet out and he floundered, with his chest heaving for air. He struggled back to the shallow edge and stood quietly while his lungs eased their frantic labour. Smoke rolled around him and he kneeled to keep his head close to the water and the layer of clear air just above it. Fire flared on the rim of the forest to the right and moved toward him and the heat grew until it drove him into the deeper water. He stood stretched upward with his head alone above the surface and looked out over the lake through the rolling smoke clouds. Fifty yards from shore a huge rock showed, humping out of the water like the low ridged back of some vast immobile beast. He swam slowly to it, fighting the drag of his clothes and boots, and crawled up on it and lay flat, while his tired muscles jumped and knotted and relaxed to rest.

The man lay on the rock and watched the fire work its way along the shore. He saw flames spire swiftly up one tree and leap to the next and sometimes, driven by the surge of their own tremendous draught, lunge to engulf several trees at once. The roar of the burning drowned all

He turned his head back to the rock and his body stiffened—the bear was looking at him, its head raised.

possible other sound. It was nothing heard, little more than a slight prickling on the back of his neck, that turned his eyes to the water past the other end of the rock. Only the broad head showed, with the muzzle cutting the water, as the great bear swam toward the rock. Quietly the man slipped into the water, stretching out in it with one hand holding to the stone while the other took the knife from its sheath on his belt. Silent in the water, he saw the bear's head rise over the rock opposite him, not more than twenty feet away, the forepaws stretched for footing, the massive shoulders emerge into view. He watched the bear turn broadside and shake and send the drops spattering clear across the rock. He watched it settle on its haunches, facing the flaming shore-line, and let its forepaws slide forward until the broad belly rested on the rock and the big head sank on them. He moved cautiously to look out over the rest of the lake. Through the clear area just over the surface he saw that it was almost ringed with fire and there was no other haven showing above the water. He turned his head back to the rock and his body stiffened. The bear was looking at him. Its head was raised and swung toward him and the small eyes watched. His knees began to flex under him for a swift thrust outward from the rock but the bear remained motionless and while he waited, taut in tenseness, he saw the big mouth open and stretch in a yawn and the white of the great teeth and the lips drawing lazily back and the muzzle crinkling. The jaws closed and the head swung away and dropped on the forepaws again.

The hot air, uncomfortable but not unendurable, beat against the man's face and the chill of the water sank into his body. Cautiously he reached and put the knife between his teeth and placed both hands on the rock and began to draw himself forward and up on it. The bear's head rose and swung toward him and the small eyes watched. He waited and the bear did not move and he inched forward until at last he was on his hands and knees on the rock. Slowly he shifted position until he was sitting crosslegged,

147

ready for an instant scrambling push striking into the water. The bear watched and when he was settled the big head swung straight again and sank down. Gradually the man's muscles softened and the instant alertness eased out of them. The hot air dried his clothes, and the fingers holding the knife now in his right hand relaxed. The smoke clouds rolled and made a strange unnatural dusk and the fire roared through it along the shore. The man's back and buttocks ached with the strain of his position on the hard rock. Slowly he shifted again until he was stretched full length on his side with his face toward the bear and his head pillowed on his left arm. The bear's ears twitched upright but the big head did not move and in a moment the ears eased limp again. The heat in the air lessened slightly and the fire roared dwindling along the shore. Far off it reached the edge of the gorge of the stream running out of the valley and sought to leap across and failed and fell back and was content with the timber it had taken.

The sun, hidden behind the smoke clouds, dropped behind the westward heights and the remaining flames around the lake sent weird lights dancing in the murky dark over the water. The man's eyes closed and opened abruptly and closed again and at last remained closed. The wind died and the smoke trailed away in wisps and the high stars wheeled in the clearing sky above the two silent figures pinpointed together on their rock in the heart of the soaring immensity of the timeless mountains.

The man woke suddenly in the grey dawn of the light before sunrise. He had rolled over in his sleep on his back and the knife had slipped from his opened hand. As awareness flooded him he fought the stiffness in his muscles to turn quickly on his side and fumble for the knife handle. The seeking fingers halted before they found it. The rock stretched away from him empty and open to the sky. The bear was gone. He pushed to his feet and stooped to take the knife and stood straight. The sound of splashing water turned his head toward the near shore. The bear was emerging from the lake on to a short sandy spit. Against the background of rising slope with charred trunks thrusting above blackened floor and thin wisps of smoke still spiralling lazily, it was a miracle of enduring life, enormous and indomitable in the half-light in defiance of the barren desolation. It started inland and drew back with quick mincing steps. There were hot embers under the ashes and flames ready to break forth flickering strong in many places at the push of any breeze.

The man slipped into the water and swam to the sandy spit. Working from there he made systematic forays into the deeper water until he found the rifle. He washed away the bottom muck and broke it open to blow the barrel and firing chamber clean. Shivering in the first rays of the sun, he moved along the shoreline as the bear had done, stepping slowly but swinging his arms vigorously to warm his muscles.

Hidden in an aspen thicket a short way out on the parkland above the stricken forest, the great bear stood over the carcass of a whitetail doe that had fallen in the flight of fear into the upper gorge and broken its neck. The bear had dragged the carcass to the open of the parkland and into the thicket. The big head lifted and the small eyes peered through the thicket. The man was passing, sixty yards away. A low rumble sounded in the bear's throat, soft and deep, not audible to the man and not meant to be. He strode on with the tireless stride of a man long used to the mountains. The bear watched him, its head turning slowly to follow his passing, and when his figure grew small in the distance the big head dropped to feed again.

August

In the clear light of early morning the man stood by the pool and looked at the shallow pan in his hands. The bottom of it was almost covered with the dull gleaming flakes.

149

The pool silt had become richer as he worked deeper into it. He took the leather pouch from a pocket and shook the flakes into it. This was his third panning of the morning and already the pouch was full. He went to his camp and behind it among the trees and stopped by a flat stone. He heaved at the stone to raise one side and braced it against one leg while he set a piece of stout branch to prop it up. In a hollow underneath lay a five-pound salt bag filled to plumpness and another partly filled. He emptied the pouch into the second bag and lowered the stone into place. He went back by the pool and stood slapping the pan gently against his thigh while he looked out over the valley. The air was fresh on his face and mystic cloud shadows wandered on the mountain wall at the head of the valley. He dropped the pan on the sandbar and took the rifle from the grassbank and strode off down the valley with the sun warm in his face. He was close to the valley entrance,

where the big boulders of an ancient rockslide had rolled out to become bedded in the ageless sod, when he met the bear, suddenly, coming toward him around one of the rocks.

The bear stopped and the man stopped, thirty feet apart. Slowly the man swung up the rifle so that his left hand could grip the barrel and his right forefinger slipped around the trigger. The bear watched him and the low rumble, soft and deep, formed in its throat. Slowly the man stepped to the left, moving in a half-circle, always facing the bear, yielding the right of way. The bear watched him, turning its head to follow him. When he completed the half-circle the man

150

turned, deliberately turned from the bear, and his will clamped hard on his muscles to hold them to a steady walk away. When he had travelled some forty feet he looked back. The bear had gone forward on its own way and its big, ridiculously tiny-tailed rump was toward him as it overturned scattered stones and sniffed for the scuttling insects.

Five hours later, in the early afternoon, the man returned to his camp, back-packing the dressed carcass of a small whitetail buck. Across the valley the great bear lay on the ledge and watched him. He could see it there, a dark shape on the stone, while he skinned the deer and pegged out the hide for drying. He built a big fire of dry wood and while he waited for it to turn down to glowing embers he began cutting the meat into strips. He looked across the valley and saw the bear rise and disappear into the dark recess of the crevice and he nodded to himself. He knew its habits now.

The man raised poles in a rack over the fire and hung the strips of meat on it. He piled green wood on the fire and retreated from the smoke and sat resting with his back against a tree looking out across the valley.

The stream gathered speed as it left the valley and skipped in stony steps down past the edge of the burned-out forest where new green was beginning to rise above blackened ground. It dropped, gaining momentum, into the deepening gorge that took it farther down and where it raced and whirled in rock pools and raced on. The man stood on the low cliff edge overlooking the gorge. Thirty-five feet below him the great bear lay beside the stream. Its new coat was lengthening and a pale silvery cast was beginning to touch the tips of the thick-grown hairs. It lay limp and relaxed on the pebble strand. Suddenly a forepaw darted and flipped a fat trout flashing through the air and the bear leaped from its lying position to seize the fish as it landed flopping a dozen feet away. Lazily the bear fed, then wandered up the stream to where a smooth rock slanted straight into the water. Standing at the top of the

A forepaw darted and flipped a fat trout through the air.

slant, it gave a small bounce and went forward on its belly on the rock with legs outstretched and slid splashing into the stream. The man leaned over the cliff to watch and a soundless chuckle shook him. Lazily the bear climbed again to the top of the smooth rock and rolled over on its back and slid down, tail first, thick legs waving. Its rump struck the water with a spattering smack and the chuckle in the man grew into sound. The bear whirled and rose in the water and looked up. It looked away and inspected the opposite bank in plain pretence that the man was not there. Its head dropped and it shuffled away down the gorge and out of sight around the first turn.

The chill of the night lingered, gradually giving way to the sun's warmth. The morning air was crystal in its distinct clarity. The man stood by the pool and looked at the pan in his hands. There were only a few scattered flakes in it. The pool was almost worked out. He started to walk along the stream, studying its flow and occasional silt banks. His steps slowed and at last stopped and he looked out over the valley. New colour was showing on the clumps of low bushes that dotted the valley floor. Berries were ripening there and along the climbing sides of the valley. Far by the opposite slope he saw the bear rise out of the bushes, settling back on its haunches like a big sitting squirrel, stripping berries into its mouth with its long foreclaws. He strode back to his camp and tossed the pan to one side and lifted the flat stone. Three full salt bags lay there now and a fourth partly filled. He emptied the leather pouch into the fourth bag and lowered the stone in place. Rifle in hand he wandered out through his side of the valley, tasting berries along the way.

September

The green of the valley was changing, darker with a brown cast in barely discernible splotches. The thin cutting edge of fall was invading the air. Among the trees behind the

153

man's camp the flat stone lay undisturbed with grass blades curling over it. The camp itself was neat and orderly. Firewood was stacked in a long pile. A little to one side the pan lay, no longer glinting bright, spotted with dirt and rust. Where the tree fringe abutted the open of the valley the man sat, cross-legged in the sun. Across his lap was a deerskin, tanned with lye from wood ashes and worked to fairly smooth flexibility. Carefully he sliced into the leather, cutting doubled patterns for moccasins to replace his worn boots.

Across the valley, working along the base of the slope and up a short way, the great bear was digging for ground squirrels, ripping into the soil several feet with half a dozen powerful strokes and lying flat on its belly for the final reaching, scraping thrust. The increasing richness of the fur with its silver tipping shone in the clear light. Alternately the man bent to his cutting and raised his head to watch the bear. Suddenly, with the suddenness of decision, he rose and strode back among the spruce and juniper and about, until he found a level space between the trees to his liking. Here he laid out a rough rectangle, scratching the lines with his boot heel. He marked off space inside for a bunk and another rectangle, small and against one end of the other, for a fireplace. He studied his design and nodded to himself and looked around, estimating the standing timber close by. He strode to his shelter and crawled to the low end to inspect what remained of his staple supplies. He came out carrying a small pack and closed the open end of the shelter with its log barrier. He strode to the flat stone and filled the leather pouch from one of the bags. A few moments later he was striding eastward out of the valley with the rifle in one hand, the lead rope of the burro in the other.

A cool wind whipped down the valley, whispering of the winter still hidden far up in the soaring peaks. It moved over the changing green that was darker with the brown splotches plainer and spreading. It moved out the valley entrance and down the rolling slope where the man strode steadily forward, facing straight into it. He was leading a loaded pack horse now and the burdened burro trotted behind. At the crest of the slope he stopped and searched his back trail for long minutes. His head rose higher and his stride lengthened as he passed through the valley entrance and the horse and the burro followed.

Three miles away on the ridge overlooking the last slope, ten feet back in the timber that topped the ridge, two men stood in the tree shadows and watched the three figures entering the valley. The taller of the two, lean even in his thick mackinaw jacket, had a narrow hatchet face gashed by a thin-lipped mouth. The other, shorter but bulking thick from shoulders to hips, had burnt-out eyes in a round bullet head. The thin-lipped one snapped his fingers and nodded to the other. Together they went back deeper into the timber and mounted the two horses there and rode out and down the ridge, circling to the right toward the high shoulder of climbing rock that would give them a view out over the valley.

Restless on its rock ledge, the great bear lay on the stone and watched the empty camp across the valley. Its ears twitched and the big head rose and swung to the right. It saw the man entering the valley and the horse and burro following. It saw the man stop and look toward it and wave his arms and start forward again. The low rumbling, soft and deep, rolled out from the ledge and died away in the afternoon wind. Quietly the bear watched the man stride toward his camp and begin untying the packs. Quietly it rose and padded on the stone into the darkness of the crevice.

Vigour flowed through the man. The afternoon air of his valley flooded his muscles with strength. His axe leaped into his hands and he felled four trees of the right foundation size and lopped away the branches and cut the logs to

155

the lengths he wanted and notched them; using the axe handle for a measure he took three pieces of rope and used the three-four-five rule to square the corners as he fitted the logs together. As he straightened from checking the fourth joint he saw first the heavy boots, and as his eyes swept upward he saw the small wicked muzzle of the rifle bearing on his belly and the thin-lipped gash of a mouth in the narrow face.

The two men wasted no time. They asked their questions and when he did not answer they roped him to a thick tree. They searched through his camp and came back by him and built a fire and when this was blazing strong they took his rifle and emptied the magazine and laid it with the barrel reaching into the flames and waited for the metal to heat.

The man stood tight against the tree and the pale hazel of his eyes was startling against the dead bloodless brown of his broad wind-burned face. He stared out over the valley and his gaze moved upward and stopped two hundred yards up the opposite slope, and the beginning of living colour crept into his face. The muscles along his jaw were ridged hard and he waited, cautious in his cunning, until the hot steel was close to his flesh before he spoke. He spoke quickly and bobbed his head toward the far slope. The two others turned. They saw the ledge and the uneven dark outline of the crevice. They spoke briefly together and the burnt-eyed one swung abruptly and started across the valley and the thin-lipped one sat hump-kneed on the ground and picked up his rifle and set it across his lap.

The man tight against the tree and the thin-lipped one hump-kneed on the ground watched the other move out and across the valley floor. They saw him stop at the base of the opposite side and look around for the trail and find it. They saw him start up, hurrying now, and reach the ledge almost running and disappear into the crevice.

Time passed and they watched, each in his own intentness, and nothing moved across the way. The ledge under

They wasted no time—where had he hidden the gold?

its overhanging rock slept in its own quietness in the afternoon sun. The thin-lipped one rose and unloosened the rope holding the man to the tree and ordered him ahead and prodded him in the small of the back with the rifle. The man led and the thin-lipped one followed and they started across the valley floor.

Deep in the crevice darkness the great bear stood over the crumpled body. The big head with the small eyes, red-rimmed now, swung slowly from side to side. The sound of running steps had brought it from sleep into instant alertness. The forward leap out of the inner darkness into the dimness near the crevice entrance and the incredibly swift slashing stroke of forepaw had been instinctive reactions to the challenging affront of invasion. Silently it had dragged the body back into the protective darkness and stepped over it, facing the entrance. The scent of the body, familiar yet unfamiliar, rose in its nostrils and caution at an experience never before known held it waiting in the darkness, listening for further sound.

Striding steadily, the man led the way up the trail. His face was a fixed mask and his muscles bunched in tight tension. When the bear broke from the crevice, red-rimmed eyes blinking for swift focus in the sunlight, the man leaped sideways off the trail and down the steep slope, falling and rolling over the sharp rocks and hard against the trunk of a sturdy spruce. He scrambled to his feet and jumped for the first limb and swung his legs in to the trunk and began climbing.

Above him on the trail the thin-lipped one swung up the rifle and fired and the bullet thudded into the bear's left shoulder and scraped the bone and bore back along the side under the skin. In a silent rush the great bear drove down the trail and the thin-lipped one screamed and turned to run and a crashing forepaw crushed his spine forward into his breastbone and raked tearing down through the muscles of his back. The big jaws closed on the already lifeless body and shook it and flung it away.

Close against the trunk, the man peered through the thick branches of the spruce. Below him the great bear quartered the ground like a huge dog on a hunt, moving with a silent flowing deadliness, raising its head often to test the wind. It limped slightly, favouring its left foreleg, and the recurrent pain from the flesh wound in the shoulder swelled the steady rage within and brightened the reddened rims of the eyes. It worked back along the trail near the valley floor and looked across at the man's camp. Abruptly it swung and with steady purpose went up the trail to the ledge and passed along the slopeside and faded into the tangled growth near the head of the valley.

Safe in his spruce, the man watched it go and disappear from his sight. He waited. At last he climbed to the ground and scrambled up to the trail and grabbed the rifle there. Quickly he ejected the spent cartridge shell and pumped another cartridge into the firing chamber. Quickly he checked the magazine and saw it was almost full. Cautious and alert he slipped down and started across the valley.

*As the bear emerged, the captive leaped aside and the
thin-lipped one raised his rifle and fired.*

The packhorse and burro grazed by the camp, quiet now after the brief startling from the single shot across the way. In the fringe of trees behind them and around the camp nothing stirred except the wind whispering its endless murmur through the evergreen branches. As the man approached, downwind, he stopped often to peer forward and swing his head to scan the whole long fringe of trees, searching with his eyes every possible cover. It was the drumming of the horse's hoofs as it pounded to the length of its picket rope and jerked around, strangling, that whirled him toward the sound. The great bear streaked toward him out of thicket shadow and he fired in the instant, instinctively—aiming as rapidly as he could pump the gun. The first shot bored into the junction of neck and right shoulder and shattered the bone there and the second smashed into the massive breast and ripped back through the lungs. The great bear drove ahead, uneven in bounding stride with a deep coughing tearing its throat, and the third shot struck through the mouth and back into the spine. The man leaped aside and the bear's rush took it past and it crumpled forward to the ground. The man stood by the bear's body and stared down. It was smaller with the life gone. The muscles of the man's shoulders shook a little and he swung his head slowly from one side to the other and the flat planes of his face were hard as the rock formations ringing the valley.

He stood by the rectangle of notched logs a long time. Quietly he turned and went to the flat stone and took the plump salt bags from under it and carried them over by his shelter and began to prepare his packs. Half an hour later he strode across the valley floor and the packhorse and the burro followed. The sun, dropping below the far peaks, was behind him. The chill rising wind beat against his back. Unbelievably small in the vastness he strode out of the valley, and with him went a new loneliness and a sense of something lost.

The Shark Cage

JAMES ALDRIDGE

BEN AMINO had lost his left arm—from elbow to wrist—to
a shark. The shark had attacked him underwater in a
remote Egyptian bay along the Red Sea coast, where he
had been taking underwater films for an American film
company. By some miracle he had managed to reach the
surface of the coral reef in a bloody heap. By some greater
miracle, his son Davy had flown him, unconscious, back
to Cairo in the small Auster aeroplane.

Apart from the responsibility of getting his father to a
hospital, it had been a terrorizing experience for a boy
who had never flown a plane by himself before. And Ben
Amino had realized it was not going to be easy to change
suddenly from a withdrawn and short-spoken father to a
grateful but uncertain parent who must try to find a way
of penetrating the barrier his son had erected against him.

"This time," Ben told his son, "I'm going to build a shark cage."

"What's that?" Davy asked suspiciously, not commenting at all on his father's intention of returning to Shark Bay.

"It's a metal cage," Ben said in his impatient way.

Then he corrected himself. He must try to change even the tone of his voice, although it was going to be difficult for a man of forty to express himself gently when he had never been inclined that way.

"It's a small iron cage big enough for a man to stand up in underwater so that he can photograph sharks in safety," he explained. "You're inside, and they're outside. Cousteau has one on his ship. But mine will have to be much smaller, and light enough to carry in a small aircraft and dismantle too."

"How can you fly with one arm?" Davy asked him.

"It's my left arm that's gone," Ben told him. "Which doesn't matter on the Auster. I can use my right on the throttles. That's what counts. . . ."

"Are you allowed to fly an aeroplane with only one arm?"

"They don't know about it," Ben said. "It's eight months since it happened. And there was no accident to the plane. They have no reason to know I lost an arm. My next medical check isn't due until November, and we'll be gone from Egypt by then. I can get the plane all right whether I have a false arm or not. They won't know. . . ."

He was making it seem so easy, when he suddenly realized that Davy was trying to make it difficult.

Davy did not want to go back to Shark Bay. He did not want to face again the terror of seeing his father rising bloody and mangled from the sea. He did not want to remember his terrified efforts to get his father into the plane, to start the plane, to get it off the ground, to fly it on course; to find the airfield, and finally to put the plane down among the airliners without smashing it to pieces.

"This time," Ben assured him again, trying to be patient

with Davy's desire to retreat from him, "there will be no accidents. I promise. . . ."

How could he promise such a thing? Yet it was the least he could do.

Ben still had only a hazy idea of the whole project. The last time he had photographed sharks under water for the Universal Film Company he had hoped to collect enough money from his shark films to take the boy home, to try to set him up in a decent school, or to arrange for someone to look after him. But eight months of hospitals and doctors and keeping the flat in Cairo until he was out of hospital had eaten away all his stake money. There was not enough left now to pay his and the boy's fares back home, and to live there a few months while he found some sort of work for an ex-bush-pilot with one arm and no wife.

"D'you want to come and see the cage being made?" he asked the boy.

"Yes!" Davy said seriously.

"Come on then," he said, trying to sound light-hearted about it.

Ben had drawn a rough plan of the cage, and he had persuaded a native blacksmith in a big car-repair shop to attempt it. The Greek foreman had agreed (with a pound in his pocket) and the Egyptian smith and his assistant, who was even younger than Davy, began working the angle iron and mild steel strips into four separate walls of a cage.

"It would be better to have the door on top," the smith told him before beginning to weld the flat strips to the angle iron on the greasy garage floor.

"I might not have the strength to push it up under water," Ben argued, making the gesture of pushing above his head with his one and half arms.

"But this door is too big, too long," the smith said with a shrug. "It will be stiff."

"It'll do," Ben insisted.

He tried to explain the construction plan to Davy, but

163

the boy seemed so uninterested in explanation that Ben did not pursue it, and he allowed the boy to watch with his own eyes. Ben had already noticed that his son observed everything; but he disliked being taught.

Ben kept his eye on it to be sure it was done properly. He watched the smith cutting and welding and drilling, assisted by the Arab boy, Mahmoud, who never said a word, although he worked like a man. The boy had perfected the helper's art. He knew when and where to hold the thin steel strips for the smith to cut and drill. If the smith needed a hammer or a cold-chisel it was in the smith's hand before he could ask for it—like a surgeon being supplied by a well-drilled team of assistants.

As the cage took shape Ben asked his son what he thought of it.

"How will you keep it standing up underwater?" Davy asked.

"I'll weight the floor and lash the sides to the coral," Ben said.

The smith broke a drill with a loud crack, and while he was hunting for another one in his tool box he told Mahmoud to weld the door strips together. Ben and Davy watched the Arab boy light the acetylene torch, adjust the flame to its blue point, adjust his cracked goggles, and begin welding the last of the mild steel strips to the door frames.

"Plenty of weld!" Ben warned the boy.

Mahmoud grinned. "*Iowa, ya bey*," he said.

But Ben watched him carefully to be sure that the welding was not slip-shod. He stood over the boy until he realized that Davy had deliberately walked away. What for? Ben looked at Davy's back and guessed it was a strange act of loyalty to the Arab boy, who was obviously quite capable of welding the door without any adult supervision.

Once it was built, the next problem was transporting the cage in a small hired aeroplane without frightening the

From inside the cage, Ben would photograph the sharks.

people who owned the plane. The less they saw of the strange iron cage the better. Even dismantled, it was far too cumbersome and wide to fit into the fuselage of an Auster.

The only way to carry it would be to lash it along the bottom of the fuselage on the outside. But that would have to be well arranged, otherwise it might shift in flight, with disastrous results.

Ben had his friends among the Egyptian aeroplane riggers at the little airfield, and he explained what he wanted to one of them who was called Salaam by his friends because of his habit of saying: *Ya Salaam* (Good gracious!) to all events, be it a successful operation on an aeroplane or some serious crash on the airfield.

"*Ya Salaam!*" Salaam said to Ben when he saw the cage. "You can't fly that on the Auster."

"Why not?" Ben asked. "She'll lift the weight easily enough. . . ."

Salaam shook his head and "Ya Salaamed" and showed Ben the thin tubular fuselage of the Auster braced only by wooden stringers.

"They must be elastic in flight," Salaam said. "If you lash a rigid steel weight to them you will put too much local strain on the tail. And then . . . *Ya Salaam!*"

Ben might fly it all right, but it would dangerously weaken the whole structure of the plane.

"But there's a Beechcraft in the hangar," Salaam told him. "It will be better."

The Beechraft was an efficient and tough American plane with a big engine. This one had been bought up by the Egyptians from the oil company which Ben had originally worked for. He had been flying oil geologists over the Egyptian deserts in Beechcrafts and Fairchilds, but now they were beat-up and rotting in the hangars.

"Under here, you see?" Salaam said, under the fuselage of one of the Beeches.

Ben saw and remembered the four eyebolts on the fuselage which were used for tying down a plane in the open

166

desert in case of high winds.

"Perfect," Ben said.

Salaam opened a panel in the back of the fuselage and showed him where he could attach two more brackets to which he could lash the cage.

"What about the engine of this one? It used to take oil like a sieve," Ben said.

"It will be all right for another twenty hours, and I have some very heavy oil."

He was safe with Salaam, and he felt half-way there.

It had not been unusual in Ben's Canadian days to fly small planes with long lumps of mining equipment lashed outboard to the fuselage. But this old Beechcraft was very slack on the controls, and its engine lost compression even in take-off, so that he felt as if he were flying the shark cage itself.

"All right?" he asked Davy.

Davy was white, and Ben did not know if that was caused by the hot air bumps over the desert or by Davy's natural fear of aeroplanes, or by some other anticipation of danger yet to come at Shark Bay.

"Can't you go up higher," Davy asked, "where there aren't any bumps?"

"We're climbing as fast as we can," Ben shouted over the unimpressive roar of the worn-out engine. "That shark cage is too far forward. . . ."

Even with full tail-trim adjustment the Beechcraft was nose heavy. Ben held the stick well back, but his false left arm was already cutting into his flesh as a result. He had to keep the plane delicately balanced; if he pulled the stick back too far the nose would suddenly lift, and then she would probably spin out of control.

"There are peppermints in my pocket," Ben said. "Get them out."

Davy put his hand in Ben's shirt pocket and took out the roll of peppermints. He put one in his father's mouth because Ben dare not let anything go.

167

"Do you feel sick?" Ben asked.

Davy shook his head, and Ben realized he shouldn't have asked that question. It probably invoked bad memories of the last flight, when Davy had been very sick. But this time Ben had given him some air-sick pills.

"Do you want to feel it?"Ben asked, nodding at the stick.

Davy shook his head and looked at his father's aluminium arm, and at the leather-covered alloy hand. Where the false arm joined the real one at the elbow there was already a large red wound which was beginning to bleed. It looked raw; but when Davy glanced at his father's face to see how he could bear it, Ben simply looked back, impassive.

"Like trying to steer a heavy freight train," Ben shouted.

He made light work of it, but he felt as if he were holding the plane aloft in the air with his bad arm, which was beginning to feel the strain.

"There it is," Ben shouted thankfully when they came over a white bay among the ten thousand others along the naked green line of sea and desert.

Ben had heard from an Egyptian marine biologist of this new bay, which was supposed to be full of both sharks and large manta rays. It also was called Shark Bay, as they all were, and like the others it was simply a curved strip of inaccessible coral sand rimmed by featureless desert, impossible to approach except by light plane or from the sea.

"Hold on tight," Ben shouted as they began to go down. "She'll bump. . . ."

The approach was simple. But the moment they levelled off over the white and yellow sand the surface changed aspect from an apparently smooth stretch to an incredibly lumpy one.

The moment the plane touched down, something underneath seemed to slip out of place, and the plane slewed round in a vicious curve. They heard a heavy rip in the

The plane slewed round in a vicious curve.

fuselage, and the crash of something coming through into the after compartment. The plane bumped up once and then came down to a dead stop with another sad crashing noise below. . . .

"Are you all right?" Davy asked his father. "What's happened?"

Ben's false arm had almost been ripped off by the sudden jerk of the stick forward, and he was obviously in pain. He was tearing at the straps which bound the false limb to the real one, and he worked desperately until he had freed his raw flesh from the torture of metal and leather.

"Blast this thing," he said angrily. "It's worse than no arm at all."

He was cursing it until he saw his son's face. Then he remembered himself, and he calmed down. But when he saw this old terror in the boy's face, he asked himself if he was doing the right thing—dragging his son back over this frightening experience. Yet, from the beginning, the idea resolved itself into a necessity for both their sakes.

Ben was not a subtle man, and doggedness was the only way he knew of overcoming his difficulties.

"It'll be all right," he told Davy and jumped out to inspect the damage.

It was not serious. The edge of the shark cage had sliced off a large lump of coral protruding from the sand. It was this lump which had smashed through the fuselage and made such a noise. If the coral had not been so neatly sliced off, it might have gone through the tail plane, with irreparable results.

"Nothing much," Ben the improviser said. "We can patch the fuselage. . . ."

But Davy had already gone to the sea's edge, where he was dipping his hot face in the water and rubbing it over his hair and his neck.

"Poor kid," Ben said again.

Then he shook off that feeling. "Poor kidding" his son was not going to help anybody.

The shark cage was slightly bent from the blow on the coral, but with Davy's silent help Ben had assembled it by midday.

They waited until the sun was down, resting under the plane. Then they bolted the pieces together. Davy put the bolts in place and Ben used the wrench with his good arm to make sure that they were tight. They had hung the door on its hinges in time for nightfall.

"Do you think they can get my other arm through that?" Ben joked, admiring the cage.

"Are you going to wear your metal arm under water?" Davy asked.

"No. That's worse than having none at all," Ben said.

He did not say that he could never get the arm back on over his bruised flesh.

They slept under the plane, and this time Ben had thought of everything for his son: soft drinks and even biscuits and tinned fruit, which they ate with their fingers while Ben showed him how to identify the constellations.

In the early morning Ben reconnoitred the best place underwater for the cage, but they found it difficult to roll it over the sand to the edge of the coral reef.

"Better wear your shoes," Ben told Davy, who had cut his foot.

Ben himself was not yet used to being one-armed, and his temper was short by the time the cage was ready to tip over the edge of the reef into the twenty feet of clear water. Davy helped. He did what he was told to do— silently; but he never volunteered a move, as most boys would surely be inclined to.

"When I say push, give it all you've got," Ben told him, "and then jump clear of the ropes. . . ."

He had attached four ropes to the top of the cage. That way the cage would not fall in sideways, but would go down the right way up.

"Now push!" Ben said.

They slipped and struggled until the cage started to topple over the reef.

"Get out of the way," Ben shouted.

But Davy was already clear when the cage went in. The ropes tightened on the stakes which Ben had driven into the sand, and the cage was suspended underwater. Ben put on his mask and went down to take a look at it.

"That's pretty good, Davy," Ben said when he came out after fixing the cage where it should be on the sea floor. "Now I'll lash it to the coral and we're all set. . . ."

He noticed then that Davy had already erected the canvas shelter under which they would spend the hot part of the day. He had also carried down one half of the little air compressor, so that Ben could set it up.

"I'm finally getting somewhere," Ben decided.

The underwater camera which the Universal Film Company had sent him was built to take 35 mm wide screen film and lenses. That was the point of this expedition. The company would pay up to five thousand dollars for a thousand feet of good shark film, and an extra thousand

Ben braced the camera on the s

dollars for any shot of a big manta ray.

The camera was heavy, but Ben slung it down on one of the ropes, and then pulled on his aqualung.

"You can lie on the coral edge and watch if you like," he told Davy, showing him how he could stretch out in the few inches of water behind a bar of coral and put his face in the water over the deep edge.

"I know," Davy said.

"But don't go in with the aqualung."

Ben had brought along an extra lung. He had already shown Davy how to use it in a safe inlet behind one of the reefs, where the sharks could not enter. Davy was a good swimmer and he had easily mastered the lung.

"I won't be long," Ben said and lowered himself in with the rope.

Once he was under the silver-blue surface, he looked around hopefully to see if any sharks had appeared to

age and pushed the trigger button.

sample his bait of donkey meat. The meat was pouring out thin black streaks of blood into the clear coral sea. There were herds of small fish nosing it curiously, but nothing big in sight. He slid the camera down the rope, and he congratulated himself on his ingenuity when he entered the cage—an almost fool-proof approach and a safe position for shark filming. He closed and lashed the door, and waited.

He had to wait until after he had gone down again in the afternoon before the first sharks appeared. They came, as they always did, from nowhere. One moment there were no sharks, then mysteriously, with a wave of the hand, one was nosing at the donkey meat in front of him. By the time he had raised the camera, there were two more nearby, one of them a tiger shark with two striped pilot fish cruising over his nose bulge. Ben braced the camera on the side of the cage and pushed the trigger button. The nearest shark fled in fright. They had not yet tasted blood. When they did they would be much bolder; so he waited.

He was not upset to be back among these terrors of flesh and blood which had cut him up so badly. He felt very safe in the cage. But he did feel, quite clearly, the memorized pain in his arm where the teeth had slashed him. But he felt it in the part of the arm which was no longer there.

"This is the last time," he was saying to himself. "When I've made this stake I won't come back. It's not fair to the boy. . . ."

He knew he was too much of an improviser. That was all right for bush piloting and the sort of knock-about flying he had been doing in Egypt. In fact, looking back on it, improvisation had almost become his life. How else did a pilot like him operate or even survive? But that was not such a good method of life for a man with a son to bring up. He must (he decided, looking at the wrinkled hide of a shark not six feet away) give it some more serious thought later on. He did not want Davy to grow up the same way.

There were two sharks attacking the meat now, and as they turned away they swam by the cage without fear. He held the camera on them.

"Not me!" he said as one of them came back to look at him. "Not me. . . . ."

He had the choice of five or six in range. Some of them were basking sharks, but two of them were tigers. One was lying on the bottom near a large undersea rock of dead coral, the place where he had hoped to see the big rays. He had also anchored one of the guy ropes to it.

"Take your time," he warned himself.

The inclination was always to make the film sequences too short. He was supporting the camera with his delicate lump of serrated flesh. It hurt, but it worked. Then suddenly one of the larger basking sharks approached the cage very boldly, and when it swung away it slapped the side of the cage with its tail.

The cage teetered back and forth and almost fell over on its side; but it was held up by the ropes which he had lashed to the mushroom coral behind him. He waited for it to settle, and then he decided he had had enough for the time being. He had used up all his film.

"One more and I'm through," he told Davy when he had surfaced.

"Why did the shark knock the cage?" Davy asked.

He had been watching from the top, and Ben shrugged it off.

"Hard to say," he said. "Probably an accident. . . ."

But Davy looked unconvinced, and to encourage him out of his fears Ben told him to start packing up the gear so that they could leave the moment he came out.

He was an unlucky man, he always had been; and though he had learned to live with his bad luck, he was getting too old to survive it much longer.

He had finished filming the sharks. The meat was finished, which meant that most of them had gone. But he still waited doggedly on in the hope of a thousand-dollar manta ray appearing over the coral rock, where they liked to come to be de-loused by the smaller fish.

"Good heavens!" he said. "I'm in luck. . . ."

A shadow, a speckled moving cloud was cruising along the bottom beside the reef. It was a manta with monstrous lobed jaws, flying in a heavy and cumbersome manner as if it were blind or hurt or simply old. It was knocking small lumps of coral off the reef as it came, and the white sand below it was swirling off the bottom as it flapped its giant pointed wings in heavy propulsion.

"Come on you beauty," Ben encouraged.

It was coming right by the cage, and though he was lost in the elation of filming it, he saw that its wings, or its massive head, were going to foul the rope which he had tied from the cage to the coral rock on the sea floor.

Ben rattled the camera on the bars to divert the ray from its course, but it flew on and fouled the rope.

175

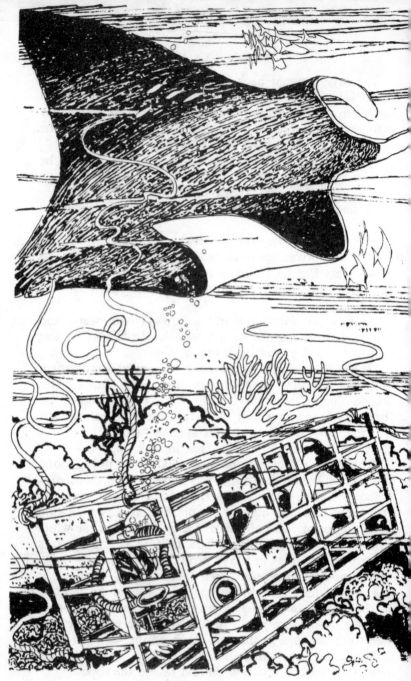

"How do I get out of this?" Ben thought.

In the shock of contact, or in the sudden and powerful lashing of the ray's wings, the cage was pulled forward by the guy rope. Ben felt it going over, as if it had been hit by a destroyer. . . .

For a moment he thought that the manta was going to drag the cage and himself out to sea. He was on his side. He knew that the moorings behind had snapped, or the coral had broken, and he felt the cage roll over and over on the bottom under great force. Then, with a sudden jerk, the ray was free of the rope and it blundered away in a fog of sand and coral dust.

"How do I get out of this?" Ben thought.

He was lying on his side in the cage. The door was flat on the sea-bed. The cage had also been pushed out of shape, and the door itself was forced in on one side. He felt like an enormous fish in a bowl. It had been a small enough prison standing up in it, but lying down like this he could hardly manoeuvre.

"If I ever get out of this one, it will be a miracle," he said.

He began to lever the cage by putting his foot through the bars on to the sea floor, trying to turn the cage over to bring the door on top. Impossible. He tried to bend the mild steel strips, but the smithy had made them too strong. He shook the door underneath, in the hope that he could break something, but Mahmoud's welding held.

"I've had it," he told himself at last.

He rolled over to see if Davy was watching. He could not see Davy's mask on the surface. Then he looked at his air gauge and cursed himself for a fool for waiting that extra five minutes—for that thousand miserable dollars.

He had no more than twenty minutes' air left, at the outside.

It was two minutes, it seemed like an hour.

He had tried everything again, and then he looked up and saw Davy's mask. Ben lay on his back and waved. He could see Davy's hand wave back. Ben made the motion with one arm of undoing the nuts which held the cage together, and he tried to show Davy that he needed the spanner.

Davy's face disappeared in an instant.

When he came back Ben saw the spanner in the boy's hand in the water.

"Don't drop it," he bubbled out through his air as if the boy could hear.

Davy dropped it, but he had tied it to a fishing cord, and he guided it by swinging it into the cage. Ben did not wait to untie it but began to reach out for the bolts.

But the round heads of the bolts were on the inside, the square heads outside. No amount of arm-twisting could bring the spanner to play on them. He looked up and shook his head. Davy was not there.

He calculated that he had fifteen minutes of air left, when he saw one of the guy ropes coming his way. Davy was paying it out to him, and he guessed that the boy was going to try his strength at pulling the cage upright. On the surface it would have been impossible, but with the cage underwater he might have a chance.

"Okay!" Ben bubbled out when he had tied the rope to the cage roof. "But hurry!"

Davy's mask disappeared, and in half a minute he saw the rope straining tight, but there was no impression on the position of the cage. This was hopeless, and when Davy's face appeared again Ben whirled his hand around and around.

"The plane," he was saying into the sea. "Start the plane. . . ."

He made the gestures of propellor-turning, of stick, of throttle, until the boy understood and disappeared again. While he waited, Ben tried to calculate what the boy would do: whether he would have enough sense to attach the rope to the tail-wheel, whether he could manage to start the engine with its tendency to flood, whether a thousand things would be done that would be right or wrong or successful, and even though he was underwater he had the

As the rope strained, the cage below heaved.

impression that he was sweating.

"Hurry up, Davy," he said and began to worry about the boy now.

If he was left down here Davy would never fly that Beechcraft off the ground. The plane was too old and too difficult for Davy to succeed a second time. This time Davy's life depended entirely on his own.

He felt the tug then.

"He's got it going. . . ."

The rope strained, but he thought it would be cut loose by one of the iron edges. He pushed it off with his good hand. He was cut to pieces already by pinches and slaps from the cage, but now that the plane was straining he knew he had a chance.

"He's got the brakes on," Ben told himself.

If they were old enough the brakes would give, and suddenly something did give.

The cage bounced along the floor, side down, and then the bottom struck the edge of the coral and it began to right itself, not right up, but near enough.

"Hold it!" Ben cried desperately.

Regardless of the results to his good hand, Ben put his arm through the side and held the cage up to the coral. The rope slacked off, and he pulled it down and got a hitch on to a coral projection and tied it roughly on to one of the steel bars.

He could already feel his air valve beginning to drag. His gauge registered less than ten atmospheres, and he was obviously dragging out the last of it.

He pushed on the cage door, but even though it was upright it would not budge. The cage was so out of shape that the door was jammed in beyond hope of moving it by the force of an arm or a leg.

He looked up helplessly again. . . .

"I'm licked," he wept, "I'm licked. . . ."

He felt as if he were losing his head, but when he saw the boy's face again—the mask, the opaque oval of eyes— he showed the boy that he could not push the door open.

It was only when he saw Davy suddenly disappear and then re-appear, body and all, under the surface, that he began to look around anxiously to see what had happened to the sharks.

"Stay up!" he tried to wave at the boy.

Davy came down awkwardly. He was too small and too buoyant for the amount of air in the big lung, but he reached the cage and hung on. Ben wanted the air in that lung badly, but he looked frantically around to be sure that there were no sharks.

There were two, but they were basking a little way off near the rock.

Davy tried to pull the door open with his hands.

Ben thought of a hacksaw, but he knew they did not have one in the tool box.

He was out of ideas and almost out of air. He watched Davy, stupidly mesmerized, as the boy tied the other guy rope to the cage door.

What now?

Davy kicked frantically to dive deeper. Ben saw the boy swimming over towards the rock with all the broken rope he could find. The sharks lying on the floor near the rock could be any kind, as far as Ben could see, and he watched his son swim carefully around the rock dragging the tied length of rope so that it swung right around the rock.

"He's going to use it as a pulley," Ben realized, sucking at the valve and wondering which lungful would be the last.

He wanted to hurry the boy, but he knew he dare not.

He watched Davy's clumsy passage over the sleeping sharks. It was a bitter moment when he realized that youth should not be exposed to danger, even in the interests of life and death. He had always committed his greatest crimes against his son, simply by assuming that everything would be all right. Nothing was all right. Life itself was a trap, and he must guard the boy against it if he ever got out of this. He must guard the boy against even the simplest risks, the remotest dangers. . . .

Ben was dragging the very last gasps out of the lung as Davy completed the circuit safely and began to surface with the length of rope.

"Let me have your lung!" Ben gestured at him.

He pointed to his gauge and shook his head and pointed to his lung and to Davy's, indicating that he must lower it down quickly. . . .

Davy nodded.

Ben felt the valve rattling and resisting heavily with every short breath he took.

He had to suck it in from the depth of his stomach muscles to get the last inch of pressure out of it. He was feeling dizzy, and he wondered what was holding the boy up. He was not going to last, he knew it. . . .

The lung came down on the end of the cord.

Ben ripped off the mouthpiece of his own and pulled the hose of the new one through the bars, jamming his face against the cage so that he could get the mouthpiece

181

through it into his mouth.

The mouthpiece was bubbling air automatically and he felt the first full drag of cold, metallic air enter his lungs.

Yet it seemed too late, because he was too exhausted by his last breathing efforts to do more than hold the side of the cage with his lump of an arm, hold the mouthpiece in with the other, and simply hang on to consciousness.

He was not aware of the tug on the cage until it began to topple over again. The rope, which was now attached to the twisted door and was then passed around the rock, began to tighten. He could see lumps of dead coral flying off the dead rock and the fish flying away and the sharks waking up.

Davy was revving up the Beechcraft and pulling on the rope with it.

Ben got a good grip on the mouthpiece of the lung with his teeth and used his good arm to hold on to the nearest lump of coral.

He could feel the strain on the rope now. He held on, feeling his flesh tearing on the coral.

Everything happened together:

The door was ripped open, the rope broke, and he lost his grip on the mouthpiece of the spare aqualung, which floated away. The cage itself began to teeter over to fall again. . . .

There was a second to get through the half-open door before it fell.

He felt the iron scrape his back as he flung his body forward. He felt the cage crack down on his heels as it fell over. He began to kick his way to the surface with bursting lungs.

Yet he could kill himself, even now.

If he did not remember to let the air in his lungs out, slowly, as he went up—the pressure of the air which he had breathed in would quickly expand as he got nearer the surface, and he would blow his lungs out.

"Let it out," he told himself, "slowly. . . ."

He burst to the top with his lips still whistling out air.

Then he gulped in the first draught of light and sun and air, right down to his diaphragm.

"Hurry!" Davy was shouting, putting his mask on to the water to see what was below. "There's a shark. . . ."

Ben knew real terror, that last of all terrors which drove men to exceed the limited capacities of normal strength and thought, and he thrashed his legs and arms and reached the coral shallows as if he were flying with his arms.

Davy helped him out, and he remembered the empty lung still on his back. He hardly had the strength to fall flat on his stomach in the hot shallow water. . . .

That was all.

He lay still and exhausted with his face in the hot shallows, feeling the sun. He heard Davy asking him, begging to know, if he was all right. He nodded slowly. He could hear the Beechcraft's engine still running. It was probably overheating.

"Turn the engine off, Davy," he managed.

The cage began to teeter over to fall again.

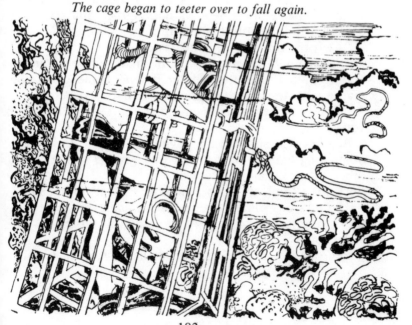

183

He heard the boy splash off, and then the silence as the rumble of the Beech's engine died in a hot cough. Ben knew he had to get up now or he would never get up.

He pulled the release buckles of the lung and the weight belt, and he crawled out of the harness. He got to his feet and reached the sand, where he lay down again on his back feeling every tear and rent in his body.

He knew then that he was a wasteful man.

But he knew it! That counted. And he would never again risk the life of the boy.

"I'm sorry, kid," he said, looking at the boy. "Are you all right?"

That solemn, frightened face was looking down at him.

"You did the right thing," Ben told him desperately.

It was more than true. Davy was not a willing volunteer, he was not much at anticipation, he would certainly never go around offering anyone generous slices of himself; but he was going to be a good man to have around when you were in a tight spot. Perhaps that was the value of improvisation, the temperament of both father and son; the dogged grip they both had on life.

"I left the camera. . . ." Ben said.

He sat up. The camera was insured and it would be nobody's loss. But the film in it—the sequence of the manta ray—was worth a thousand dollars.

"You're not going back in are you?" Davy said. "Are you?"

Ben knew he still had the pugnacity to do it, to find the other lung and go back under and get the camera. But other values began to intervene.

"I don't think so, Davy," he said. "I don't think so."

The boy was almost smiling in his embarrassment. He was trying to pity or comfort or assure his father—as far as he could.

Ben saw his son's relief, and his heart warmed to him.

Jimmy Goggles the God

H. G. WELLS

It isn't everyone who's been a god," said the sunburnt man. "But it's happened to me. Among other things."

I intimated my sense of his condescension.

"It don't leave much for ambition, does it?" said the sunburnt man.

"I was one of those men who were saved from the *Ocean Pioneer*. Gummy! how time flies! It's twenty years ago. I doubt if you'll remember anything of the *Ocean Pioneer*?"

The name was familiar, and I tried to recall when and where I had read it. The *Ocean Pioneer*? "Something about gold dust." I said vaguely, "but the precise—"

"That's it," he said. "In a beastly little channel she hadn't no business in—dodging pirates. It was before they'd put the kybosh on that business. And there'd been volcanoes or something and all the rocks was wrong. There's places about by Soona where you fair have to follow the rocks about to see where they're going next. Down she went in twenty fathoms before you could have dealt for whist, with fifty thousand pounds worth of gold aboard, it was said, in one form or another."

"Survivors?"

"Three."

"I remember the case now," I said. "There was something about salvage—"

But at the word salvage the sunburnt man exploded into language so extraordinarily horrible that I stopped aghast. He came down to more ordinary swearing, and pulled himself up abruptly. "Excuse me," he said, "but—salvage!"

He leant over towards me. "I was in that job," he said. "Tried to make myself a rich man, and got made a god instead. I've got my feelings—

"It ain't all jam being a god," said the sunburnt man, and for some time conversed by means of such pithy but unprogressive axioms. At last he took up his tale again.

"There was me," said the sunburnt man, "and a seaman named Jacobs, and Always, the mate of the *Ocean Pioneer*. And him it was that set the whole thing going. I remember him now, when we was in the jolly boat, suggesting it all to our minds just by one sentence. He was a wonderful hand at suggesting things. 'There was forty thousand pounds,' he said, 'on that ship, and it's for me to say just where she went down.' It didn't need much brains to tumble to that. And he was the leader from the first to the last. He got hold of the Sanderses and their brig; they were brothers, and the brig was the *Pride of Banya*, and he it was bought the diving dress—a second-hand one with a compressed air apparatus instead of pumping. He'd have done the diving too, if it hadn't made him sick going down. And the salvage people were mucking about with a chart he'd cooked up, as solemn as could be, at Starr Race, a hundred and twenty miles away.

"I can tell you we was a happy lot aboard that brig,

jokes and drink and bright hopes all the time. It all seemed
so neat and clean and straightforward, and what rough
chaps call a 'cert'. And we used to speculate how the other
blessed lot, the proper salvagers, who'd started two days
before us, were getting on, until our sides fairly ached. We
all messed together in the Sanderses' cabin—it was a
curious crew, all officers and no men—and there stood the
diving-dress waiting its turn. Young Sanders was a hum-
orous sort of chap, and there certainly was something
funny in the confounded thing's great fat head and its
stare, and he made us see it too. 'Jimmy Goggles', he used
to call it, and talk to it like a Christian. Asked if he was
married, and how Mrs. Goggles was, and all the little
Goggleses. Fit to make you split. And every blessed day
all of us used to drink the health of Jimmy Goggles in
rum, and unscrew his eye and pour a glass of rum in him,
until, instead of that nasty mackintosheriness, he smelt as
nice in his inside as a cask of rum. It was jolly times we
had in those days, I can tell you—little suspecting, poor
chaps! what was a-coming.

"We weren't going to throw away our chances by any
blessed hurry, you know, and we spent a whole day
sounding our way towards where the *Ocean Pioneer* had
gone down, right between two chunks of ropy grey rock—
lava rocks that rose nearly out of the water. We had to lay
off about half a mile to get a safe anchorage, and there
was a thundering row who should stop on board. And
there she lay just as she had gone down, so that you could
see the top of the masts that was still standing perfectly
distinctly. The row ended in all coming in the boat. I went
down in the diving-dress on Friday morning directly it was
light.

"What a surprise it was! I can see it all now quite distinctly. It was a queer-looking place, and the light was just
coming. People over here think every blessed place in the
tropics is a flat shore and palm trees and surf, bless 'em!
This place, for instance, wasn't a bit that way. Not common rocks they were, undermined by waves; but great

187

curved banks like ironwork cinder heaps, with green slime below, and thorny shrubs and things just waving upon them here and there, and the water glassy calm and clear, and showing you a kind of dirty grey-black shine, with huge flaring red-brown weeds spreading motionless, and crawling and darting things going through it. And far away beyond the ditches and pools and the heaps was a forest on the mountain flank, growing again after the fires and cinder showers of the last eruption. And the other way forest, too, and a kind of broken—what is it?—amby-theatre of black and rusty cinders rising out of it all, and the sea in a kind of bay in the middle.

"The dawn, I say, was just coming, and there wasn't much colour about things, and not a human being but ourselves anywhere in sight up or down the channel. Except the *Pride of Banya*, lying out beyond a lump of rocks towards the line of the sea.

"Not a human being in sight," he repeated, and paused.

"*I* don't know where they came from, not a bit. And we were feeling so safe that we were all alone that poor young Sanders was a-singing. I was in Jimmy Goggles, all except the helmet. 'Easy,' says Always, 'there's her mast.' And after I'd had just one squint over the gunwale, I caught up the bogey and almost tipped out as old Sanders brought the boat round. When the windows were screwed and everything was all right, I shut the valve from the air belt in order to help my sinking, and jumped overboard, feet foremost—for we hadn't a ladder. I left the boat pitching, and all of them staring down into the water after me, as my head sank down into the weeds and blackness that lay about the mast. I suppose nobody, not the most cautious chap in the world, would have bothered about a look-out at such a desolate place. It stunk of solitude.

"Of course you must understand that I was a greenhorn at diving. None of us were divers. We'd had to muck about with the thing to get the way of it, and this was the first time I'd been deep. It feels damnable. Your ears hurt beastly. I don't know if you've ever hurt yourself yawning or sneezing, but it takes you like that, only ten times worse. And a pain over the eyebrows here—splitting—and a feeling like influenza in the head. And it isn't all heaven in your lungs and things. And going down feels like the beginning of a lift, only it keeps on. And you can't turn your head to see what's above you, and you can't get a fair squint at what's happening to your feet without bending down something painful. And being deep it was dark, let alone the blackness of the ashes and mud that formed the bottom. It was like going down out of the dawn back into the night, so to speak.

"The mast came up like a ghost out of the black, and then a lot of fishes, and then a lot of flapping red seaweed, and then whack I came with a kind of dull bang on the deck of the *Ocean Pioneer*, and the fishes that had been feeding on the dead rose about me like a swarm of flies from road stuff in summer time. I turned on the compressed air again—for the suit was a bit thick and mackintoshery after all, in spite of the rum—and stood recovering myself. It struck coolish down there, and that helped take off the stuffiness a bit.

"When I began to feel easier, I started looking about me. It was an extraordinary sight. Even the light was extraordinary, a kind of reddy coloured twilight, on account of the streamers of seaweed that floated up on either side of the ship. And far overhead just a moony, deep green blue. The deck of the ship, except for a slight list to starboard, was level, and lay all dark and long between the weeds, clear except where the masts had snapped when she rolled, and vanishing into black night towards the forecastle. There weren't any dead on the decks, most were in the weeds alongside, I suppose; but afterwards I found two skeletons lying in the passengers' cabins, where death had come to them. It was curious to stand on that deck and recognize it all, bit by bit; a place against the rail where I'd been fond of smoking by starlight, and the corner where an old chap from Sydney used to flirt with a widow we had aboard. A comfortable couple they'd been, only a month ago, and now you couldn't have got a meal for a baby crab off either of them.

"I've always had a bit of philosophical turn, and I dare say I spent the best part of five minutes in such thoughts before I went below to find where the blessed dust was stored. It was slow work hunting, feeling it was for the most part, pitchy dark, with confusing blue gleams down the companion. And there were things moving about, a dab at my glass once, and once a pinch at my leg. Crabs I expect. I kicked a lot of loose stuff that puzzled me, and stooped and picked up something all knobs and spikes. What do you think? Backbone! But I never had any particular feeling for bones. We had talked the affair over pretty thoroughly, and Always knew just where the stuff was stowed. I found it that trip. I lifted a box one end an inch or more."

He broke off in his story. "I've lifted it," he said, "as near as that! Forty thousand pounds' worth of pure gold! Gold! I shouted inside my helmet as a kind of cheer and hurt my ears. I was getting confounded stuffy and tired by this time—I must have been down twenty-five minutes or more—and I thought this was good enough. I went up the companion again, and as my eyes came up flush with the deck, a thundering great crab gave a kind of hysterical jump and went scuttling off sideways. Quite a start it gave me. I stood up clear on deck and shut the valve behind the helmet to let the air accumulate to carry me up again—I noticed a kind of whacking from above, as though they were hitting the water with an oar, but I didn't look up. I fancied they were signalling me to come up.

"And then something shot down by me—something heavy, and stood a-quiver in the planks. I looked, and there was a long knife I'd seen young Sanders handling. Thinks I, he's dropped it, and I was still calling him this kind of fool and that—for it might have hurt me serious—when I began to lift and drive up towards the daylight. Just about the level of the top spars of the *Ocean Pioneer*, whack! I came against something sinking down, and a

Down they went, clutching and turning over.

boot knocked in front of my helmet. Then something else, struggling frightful. It was a big weight atop of me, whatever it was, and moving and twisting about. I'd have thought it a big octopus, or some such thing, if it hadn't been for the boot. But octopuses don't wear boots. It was all in a moment, of course. I felt myself sinking down again, and I threw my arms about to keep steady, and the whole lot rolled free of me and shot down as I went up—"

He paused.

"I saw young Sanders's face, over a naked black shoulder, and a spear driven clean through his neck, and out of his mouth and neck what looked like spirits of pink smoke in the water. And down they went clutching one another, and turning over, and both too far gone to leave go. And in another second my helmet came a whack, fit to split, against the niggers' canoe. It was niggers! Two canoes full.

"It was lively times, I tell you! Overboard came Always with three spears in him. There was the legs of three or four black chaps kicking about me in the water. I couldn't see much, but I saw the game was up at a glance, gave my valve a tremendous twist, and went bubbling down again after poor Always, in as awful a state of scare and astonishment as you can well imagine. I passed young Sanders and the nigger going up again and struggling still a bit, and in another moment I was standing in the dim again on the deck of the *Ocean Pioneer*.

" 'Gummy,' thinks I, 'here's a fix! Niggers?' At first I couldn't see anything for it but Stifle below or Stabs above. I didn't properly understand how much air there was to last me out, but I didn't feel like standing very much more of it down below. I was hot and frightfully heady quite apart from the blue funk I was in. We'd never reckoned with these beastly natives, filthy Papuan beasts. It wasn't any good coming up where I was, but I had to do something. On the spur of the moment, I clambered over the side of the brig and landed among the weeds, and set off through the darkness as fast as I could. I just stopped once and knelt, and twisted back my head in the helmet and had

192

a look up. It was a most extraordinary bright green-blue
above, and the two canoes and the boat floating there very
small and distant like a kind of twisted H. And it made me
feel sick to squint up at it, and think what the pitching and
swaying of the three meant.

"It was just about the most horrible ten minutes I ever
had, blundering about in that darkness—pressure something awful, like being buried in sand, pain across the
chest, sick with funk, and breathing nothing as it seemed
but the smell of rum and mackintosh. Gummy! After a bit,
I found myself going up a steepish sort of slope. I had
another squint to see if anything was visible of the canoes
and boats, and then kept on. I stopped with my head a foot
from the surface, and tried to see where I was going, but,
of course, nothing was to be seen but the reflection of the
bottom. Then out I dashed like knocking my head through
a mirror. Directly I got my eyes out of the water, I saw I'd
come up a kind of beach near the forest. I had a look
round, but the natives and the brig were both hidden by a
big hummocky heap of twisted lava. The born fool in me
suggested a run for the woods. I didn't take the helmet off,
but I eased open one of the windows, and, after a bit of a
pant, went on out of the water. You'd hardly imagine how
clean and light the air tasted.

"Of course, with four inches of lead in your boot soles,
and your head in a copper knob the size of a football, and
been thirty-five minutes under water, you don't break any
records running. I ran like a ploughboy going to work.
And halfway to the trees I saw a dozen niggers or more,
coming out in a gaping, astonished sort of way to meet me.

"I just stopped dead, and cursed myself for all the fools
out of London. I had about as much chance of cutting
back to the water as a turned turtle. I just screwed up my
window again to leave my hands free, and waited for them.
There wasn't anything else for me to do.

"But they didn't come on very much. I began to suspect
why. 'Jimmy Goggles,' I says, 'it's your beauty does it.' I
was inclined to be a little lightheaded, I think, with all

Nothing like a striking appearance to help a man in trouble.

these dangers about and the change in the pressure of the blessed air. 'Who're ye staring at?' I said, as if the savages could hear me. 'What d'ye take me for? I'm hanged if I don't give you something to stare at,' I said, and with that I screwed up the escape valve and turned on the compressed air from the belt, until I was swelled out like a blown frog. Regular imposing it must have been. I'm blessed if they'd come on a step; and presently one and then another went down on their hands and knees. They didn't know what to make of me, and they was doing the extra polite, which was very wise and reasonable of them. I had half a mind to edge back seaward and cut and run, but it seemed too hopeless. A step back and they'd have been after me. And out of sheer desperation I began to march towards them up the beach, with slow, heavy steps, and waving my blown-out arms about, in a dignified manner. And inside of me I was singing as small as a tomtit.

"But there's nothing like a striking appearance to help a man over a difficulty—I've found that before and since. People like ourselves, who're up to diving dresses by the

194

time we're seven, can scarcely imagine the effect of one on a simple-minded savage. One or two of these niggers cut and run, the others started in a great hurry trying to knock their brains out on the ground. And on I went as slow and solemn and silly-looking and artful as a jobbing plumber. It was evident they took me for something immense.

"Then up jumped one and began pointing, making extraordinary gestures to me as he did so, and all the others began sharing their attention between me and something out at sea. 'What's the matter now,' I said. I turned slowly on account of my dignity, and there I saw, coming round a point, the poor old *Pride of Banya* towed by a couple of canoes. The sight fairly made me sick. But they evidently expected some recognition, so I waved my arms in a striking sort of noncommittal manner. And then I turned and stalked on towards the trees again. At that time I was praying like mad, I remember, over and over again: 'Lord help me through with it! Lord help me through with it!' It's only fools who know nothing of dangers can afford to laugh at praying.

"But these niggers weren't going to let me walk through and away like that. They started a kind of bowing dance about me, and sort of pressed me to take a pathway that lay through the trees. It was clear to me they didn't take me for a British citizen, whatever else they thought of me, and for my own part I was never less anxious to own up to the old country.

"You'd hardly believe it, perhaps, unless you're familiar with savages, but these poor misguided, ignorant creatures took me straight to their kind of joss place to present me to the blessed old black stone there. By this time I was beginning to sort of realize the depth of their ignorance, and directly I set eyes on this deity I took my cue. I started a baritone howl, 'wow-wow', very long on one note, and began waving my arms about a lot, and then very slowly and ceremoniously turned their image over on its side and sat down on it. I wanted to sit down badly, for diving dresses ain't much wear in the tropics. Or, to put it different

Girls came in and danced about me something disgraceful.

like, they're a sight too much. It took away their breath, I could see, my sitting on their joss, but in less time than a minute they made up their minds and were hard at work worshipping me. And I can tell you I felt a bit relieved to see things turning out so well, in spite of the weight on my shoulders and feet.

"But what made me anxious was what the chaps in the canoes might think when they came back. If they'd seen me in the boat before I went down, and without the helmet on—for they might have been spying and hiding since over night—they would very likely take a different view from the others. I was in a deuce of a stew about that for hours, as it seemed, until the shindy of the arrival began.

"But they took it down—the whole blessed village took it down. At the cost of sitting up stiff and stern, as much like those sitting Egyptian images one sees as I could manage, for pretty nearly twelve hours, I should guess at least, on end, I got over it. You'd hardly think what it meant in that heat and stink. I don't think any of them dreamt of the man inside. I was just a wonderful leathery great joss that had come up with luck out of the water. But the fatigue! the heat! the beastly closeness! the mackintosheriness and the rum! and the fuss! They lit a stinking fire on a kind of lava slab there was before me, and brought in a lot of gory muck—the worst parts of what they were feasting on outside, the Beasts—and burnt it all in my honour. I was getting a bit hungry, but I understand now how gods manage to do without eating, what with the smell of burnt offerings about them. And they brought in a lot of the stuff they'd got off the brig and, among other stuff, what I was a bit relieved to see, the kind of pneumatic pump that was used for the compressed air affair, and then a lot of chaps and girls came in and danced about me something disgraceful. It's extraordinary the different ways different people have of showing respect. If I'd had a hatchet handy I'd have gone for the lot of them—they made me feel that wild. All this time I sat as stiff as company, not knowing anything better to do. And at last, when nightfall came, and the wattle joss-house place got a bit too shadowy for their taste—all these here savages are afraid of the dark you know—and I started a sort of 'Moo' noise, they built big bonfires outside and left me alone in peace in the darkness of my hut, free to unscrew my windows a bit and think things over, and feel just as bad as I liked. And, Lord! I was sick.

"I was weak and hungry, and my mind kept on behaving like a beetle on a pin, tremendous activity and nothing done at the end of it. Come round just where it was before. There was sorrowing for the other chaps, beastly drunkards certainly, but not deserving such a fate, and young Sanders with the spear through his neck wouldn't go out of my mind. There was the treasure down there in the *Ocean Pioneer*, and how one might get it and hide it somewhere safer, and get away and come back for it. And there was the puzzle where to get anything to eat. I tell you I was fair rambling. I was afraid to ask· by signs for food, for fear of behaving too human, and so there I sat and hungered until very near the dawn. Then the village got a bit quiet, and I couldn't stand it any longer, and I went out and got some stuff like artichokes in a bowl and some sour milk. What was left of these I put away among the other offerings, just to give them a hint of my tastes. And in the morning they came to worship, and found me sitting up stiff and respectable on their previous god, just as they'd left me overnight. I'd got my back against the central pillar of the hut, and, practically, I was asleep. And that's how I became a god among the heathen—a false god no doubt, and blasphemous, but one can't always pick and choose.

"Now, I don't want to crack myself up as a god beyond my merits, but I must confess that while I was god to these people they was extraordinary successful. I don't say there's anything in it, mind you. They won a battle with another tribe—I got a lot of offerings I didn't want through it—they had wonderful fishing, and their crop of pourra was exceptional fine. And they counted the capture of the brig among the benefits I brought 'em. I must say I don't think that was a poor record for a perfectly new hand. And, though perhaps you'd scarcely credit it, I was the tribal god of those beastly savages for pretty nearly four months.

"What else could I do, man? But I didn't wear that diving-dress all the time. I made 'em rig me up a sort of holy of holies, and a deuce of a time I had too, making them understand what it was I wanted them to do. That indeed was the great difficulty—making them understand my wishes. I couldn't let myself down by talking their lingo badly—even if I'd been able to speak at all—and I couldn't go flapping a lot of gestures at them. So I drew pictures in sand and sat down beside them and hooted like one o'clock. Sometimes they did the things I wanted all right, and sometimes they did them all wrong. They was always very willing, certainly. All the while I was puzzling how I was to get the confounded business settled. Every night before the dawn I used to march out in full rig and go off to a place where I could see the channel in which the *Ocean Pioneer* lay sunk, and once even, one moonlight night, I tried to walk out to her, but the weeds and rocks and dark clean beat me. I didn't get back till full day, and then I found all those silly niggers out on the beach praying their sea-god to return to them. I was that vexed and tired, messing and tumbling about, and coming up and going down again, I could have punched their silly heads all round when they started rejoicing. I'm hanged if I like so much ceremony.

"And then came the missionary. That missionary! It was in the afternoon, and I was sitting in state in my outer temple place, sitting on that old black stone of theirs when he came. I heard a row outside and jabbering, and then his voice speaking to an interpreter. 'They worship stocks and stones,' he said, and I knew what was up, in a flash. I had one of my windows out for comfort, and I sang out straight away on the spur of the moment. 'Stocks and stones!' I says. 'You come inside,' I said, 'and I'll punch your bloom-

"Hullo," I said. "How's the trade in calico?"

ing head.' There was a kind of silence and more jabbering, and in he came, Bible in hand, after the manner of them— a little sandy chap in specks and a pith helmet. I flatter myself that me sitting there in the shadows, with my copper head and my big goggles, struck him a bit of a heap at first. 'Well,' I says, 'how's the trade in calico?' for I don't hold with missionaries.

"I had a lark with that missionary. He was a raw hand, and quite outclassed with a man like me. He gasped out who was I, and I told him to read the inscription at my feet if he wanted to know. Down he goes to read, and his interpreter, being of course as superstitious as any of them, took it as an act of worship and plumped down like a shot. All my people gave a howl of triumph, and there wasn't any more business to be done in my village after that journey, not by the likes of him.

"But, of course, I was a fool to choke him off like that. If I'd had any sense I should have told him straight away of the treasure and taken him into Co. I've no doubt he'd have come into Co. A child, with a few hours to think it over, could have seen the connection between my diving dress and the loss of the *Ocean Pioneer*. A week after he left I went out one morning and saw the *Motherhood*, the salver's ship from Starr Race, towing up the channel and sounding. The whole blessed game was up, and all my trouble thrown away. Gummy? How wild I felt! And guying it in that stinking silly dress! Four months!"

The sunburnt man's story degenerated again. "Think of it," he said, when he emerged to linguistic purity once more. "Forty thousand pounds' worth of gold."

"Did the little missionary come back?" I asked.

"Oh yes? Bless him! And he pledged his reputation there was a man inside the god, and started out to see as much with tremendous ceremony. But there wasn't—he got sold again. I always did hate scenes and explanations, and long before he came I was out of it all—going home to Banya along the coast, hiding in bushes by day, and thieving food from the villages by night. Only weapon, a spear. No clothes, no money. Nothing. My face was my fortune, as the saying is. And just a squeak of eight thousand pounds of gold—fifth share. But the natives cut up rusty, thank goodness, because they thought it was him had driven their luck away."

The Password

V. H THOMAS

I SUPPOSE it would be stretching a point to say that I *won* the war. Lots of others have already claimed that distinction anyway. Let's say rather that, by hesitating over something I ought to have done, I helped preserve one of the vital instruments of our ultimate victory. Still sounds a bit steep, eh? Then read and judge for yourself.

This story begins in an Army camp just outside Reading. I had been in the Army for seven months, and when the Low Countries were swooped upon by Hitler had been all set to join the B.E.F. Now a long spell in the U.K. loomed ahead.

One hot, Friday afternoon the whole camp was detailed to parade on the square. Cooks, defaulters, sick—the lot. The C.O. was there, and the Adjutant, armed with a large notebook and pencil. They passed down the ranks, picking out a man here and a man there, until a full fifty of us were standing "one pace forward".

"Get your teas," said the C.O., "and be back here at 17.00 hours with full kit, arms and blankets."

We piled into a couple of buses, but it wasn't until we were clear of Reading that the officer-in-charge told us that we were on our way to guard the Prime Minister during his week-end stay at Chequers. This was tough on the boys who'd been looking forward to the bright lights of Broadway, but promised, nevertheless, to be a break from camp routine.

Chequers stands in the heart of woody Buckinghamshire. A delightful spot at any time, and in that lovely summer of 1940 it was a sheer paradise.

We pitched our tents under the trees about a quarter of a mile from the house. The Prime Minister had arrived already, so we posted sentries and established Bren positions without delay. Apparently the P.M. liked to be seen without seeing and instructions were given that we must move about as unobtrusively as possible. A password was instituted—"Tofrek"—one of the regiment's battle-honours.

I drew the 23.59–02.00 hours shift, and midnight found me skirting the terrace with its lovely formal gardens and quaint old summer-houses. Everyone outside Chequers seemed very much awake, for there had been a constant stream of official cars and dispatch-riders, coming and going since early evening.

But by 01.30 hours the traffic had died down a bit, and I had draped myself in a leisurely fashion round one of the tall trees fringing the croquet-lawn. I thought about a quick smoke, and was just getting out my matches when the door of the house opened and, framed in the light beyond, stood a stout figure in a dinner-suit, flanked on one side by the glowing end of a cigar, and on the other by a glass of something strengthening.

Winston in person it was, and with him was General de Gaulle. They walked across the lawn, engaged in earnest conversation. They were discussing the German Navy, Winston sprinkling his colourful English with pinches of a French all his own and de Gaulle making his contribution in a low, bell-like voice.

They were approaching my tree now, and with a start I realized that my only way out was to scramble noisily up the steep bank behind me. Alternatively, I must move forward and join the party. Both manoeuvres had their disadvantages. Then again, wasn't I supposed to challenge them?

True, I knew they were the P.M. and de Gaulle respectively, but Army regulations made no provision for profoundly intelligent deductions like that. Right then:

"Halt, who goes there?"

I tried to sound masterful, but my voice was curiously high-pitched.

The two stopped in their tracks. Winston spoke:

"Prime Minister here."

"Will you give me the password, please, sir?"

There was an ominous silence, and upon my slim, twenty-two-year-old shoulders there descended an awful responsibility. I had asked for the password, and neither of them knew it! In accordance with my orders, they must, therefore, be shot at. Well, here was a thing.

"Prime Minister here," said Winston again, a bargainer to the last.

Here was a great man, orator, statesman, author and pride of a nation, but nothing could save him. It was all written down in the book, and that was that. I fingered the well-oiled bolt of my rifle. Here we go. . . .

"Tofrek," called a pleasant feminine voice.

"Eh?"

"Tofrek."

"Pass, friend," I gulped weakly.

The P.M. and the General moved toward me, and with them was the Premier's young daughter, Mary, the unseen owner of the voice which had given me the password when the two great men stood dumb.

Winston, in affable mood, patted me on the shoulder, bade me: "Look after me well," and the trio turned and went back to the house.

I learned afterwards that Miss Churchill had moved out to join her father at the moment I was grappling with my great problem under the tree.

Well, there you are. Now what were you saying?

They stopped in their tracks. Winston spoke:
"Prime Minister here."

The Spotted Devil of
Gummalapur

KENNETH ANDERSON

ALTHOUGH EXAMPLES of panthers turned man-eaters are comparatively rare, when they do occur they depict the panther as an engine of destruction quite equal to his far larger cousin, the tiger. Because of his smaller size he can conceal himself in places impossible to a tiger, his need for water is far less, and in demoniac cunning and daring, coupled with the uncanny sense of self-preservation and stealthy disappearance when danger threatens, he has no equal.

Such an animal was the man-eating leopard of Gummalapur. This leopard had established a record of some forty-two human killings and was held in awe throughout an area of some 250 square miles over which it held indisputable sway.

Before sundown the door of each hut in every one of the villages within this area was fastened shut. Not until the sun was well up in the heavens next morning did the timid inhabitants venture to expose themselves.

206

Finding that its human meals were increasingly difficult to obtain, the panther became correspondingly bolder, and in two instances burrowed its way in through the thatched walls of the smaller huts, dragging its screaming victim out the same way, while the whole village lay awake, trembling behind closed doors, listening to the shrieks of the victim as he was carried away. In one case the panther, frustrated from burrowing its way in through the walls, which had been boarded up with rough planks, resorted to the novel method of entering through the thatched roof. In this instance it found itself unable to carry its prey back through the hole it had made, so in a paroxysm of fury had killed all four inhabitants of the hut—a man, his wife and two children—before clawing its way back to the darkness outside and to safety.

Such was the position when I arrived at Gummalapur, in response to an invitation from Jepson, the District Magistrate, to rid his area of this scourge. Preliminary conversation with some of the inhabitants revealed that they appeared dejected beyond hope, and with true eastern fatalism had decided to resign themselves to the fact that this *shaitan*, from whom they believed deliverance to be impossible, had come to stay, till each one of them had been devoured or had fled the district.

Indeed, they spoke in whispers as if afraid that loud talking would be overheard by the panther, who would single them out for revenge.

That night, I sat in a chair in the midst of the village, with my back to the only house that possessed a twelve-foot wall, having taken the precaution to cover the roof with a deep layer of thorns and brambles, in case I should be attacked from behind by the leopard leaping down on me. It was a moonless night, but the clear sky promised to provide sufficient illumination from its myriad stars to enable me to see the panther should it approach.

The evening, at six o'clock, found the inhabitants behind locked doors, while I sat alone on my chair, with my rifle across my lap, loaded and cocked, a flask of hot tea nearby, a blanket, a water-bottle, some biscuits, a torch at hand, and of course my pipe, tobacco and matches as my only consolation during the long vigil till daylight returned.

With the going down of the sun a period of acute anxiety began, for the stars were as yet not brilliant enough to light the scene even dimly, but by seven-fifteen p.m. they shed a sufficiently diffused glow to enable me to see along the whole village street, although somewhat indistinctly. My confidence returned, and I began to think of some way to draw the leopard towards me, should he be in the vicinity. I forced myself to cough loudly at intervals and then began to talk to myself.

By nine p.m. I got tired of it, and considered taking a walk around the streets of the village. After some deliberation I did this, still talking to myself as I moved cautiously up one lane and down the next, frequently glancing back over my shoulder. I soon realized, however, that I was exposing myself to extreme danger, as the panther might pounce on me from any corner, from behind any pile of garbage, or from the rooftops of any of the huts. Ceasing my talking abruptly, I returned to my chair, thankful to get back alive.

Time dragged by. Midnight came and I found myself feeling cold. By two a.m. I found I was growing sleepy. Hot tea and some biscuits, followed by icy water from the bottle dashed into my face, revived me a little, and I fell to talking to myself again, as a means of keeping awake thereafter.

At three-thirty a.m. heavy cloud covered the heavens and obscured the stars, making the darkness intense, and it would have been quite impossible to see the panther a yard away.

Next day I conceived a fresh plan for that night. I explained the plan to the villagers, who, to my surprise, entered into it with some enthusiasm. A hut was placed at my disposal immediately next to that through the roof of which the leopard had once entered and killed the four inmates. A very life-like dummy was rigged up, made of straw, an old pillow, a jacket, and a *sari*. This was placed within the doorway of the hut in a sitting position, the door itself being kept half-open. I sat myself behind a low parapet of boxes, placed diagonally across the opposite end of the small hut, the floor of which measured about twelve feet by ten feet. At this short range, I was confident of accounting for the panther as soon as it made itself visible in the doorway.

The hours dragged by in dreadful monotony. Suddenly the silence was disturbed by a rustle in the thatched roof which brought me to full alertness. But it was only a rat, which scampered across and then dropped with a thud to the floor nearby, from where it ran along the tops of the boxes before me, becoming clearly visible as it passed across the comparatively light patch of the open doorway.

I kept awake, occasionally smoking my pipe, or sipping hot tea from the flask, but nothing happened beyond the noises made by the tireless rats, which chased each other around the room, and even across me, till day dawned, and I lay back to fall asleep after another tiring vigil.

The following night, for want of a better plan, and feeling that sooner or later the man-eater would appear, I decided to repeat the performance with the dummy. Shortly after one a.m. a sharp wind sprang up, and I could hear the breeze rustling through the thatched roof. This rapidly increased in strength, till it was blowing quite a gale. The rectangular patch of light from the partly open doorway practically disappeared as the sky became overcast with storm clouds, and soon the steady rhythmic patter of rain-drops, which increased to a regular downpour, made me feel that the leopard, who like all his family are not over-fond of water, would not venture out on this stormy night, and that I would draw a blank once more.

By now the murmuring voices from the neighbouring huts had ceased or become inaudible, drowned in the swish of the rain. I strained my eyes to see the scarcely perceptible doorway, while the crouched figure of the dummy could not be seen at all, and while I looked I evidently fell asleep,

Suddenly the dummy moved and vanished through the door—
I jumped up but failed to get a shot.

tired out by my vigil of the two previous nights.

How long I slept I cannot tell, but it must have been for some considerable time. I awoke abruptly with a start, and a feeling that all was not well.

The rain had ceased and the sky had cleared a little, for the oblong patch of open doorway was more visible now, with the crouched figure of the dummy seated at its base. Then, as I watched, a strange thing happened. The dummy seemed to move, and as I looked more intently it suddenly disappeared to the accompaniment of a snarling growl. I realized that the panther had come, seen the crouched figure of the dummy in the doorway which it had mistaken for a human being, and then proceeded to stalk it, creeping in at the opening on its belly, and so low to the ground that its form had not been outlined in the faint light as I had hoped. The growl I had heard was at the panther's realization that the thing it had attacked was not human after all.

Switching on my torch and springing to my feet, I hurdled the barricade of boxes and sprang to the open doorway, to dash outside and almost trip over the dummy which lay across my path. I shone the beam of torchlight in both directions, but nothing could be seen. Hoping that the panther might still be lurking nearby and shining my torch-beam into every corner, I walked slowly down the village street, cautiously negotiated the bend at its end and walked back up the next street, in fear and trembling of a sudden attack. But although the light lit up every corner, every roof-top and every likely hiding-place in the street, there was no sign of my enemy anywhere. Although I searched for it through all the streets of Gummalapur that night, it had vanished as mysteriously as it had come.

It was therefore obvious that I would have to change my scene of operations, and so, after considerable thought, I decided to move on to the village of Devarabetta, diagonally across an intervening range of forest hills, and some eighteen miles away, where the panther had already secured five victims, though it had not been visited for a month.

211

The inhabitants were preparing to shut themselves into their huts when I appeared, and scarcely had the time nor inclination to talk to me. However, I gathered that they agreed that a visit from the man-eater was likely any day, for a full month had elapsed since his last visit and he had never been known to stay away for so long.

Time being short, I hastily looked around for the hut with the highest wall, before which I seated myself as on my first night at Gummalapur, having hastily arranged some dried thorny bushes across its roof as protection against attack from my rear and above.

Devarabetta was a far smaller village than Gummalapur, and situated much closer to the forest, a fact which I welcomed for the reason I would be able to obtain information as to the movements of carnivora by the warning notes that the beasts and birds of the jungle would utter, provided I was within hearing.

The night fell with surprising rapidity, though this time a thin sickle of new moon was showing in the sky. The occasional call of a roosting jungle-cock, and the plaintive call of peafowl, answering one another from the nearby forest, told me that all was still well. And then it was night, the faint starlight rendering hardly visible, and as if in a dream, the tortuously winding and filthy lane that formed the main street of Devarabetta. At eight-thirty p.m. a sambar hind belled from the forest, following her original sharp note with a series of warning cries in steady succession. Undoubtedly a beast of prey was afoot and had been seen by the watchful deer, who was telling the other jungle-folk to look out for their lives.

Time passed, and then down the lane I caught sight of some movement. Raising my cocked rifle, I covered the object, which slowly approached me, walking in the middle of the street. Was this the panther after all, and would it walk thus openly, and in the middle of the lane, without any attempt at concealment? It was now about thirty yards away and still it came on boldly, without any attempt to take cover or to creep along the edges of objects in the usual manner of a leopard when stalking its prey. More-over, it seemed a frail and slender animal, as I could see it fairly clearly now. Twenty yards and I pressed the button of my torch, which this night I had clamped to my rifle.

As the powerful beam flashed across the intervening space it lighted a village cur, commonly known to us in India as a "pariah dog". Starving and lonely, it had sought out human company; it stared blankly into the bright beam of light, feebly wagging a skinny tail in unmistakable signs of friendliness.

Welcoming a companion, if only a lonely cur, I switched off the light and called it to my side by a series of flicks of thumb and finger. It approached cringingly, still wagging its ridiculous tail. I fed it with some biscuits and a sand-wich, and in the dull light of the star-lit sky its eyes looked back at me in dumb gratitude for the little food I had given it. Then it curled up at my feet and fell asleep.

Time passed and midnight came. One o'clock, two and then three o'clock passed in dragging monotony, while I strained my tired and aching eyes and ears for movement or sound. Fortunately it had remained a cloudless night and visibility was comparatively good by the radiance of the myriad stars that spangled the heavens, a sight that cannot be seen in any of our dusty towns or cities.

And then, abruptly, the alarmed cry of a plover, or "Did-you-do-it" bird, as it is known in India, sounded from the nearby muddy tank on the immediate outskirts of the village. "*Did-you-do-it, Did-you-do-it, Did-you-do-it, Did-you-do-it*," it called. No doubt the bird was excited and had been disturbed, or it had seen some-thing. The cur at my feet stirred, raised its head, then sank down again, as if without a care in the world.

It dashed round the corner and charged me.

The minutes passed, and then suddenly the dog became fully awake. Its ears, that had been dropping in dejection, were standing on end, it trembled violently against my legs, while a low prolonged growl came from its throat. I noticed that it was looking down the lane that led into the village from the vicinity of the tank.

I stared intently in that direction. For a long time I could see nothing, and then it seemed that a shadow moved at a corner of a building some distance away and on the same side of the lane. I focused my eyes on this spot, and after a few seconds again noticed a furtive movement, but this time a little closer.

Placing my left thumb on the switch which would actuate the torch, I waited in breathless silence. A few minutes passed, five or ten at the most, and then I saw an elongated body spring swiftly and noiselessly on to the roof of a hut some twenty yards away. As it happened, all the huts adjoined each other at this spot, and I guessed the panther had decided to walk along the roofs of these adjoining huts and spring upon me from the rear.

I got to my feet quickly and placed my back against the wall. In this position the eave of the roof above my head passed over me and on to the road where I had been sitting, for about eighteen inches. The rifle I kept ready, finger on trigger, with my left thumb on the torch switch, pressed to my side and pointing upwards.

A few seconds later I heard a faint rustling as the leopard endeavoured to negotiate the thorns which I had taken the precaution of placing on the roof. He evidently failed in this, for there was silence again. Now I had no means of knowing where he was.

The next fifteen minutes passed in terrible anxiety, with me glancing in all directions in the attempt to locate the leopard before he sprang, while thanking Providence that the night remained clear. And then the cur, that had been restless and whining at my feet, shot out into the middle of the street, faced the corner of the hut against which I was sheltering and began to bark lustily.

This warning saved my life, for within five seconds the panther charged around the corner and sprang at me. I had just time to press the torch switch and fire from my hip, full into the blazing eyes that showed above the wide-opened, snarling mouth. The ·405 bullet struck squarely, but the impetus of the charge carried the animal on to me. I jumped nimbly to one side, and as the panther crashed against the wall of the hut, emptied two more rounds from the magazine into the evil, spotted body.

It collapsed and was still, except for the spasmodic jerking of the still opened jaws and long, extended tail. And then my friend the cur, staunch in faithfulness to his new-found master, rushed in and fixed his feeble teeth in the throat of the dead monster.

And so passed the "Spotted Devil of Gummalapur", a panther of whose malignant craftiness I had never heard the like before and hope never to have to meet again.

I took the cur home, washed and fed it, and named it "Nipper".

Corny's
Nightmare

RICHARD
ARMSTRONG

EVERY SEAFARING man has his own private worry, a nagging anxiety about something awkward or crazy or just plain stupid that could easily happen to him but never does. With Joe Cornforth it was the fear of missing his passage, of arriving on the dockhead somewhere and finding his ship gone on without him.

In Corny this was a queer thing because he wasn't the worrying sort. One look at him was enough to convince anybody about that. He was a short, thick-set fellow with a round, fat face and a nose like a three-cornered piece of sponge rubber stuck on it among the freckles. His hair was red and nobody—not even his own mother—had ever accused him of being good looking. He was as tough as he looked but this phobia about losing his ship was real enough and he reckoned he picked it up, like an attack of measles or a family of fleas, in a place called La Spezia.

He was in the *Kariba* at the time, sharing the half-deck with Jonty Lammerton and Dave Faulkner. They were good shipmates, and there were worse places to be in with them than La Spezia in the springtime. It is a great natural harbour with a sizable town at the head of it. There are steep hills covered with vineyards and olive groves all

216

round, and away to the northward, a glimpse of snow mountains high above the clouds. The town itself is white and clean with shade trees in the streets and comical little tram-cars that run in pairs and make a crazy clatter which nobody seems to hear; and there are lots of cafés with little round tables and chairs arranged on the wide pavement outside them.

They were sitting there—Dave, Jonty and Corny—on the terrace of their favourite café at the end of the last afternoon ashore and Corny was binding bitterly.

"My first complaint," he said when invited to lay off his grievances, "is that we're spent up and can't have another round of drinks; the second is that we've got no car-fare and that means a three-mile walk back to the ship; and the third, I've got the anchor watch from eight o'clock till midnight which, as we are sailing at daybreak, means I get a lousy four and a half hours sleep."

"So what!" demanded Jonty. "I'm on at midnight and I'll get less than that."

"It's my troubles we're discussing, not yours," retorted Corny coldly. "And the fourth one is my supper, if you can call it that. The second steward—"

217

"I thought he was a pal of yours," interrupted Dave.

"Be your age, Davey boy!" Corny tried hard to look insulted. It wasn't easy with his kind of face. "Morgan the Mouch is nobody's pal. He'd beat your brains out for half a crown and I'll lay six to four he leaves me only half a pint of wobbly cocoa and one cheese sandwich. It'll be curling up all round the edges and smell like a wad of mouldy hay."

"There's worse smells than that." Jonty drained his glass and stood up. He was only of average height but broad across the shoulders—like a middle-weight boxer with a deep chest and big hands. In a beauty competition Corny would just about beat him for the wooden spoon. Nobody had ever heard him laugh, but he had a grin that split his face from ear to ear like a gash in an old boot. He was the senior of the three and whenever orders were necessary, he gave them. "Time we got going," he said now and set off towards the wide road that ran like a white ribbon right round the bay. Dave and Corny drank up and followed, hurrying to catch up with him.

Corny's estimate of the distance was fairly accurate and they had covered about a third of it when the careers of all three of them were almost cut short by a truck coming up from behind. It was a big thing with a high body and a tattered canvas hood and, hearing it rattling like a bag of hammers from about a quarter of a mile away, they got into single file to give it room to pass. But the scar-faced man with a walrus moustache who was driving it wanted all the road and the *Kariba's* apprentices survived its passage only by a last-minute dive into the ditch.

"Of all the crazy, cock-eyed nincompoops!" growled Dave, picking his long legs out of the coarse grass and nettles and brushing himself down. "He ought to be locked up!"

"Maybe he couldn't help it," said Jonty. "That truck's a proper old load of junk. You okay, Corny?"

"Yeah, I think so." Corny was sitting where he had landed staring after the truck with his mouth open. He

218

They had to jump for it as the truck roared past.

watched it bumping and swaying and anybody with half an eye could see he was hoping it would fold up and collapse in a heap. Instead it ran on for a couple of hundred yards and, still going flat out, suddenly hauled right across the road and disappeared up a side-turning on the left. Corny spat in the dust and glared at his room-mates. "Did you see what I saw?" he demanded.

"You mean the bunch of thugs in the back?"

"I mean one of them. It was Morgan the Mouch!"

"Who are you kidding!" Jonty's voice was completely disbelieving. "What would Morgan be doing with a bunch of hoodlums like that?"

"Your guess is as good as mine," snorted Corny. "But he was there in that truck. I saw him and I'll swear to it."

"So what!" demanded Dave and sorting themselves out, they pushed on towards the ship. She was moored alongside the quay right on the far side of the harbour from the

219

town and when they got there, Corny was still brooding morosely about the second steward.

"I know!" he said, as they climbed the gangway. "They're going to murder him. Morgan the Mouch, I mean. They're taking him up into the hills and we'll never see him again. They'll slit his throat right across from port to starboard and dump him down a dark ravine."

"You've got a hope!" said Jonty.

"And a vindictive nature with it," added Dave; then the supper bell put an end to the back-chat and when Corny took over the watch from the stand-by man at eight o'clock, he had forgotten all about Morgan the Mouch.

Corny never fooled around on the job. He took responsibility seriously and never tried to pass the buck. From eight o'clock the ship was in his charge and, taking nothing for granted, he began by making sure she was okay. First, he checked the lights and lashings on the gangway; then he tested the moorings fore and aft; and finally, he saw the decks were clear and safe to move about on in the dark. This kept him going until about nine o'clock and from then till half-past ten he was busy checking the crew back on board.

With the ship sailing at five in the morning nobody was very late and by ten-forty-five all hands were ticked off and safely stowed. Morgan, to Corny's secret sorrow, was among the early birds and arrived just after eight.

At eleven o'clock, every berth in the ship was dark and she was as quiet as a mortuary at midnight. The pot of cocoa and the mouldy sandwich occupied Corny till seven bells—twenty minutes past the hour—and then with his watch almost finished he set off on the rounds for the last time.

The moon was still down and the night dark and soft as black velvet but he knew the ship so well he didn't even bother to take the torch out of his hip pocket; and, starting amidships on the port side, he ambled across the foredeck then climbed lazily up on to the fo'c'sle head. For a moment or two he stood there watching the lights of the town, dwindled by distance, across the bay; then he checked the moorings and, crossing to the starboard side, slid down the ladder and headed aft again.

He was unconcerned, unsuspecting and, whistling softly through his teeth, had his mind pleasantly divided between thoughts of his bunk and speculation about breakfast next morning; he saw nothing and heard nothing but before he had taken three steps from the foot of the ladder, he was grabbed from behind, a knee jammed into the small of his back and an arm flung round his throat. Helpless and realizing instantly the futility of any struggle, he took a deep breath and prepared to yell; but his attackers were waiting for that too and the moment he opened his mouth one of them stuffed a wad of cotton waste halfway down his gullet. That left him gagged and half-choked into the bargain and he was dragged backwards into one of the compartments under the fo'c'sle head.

Everybody lived aft in the *Kariba* and this part of the ship, right up in the bows, was divided into lamp-locker, bosun's store, carpenter's shop and paint-locker. The smell of turps and patent dryers was enough to tell Corny he was in the latter, then as the door clicked shut, somebody snapped on the light and that confirmed it.

The light also wised him up about his assailants. Apart from the thug with the head-lock on him, there were three of them. Number one was a great, moon-faced lummox in jeans and a dirty T-shirt. He had a big slobbery mouth and from the goofy look in his eyes, Corny guessed he was a punchy—a once promising heavy-weight who had fought too many bouts too quickly and gone over the hill before his time. Number two was a dapper little man in a silk suit, a panama hat and a beautiful pair of black and white buckskin shoes. His eyes were small and close-set, and had neither brows nor lashes to them; his mouth was practically lipless and his two top front teeth stuck out like those of a rat. In fact all in all he bore a strong resemblance to the whole family of rodents, and the sight of an open flick knife in his hand sent cold shivers down Corny's

221

He was dragged into the paint-locker, gagged and half-choked.

spine. He swung his head to look at number three who proved to be no other than the second steward, otherwise known as Morgan the Mouch.

Corny needed no diagram now to tell him what was cooking. The stuff stowed on the shelves and in the racks around the paint-locker was worth a pile of money in any sort of currency and these beauties were out to loot it.

Twisting his head round at considerable risk of breaking his neck, Corny now got a gander at the fourth man. It was the fellow with the walrus moustache and the fancy scar who had driven the senile truck. He had over-developed forearms like Pop-eye-the-sailor and reeked of stale sweat and garlic.

Corny had all he wanted to know now. It was plain that Morgan had planned the job; none of the others would know the lay-out of the ship and her exact routine; but he wasn't the leader. He didn't have that kind of drive or ruthlessness. Ratface was running the show, and while they were waiting for him to tell them what to do next, Corny decided the time had come to put in a counter-attack. He had gone all limp in preparation for it the moment he was grabbed. Consequently, the Walrus had no idea what he had hold of, and when the slack body in his arms suddenly stiffened and cut loose, the shock almost unmanned him. Corny's first move was to hack back at his captor's shins. He landed first time, and if he had been wearing sea-boots instead of plimsols the fellow would have needed a wooden leg to see him out the rest of his life. As it was, he let out a yell, dropped his prisoner like a hot brick and started hopping about the paint locker on one leg. It was his unlucky day and his third skip kicked over a small paint-pot someone had been too tired to empty. It was half-full of black paint which slopped over Ratface's fancy shoes and spouted twelve inches or more up the legs of his beautifully pressed silk pants.

Meanwhile Corny, free for the moment, stepped back to give himself room and socked most foully the spotty-faced Welshman. "Oouch!" said Morgan, or words to

that effect and folded like a wet straw.

Head down, Corny now plunged for the door but before he could get it open, the Goofy one pulled him off it with a hand like a ham. The poor sap was as strong as an ox; for a moment he held Corny dangling at arm's length then dropped him on the deck and pinned him down with a foot the size of an elephant's. Deciding that for the moment the odds were against him, Corny stopped struggling and resumed the waiting game.

"Tie him up! Hands and feet!" snapped Ratface. His accent came straight from the New York water-front, and he had obviously mis-spent a considerable part of his life in the land of the free. He watched Walrus lash up Corny, then turned on Morgan, now painfully unwinding himself,

and the pair of them went into a huddle.

Lying there, bound and gagged just inside the door, Corny listened carefully. He gathered that Morgan, going on the apprentice's reputation for dodging the column, had expected him to be keeping his watch stretched out on a bench in the galley; and his sudden appearance on the foredeck had taken the gang completely by surprise. It had also presented them with a problem they could have done without. What to do with the prisoner?

224

Morgan, half-way to panic, was for tying a heavy weight round his ankles and sliding him overboard into the harbour, but Ratface would have none of it. That would be murder, and he wasn't putting his neck in a noose for a few lousy drums of paint.

"Well, you can't leave him here. He'll give me away as soon as he's found," snarled Morgan, chewing at his finger-tips. "And besides, he saw us turn off the coast road this afternoon and he'll have half the police in Italy round your necks by daybreak."

"Okay then, we'll take him with us and hold him till we've cashed in, then turn him loose way back in the hills. Now go and get your traps, quick."

"Me?" Morgan's eyes popped. "What for? I'm sailing at day-break. You pay me my cut and I stay."

"The ship's sailing, but not you, pal." Ratface tapped the Mouch on the breastbone with the point of his flick-knife. "You . . . you're coming with us. I'm taking no chances of you turning chicken and spilling the beans."

This shook Morgan rigid and he tried all ways to make Ratface change his mind; but the little hoodlum had his number, and in the end he went aft, white-faced, to pick up his dunnage.

Meanwhile Corny's brain was working overtime on the possibilities. One thing was certain; the gang would clean out the paint-locker and get clear of the ship with its contents before midnight. Nothing was going to stop them doing that or taking him with them when they went. This meant that with nobody to call him, Jonty, who had the middle watch, would go on sleeping his foolish head off until daybreak; then there would be a great big whale of a row, Corny, the paint and Morgan the Mouch would be found missing, the police would be informed and the *Kariba* would sail. She might be held up for half an hour or so, but she would sail that morning and he, Corny, would be left, lost and forlorn, in the Apennine Hills.

This was the moment when the fear about missing his passage first entered his life to stay with him for ever after.

He turned his attention now to the hoodlums, weighing them up in turn. Morgan, he decided, didn't count. He was a sucker and needed his brains examined for getting involved in a racket like this; but he wasn't bad; just a blow-hard, a big-head. Walrus too was a hard-boiled egg with a soft centre and in spite of his apparent toughness, like the Welshman, he would be a push-over in the crunch. But Goofy was dynamite. He was too far gone round the bend to know his own strength and he wouldn't scare; there was nothing left in him up topside to be scared with —no sensitivity, no coherent memory and no reasoning power. He would tear a man limb from tree and never know he was doing anything wrong. There was only one thing to do with Goofy and that was to keep out of his way. This left Ratface and his flick-knife—a dangerous combination but capable of being handled. The unknown factor was the nature and scope of the dapper little man's power over the Goof, and if ever it came to a show-down, the first thing to do would be to separate these two and keep them apart.

But there was no chance of starting anything now; and so far as he could see Corny reckoned his only hope was that Jonty would wake by instinct around about eight bells or soon enough after to work out what had happened, organize a pursuit, catch up with the thugs, release him and get back to the ship before she sailed. His part would be to lay a trail that couldn't be missed, and he concentrated now on the problem of how to do it.

While all this was going on, Walrus and the Goof were working like stoats clearing the racks and shelves. In their toing and froing both of them had trod in the spilled black paint and thereafter every step they took left a foot-print. The deck was covered with them and Corny stared at it unable to believe that such a small quantity of paint could make such a mess. It seemed to him there was a message in this for him somewhere, but he was still groping for it when the Goof, with the last drum of white lead gone, picked him up like a child and carted him out into the

Lying limp, he felt himself slid down a ladder.

night.

If there had been half a chance, Corny would have put up some kind of a fight then. He thought about it, but with his hands and feet tied and that wad of waste in his mouth, it wasn't on, so he rode it and continued his thinking about paint.

Lying limp, he felt himself slid down a ladder the gang had rigged off the foredeck on to the quay and then flung like a bundle of dirty washing into the back of what he guessed to be the same old jalopy that had crowded him into the ditch that afternoon.

"Here," he told himself morosely, "the trail of footprints will end and the way hereafter will be unknown. If only one of them with paint on his shoes couldn't find room and had to run behind. . . ."

There wasn't a hope, of course, and he was on the point of turning his mind on to a different line of thought when Ratface and Morgan the Mouch climbed aboard, one of them switching on a torch to show the way. Nobody in the business had sharper eyes or nimbler wits than Corny and that brief light revealed to him three things that clicked together in his mind like pieces of well-oiled machinery. They were first, that the floor of the truck was rotten and full of holes; second that his feet had come to rest against a ten-gallon drum of bright yellow funnel paint; and third that the three metal clips set round the rim of the drum to hold the lid secure were either broken off or out of place. This meant that if the drum fell over on its side the sheer weight of its contents would force off the lid, the paint would gush out and begin to drip through the rotten floorboards, leaving a trail wherever the truck went and nobody aboard would know a thing about it.

By the time Ratface was settled on top of the loot and the truck was under way, Corny had it all worked out. There were other drums standing behind the one that mattered, so it was no use tipping it over by pushing away from him. What he had to do was to pull the thing towards him and wasting no time worrying about what all that paint was going to do to himself, he got his heels hooked on to the rim of the drum and started rocking it to and fro in the darkness. It took all his strength to get it going but he managed it and when the truck turned sharp left off the quay on to the coast road, the lurch did the rest. The teetering drum toppled over on to Corny's legs, off came the unsecured lid and a great flood of cold, slimy, smelly paint gushed out.

Sitting up to his waist in it, Corny leaned back with a little sigh of relief. He had done *his* piece; the rest was up to his room-mates; and now the only fly in the ointment was this nagging anxiety about the ship sailing. They had five hours, he reckoned, and as the truck rattled and banged its way round the bay, he started doing mental arithmetic, changing the hours into 300 minutes which didn't look too good; then into 18,000 seconds which sounded a lot more but didn't last. . . .

As it turned out Jonty's instincts were right off form and two of the five hours had gone before he even woke. It took him another fifteen minutes to discover that Corny was adrift and the paint-locker looted; then he had to work out what had happened and rouse out Dave. The long fellow didn't like it a bit.

"Okay, Corny's mislaid himself, so what!" he said. "Go and tell the Mate or the Old Man; go and get lost with him yourself but include me out. I'm not on till four o'clock and I need my sleep."

Jonty got him awake at last and when he had wised him up they faced the big decision together. If they called the Mate and reported what had happened, he would immediately inform the police who would set their thief-catching machinery in motion. But they would hardly get started looking before daybreak and though they might in the end locate Corny and recover the loot, long before they did so the ship would have sailed and poor old Corny would be left on the beach. Apart from his feelings, this would set him back six months in his career and that could not be allowed.

"We've got to find him somehow ourselves," said Jonty.

"Yeah!" agreed Dave, "and it's got to be before the ship sails. Now tell me how? We've got less than three hours and Italy's a sizable dump. I mean where do we start looking?"

Jonty was racking his brain and suddenly he stiffened like a pointer. "You get rigged and wait here," he said. "I've got a hunch."

He slipped away soundlessly in his plimsols and in two minutes flat he was back with his mind made up and a gleam in his eye.

"Morgan the Mouch has jumped the ship!" he announced. "He's gone, bag and baggage. Suppose he did it; the paint-locker I mean; him and that bunch of spivs he was with this afternoon. . . . Remember that old jalopy they were in? It turned off the coast road and headed for the hills, but it can't have gone far because he was back aboard just after eight. I saw him."

"You mean they might have a hide-out somewhere down that cart-track? Thing is could we find it again?"

"If we can't and get wandered we'll be up the same creek as Corny but it's worth trying. Come on! Grab a torch and get going, brother."

"What about the ship?" protested Dave. "There'll be an unholy row about leaving her."

"We'll have to wear that," answered Jonty. "I've wakened the bosun but told him nothing. He'll find out what's happened after we're clear of her."

The moon had not quite topped the hills when they started but there was already a lot of light from it and, after Jonty had pointed out the footprints in black paint and the wheel-tracks in the dust, they set off along the quay at a brisk trot. Then, turning into the coast road, they struck the beginning of Corny's trail. There it was, about a bucketful of the stuff, right in their path, bright yellow and gleaming in the light of their torches.

"Funnel paint!" grunted Dave. "Trust old Corny!"

After that there was no need to speculate or work things out. There were several turns off towards the hills but the moon lifted clear as they went and the trail, thick, shining and unmistakable, led them unerringly and as fast as they could go into the right one.

It was a rutted cart-track, running first through an area of rough scrub and then, after forking a couple of times, climbing steeply into the mouth of a narrow ravine. It was really a blind canyon, terraced for vines. Full in the moonlight it lay and there in the bottom of it was the jalopy backed into a dilapidated open-sided shed. The loot was still in it and the truck was fairly plastered with yellow funnel paint; so was the shed, the grass underfoot and the undergrowth all around it; but they found the trail again zig-zagging up the terracing behind.

"Lavish with it! That's Corny all over," panted Jonty

"Funnel paint!" grunted Dave. "Trust old Corny!"

without stopping. "What's the time?"

"Quarter to four," answered Dave. "Even if we started back now we'd have to go faster than we came to make it. We've got to fetch somewhere soon!"

They drove themselves on and then, at last, swinging round what must have been the tenth hairpin bend in that crazy three-foot wide path, they came on a little plateau. It wasn't as big as a cricket pitch, and right on the edge of it, built so that it projected into thin air over the ravine, was a tumble-down topsy-turvy house. It was piled up all ways but they wasted no time admiring it, for there, in the bottom of it, was a sun-bleached double door on great rusty hinges and the trail ran right underneath it. The place was some kind of cellar or store and Jonty approached it cautiously.

"Corny!" he hissed through the overlap. "Are you there, Corny? It's us; Dave and Jonty!"

"You've taken your time about it, haven't you!" came back Corny's grumbling voice. He had got rid of the gag and was working on the line around his ankles. "For Pete's sake, where've you been?"

"It's him all right and still no gratitude," said Jonty over his shoulder. He examined the door. It was fastened with an iron bar and a padlock as big as his fist. "There's more spring in that than in a yo-yo and anything lighter than a three-ton truck would just bounce back from it."

"Try this!" said Dave, who had been nosing around on his own account and now thrust into his room-mate's hands a sapling about ten feet long and six inches diameter.

It was wedge-shaped at the butt from the axe that had felled it and Jonty worked it in between the two halves of the door about waist high. He took his time and did it so well that it held right away and when he and Dave threw their weight on it, the rusty screws holding the locking bar began to give immediately under the strain. They drew like the stalks out of rotten pears but the noise they made coming out would have wakened even Corny on his watch below, and as the door swung open, somebody started banging about in the house above them, obviously investigating the disturbance.

"Quick!" snapped Jonty, dashing into the cellar; then the light of his torch picked up Corny and he stopped and stared. The prisoner was plastered with yellow paint from head to foot; it was on his hands, up his arms, over his face, in his hair and fairly oozing out of his clothes. Jonty gulped and swallowed. "Holy Cow!" he gasped. "Who did that to you?"

"I did it myself, you nit. It was the only way I could lay a trail for you," answered Corny.

Dave was already cutting the lashings on Corny's hands and feet and as soon as he was free, Jonty grabbed a gunnysack and pulled him on to his feet. "Here!" he said, throwing him the sack. "Wipe off the thickest of it as we go."

Acutely aware now of time running out on them and the

mounting danger of interception, they slipped out into the moonlight; and there, sure enough, right at the beginning of the narrow path hacked out of the wall of the ravine, stood the huge figure of the punchy whom Corny had labelled the Goof.

"Keep away from him, fellows! He's dynamite!" Corny yelled and at the same time he noticed that the great lummox, instead of standing square in the middle of the path, was hugging the wall on the inside. He seemed to be straining away from the edge and suddenly Corny understood. This was the Goof's weak spot, his *Achilles heel*; he was scared of heights!

That was enough. With Corny there was never much perceptible interval between thought and action and now there was none at all. Even as the fact about the Goof registered in his mind, he flung the paint-smeared gunnysack into the slobbering face and leapt for the edge of the terrace. "Follow me!" he bawled as he went over, and for once Jonty and Dave obeyed him without question.

Braking here and there wherever an outcropping ledge, a tuft of coarse grass or the roots of a stunted bush offered a momentary hand or foothold, they half fell, half slithered down the almost sheer side of the ravine into its floor.

That must have been the quickest unroped descent of a two-hundred foot rockwall on record and the craziest; the odds were heavy on all three of them collecting a broken leg or a fractured skull apiece; but, though they lost several square feet of skin between them and got enough bruises to keep them black and blue for a month, they landed mobile and roaring to go.

Jonty cocked his ear as he came erect. High up on the terracing behind them he could hear the pounding of the Goof's big feet as he raced down the zig-zag path. He was shouting animal cries of rage and the high-pitched singsong voice of Morgan the Mouch was cheering him on.

"Head for the truck!" Jonty grunted. "Luckily I learned to drive last time home. I reckon we've got just on five minutes start on that big ape and that will do us nicely."

·He flung the paint-smeared gunny sack into the slobbering face.

Their other dead-line—daybreak—was less than half an hour away when they reached the open shed and climbed into the cab of the truck; then it seemed to take Jonty for ever to find his way about among the controls. The pursuit was already crashing through the undergrowth towards them before he got the engine running but he took no chances of stalling her. Revving her up to a real old roar, he eased in the clutch and she started to roll. If there was ever an old heap she was it but he nursed her all in one piece across the rough ground, then when she hit the cart track and settled into the ruts, he put his foot down and kept it there. Rocking and rolling alarmingly, but by some miracle holding the road even on the tightest of the many curves, she headed for the bay, gathering speed as she went.

"You're doing fine, brother," said Corny, still leaving smears of yellow paint on everything he touched. "Keep her going and we'll make it!"

And make it they did; but only just.

The sky beyond the lift of the hills at their backs was already growing light with the dawn when they passed the first fork and as they swung crazily into the coast road, they heard the *Kariba's* syren bleating like a sheep calling her lost lambs to come home. By this time, the old jalopy was coughing like a crocodile with the croup and threatening to disintegrate at any moment; but somehow Jonty held her together and, oozing funnel paint on to the cobblestones from every crack and corner, she rattled up alongside as the bosun whistled the hands to stations.

Their welcome was a bit mixed. Jonty and Dave were due a rocket each for leaving the ship and tackling the thing on their own instead of calling the Mate; but they were also entitled to some sort of medal for recovering Corny and the paint. In the end the Old Man decided one wiped out the other and called the record square. Morgan the Mouch, written off the Articles as a deserter, was left along with the Goof and his pals to the tender mercies of the Italian police, and the ship sailed on time. But it had been a near thing for Corny and ever after, he had this phobia about getting stuck in a pool of paint and missing his passage.

The Long Night

JOSEPH E. CHIPPERFIELD

1

THE EVENTS leading up to the long night of peril Johnnie Dale was to experience began the instant the Steam Yacht, *Isfennel*, registered in Cork City, passed Knockadoon Head in the small hours of the morning, and took the deep water channel to Whiting Bay. She carried no navigation lights and a seaman stood in the bows, peering anxiously into the opaque mist that had come up with the night tide.

In a matter of minutes after passing Knockadoon Head, the constantly flashing light near the Barrel Rocks disclosed that the yacht was well set in the channel and moving more to the swing of the tide than under the power of her own engines.

A voice called: "Two points to starboard", and there was a muffled answer from the darkened bridge.

Half an hour later, the *Isfennel* dropped anchor in a gloomy stretch of water below the towering cliffs of Ardoginna. The vessel had scarcely swung a little to port when a small boat came heading towards it. There was no light shown; no voice to guide the small craft. It was a pre-arranged rendezvous, carried out on time.

As the boat tied up alongside, somebody called softly: "All well?"

There was just the slightest trace of anxiety in the tones; the pause that followed seemed very significant. In the silence could be heard the quiet lip-lapping of the sea against the sides of the vessel, and the almost inaudible creaking of oars held inactive in the rowlocks of the boat alongside.

Then, preceded by a cigarette-end flung glowing into the sea, came the reply, terse and very much to the point: "Aye . . . all is well."

It was as though those words, uttered so impersonally, was the signal for which somebody on the yacht was waiting. Soon afterwards, the task of unloading cases of small arms and ammunition began. Nobody spoke as the cases were brought up from the yacht's holds and then lowered carefully into the boat that, all too often during the process, swung away with the slow turn of the tide. It was a race against time, for in less than a couple of hours the dawn would break and the yacht was expected to be standing at anchor in Youghal Harbour, ready for Customs' clearance by seven o'clock.

When the first streaks of daylight moved slowly over the eastern horizon and brought into relief the mist-shrouded heights of mountains inland, the yacht *Isfennel* was again not far from the Barrel Rocks light, but this time her navigation lamps glimmered and her bows were turned in the direction of the East Point of the harbour.

The first move had been made. Nightfall would see a further move put into effect—and Johnnie Dale brought into contact with forces that were to greatly disturb the even tenor of his lonely existence up in the Knockmeal-down Mountains of County Waterford.

2

At twenty-one years of age, Johnnie Dale was considered by his friends in England to be a most fortunate young man. Not long down from University where he had failed to get a degree, he had suddenly surprised everybody by having published a novel that soon became a best seller. On the strength of this, he announced without warning that he was buying a cottage in Ireland and was going there to live for a year or so until he had completed another book.

Thus, with sufficient money for his immediate needs, and an Alsatian dog for company, Johnnie, now sporting a short beard that gave an austere look to his lean face, took up residence in the small, two-roomed cottage. It was situated two miles from Doon, and on an exposed ridge of the mountain, Knockshanahullion.

They said of him in the village of Araglin that he would stay but a month or two. Nobody, they argued, would stay more than that in the lonely cottage set in the very grip of the hills.

That was in the spring; by summer he was well settled in, and very friendly, so it was rumoured, with Kathleen Moore, the nineteen-year-old daughter of Mary Moore of Ballysaggart House down in Lismore. Maybe that was why he was able to withstand the loneliness . . . he and that dog of his that would have you by the throat if you as much as looked at his master.

It was just as the fires of autumn brought a blaze of riotous colour to the hills that the yacht, *Isfennel,* unloaded her illicit cargo. Twenty-four hours later, the first of the consignment of small arms was on its way to a secret hiding place in the mountains not far from Dale's cottage.

Perhaps it was a low growl from his dog, Wolf, that alerted Dale and brought him out of bed in a hurry; perhaps it was the sharp cry of pain from a man whose foot had got caught in a root of heather, bringing him face down on to the case he had been helping to carry. Whatever it was, Johnnie, after bidding Wolf to be silent, stood at his cottage window looking out on to the darkened mountain side, seeing the dim passage of men, all seeming to be labouring with difficulty over ground that was broken and split into ravines.

Johnnie's curiosity was aroused. He had heard rumours —who hadn't?— of men meeting secretly up in the hills. As far as Ireland was concerned, this was an old, old story. There was also some talk in Cappoquin and Lismore of men being trained as mercenaries for fighting in Africa. There was certainly good money to be earned by those willing to bear arms in the trouble spots of the newly liberated African States, and even larger amounts for those who were adventurous enough to take risks and smuggle guns and ammunition into such countries.

"Nonsense, of course," he thought, and was soon asleep.

Next morning, he let Wolf out of the cottage in quest of a rabbit, and the day being warm and bright, he was soon ready to set out in search of adventure himself. Whistling for Wolf, he went striding up into the mountains to see if he could find out what had brought men into the hills on an autumn night when they should have been at home in their beds. . . .

3

Wolf was soon busily engaged in sniffing the trail the men of the night had followed, and loped along with the easy manner of his kind. It was Wolf's enthusiasm that urged Johnnie on when the way became difficult. The dog certainly had a nose for following a scent, but his master was not at all sure if it was the scent of men or just that of rabbits.

Johnnie plodded on, sometimes pausing to look back over the downward sweep of moorland to where the tower of Mount Melleray Abbey rose above the trees that sheltered it.

The heather grew sparse and thin the higher Johnnie

and the dog went. Soon it had almost disappeared and all that was left was coarse mountain grass and thyme and lichen-faced boulders. The silence was such that the fluting call of a curlew brought a quicker beat to the heart. It was the silence of a world as old as time.

Then, quite abruptly, the search was at an end. Wolf gave a deep bark and stood looking up at the gaunt ruins of a mountain cabin, almost roofless and altogether windowless. In its isolation, it was forbidding and eerie. All around were boulders, scattered over the years from the heights above, and in the soft earth about the ruins were the footprints of the men who had laboured the night before.

Johnnie hesitated before entering the shattered doorway. The instant he did so he saw the cases neatly stacked under what remained of the roof. He raised the end of one, and the weight alone suggested what it contained.

The young man felt he had stumbled on something that might well bring trouble to himself. The calling of a buzzard roused him with a start and he wished himself a thousand miles away from the spot. If they saw him here, they might consider him a spy or an informer.

He called his dog to heel, and departed as quickly as he could, taking a path that struck away to the north. He must have been walking for about ten minutes before he turned a break in the mountainside and came upon the lough—a dark, awesome lough above which the cliffs rose menacing and sheer; and sitting on a boulder before the stretch of water was a man about his own age who regarded him sullenly and quite clearly with the utmost suspicion.

Johnnie gave him a nod while Wolf stood tense at his side, a low growl in his throat.

"Is he cross?" the fellow asked quietly.

"Not usually," Johnnie replied, knowing full well that Wolf was putting up the best show he could to disprove his master's words.

"Isn't the creature growlin' right now the way he'd like

"A man can be after dying here without anybody knowing."

to tear the throat out of me?"

Johnnie forced a laugh.

"He doesn't mean anything by that. . . . He's just protecting me."

The man nodded almost indifferently.

"Sure, it's just as well he doesn't or I might be takin' me gun an' puttin' a bullet through his head."

Ignoring Johnnie's look of surprise at such a statement, the man turned his gaze to the cliff, staring at it with narrowing eyes.

"It's a bad place to be walkin' in, so it is," he said slowly, clipping each word with marked significance. "Sure, a man can be after fallin' an' breakin' a leg . . . an' mebbe die without anybody knowin'. . . ."

"I suppose that could happen," Johnnie admitted.

The man then faced Johnnie, his eyes cold and calculating.

"Best be keepin' to the lower moors then," was the next astonishing remark, "an' then it couldn't be happenin' to you."

241

"What do you mean by that?" Johnnie asked sharply, stung by the underlying sneer that accompanied the last few words.

The other stood up, smiling.

"I think you know exactly what I mean. We don't like foreigners pryin' into our affairs. . . . Just remember that an' keep to the foothills."

And without another word, the man turned abruptly and walked sharply away after the manner of a trained soldier, leaving Johnnie Dale and his dog alone by the lough. The stretch of water darkened as the sun went behind a bank of cloud, and a chill wind moved down from off the mountain. But the wind was no more than the breath of a sigh that was spent as soon as it moved over the lough which was as expressionless as a mirror turned to the dark.

4

Johnnie did not lack courage when once he had grasped that he had been threatened and told to keep away from the mountain.

Even as he strolled back to his cottage, he planned immediate action. He was more than familiar with the many rumours circulating in the district, but did not know just to what extent they were justified. He now made up his mind to consult somebody about them. There was only one person to whom he could go—Mrs Moore of Ballysaggart House. She seemed to know almost everything that went on in the whole of County Waterford itself.

As soon as he had a meal, he set out with Wolf for Lismore, unaware that his progress was watched by the same fellow he had seen at the lough.

The man now held him with his field-glasses, and when Johnnie took the road slipping over the lower moors to Ballyduff, the man guessed his destination.

He shook his head angrily, Mary Moore being no friend of his or his companions who haunted the hills in the silence of the night.

Mrs Mary Moore, still very much alert despite her fifty-odd years, certainly knew most of the answers to the questions Johnnie put to her while her daughter, Kathleen, waited impatiently to have her own private conversation with the young man.

It seemed to Johnnie that Mrs Moore knew everything that made up the general gossip of the district. What was more important, she knew exactly what was going on up in the hills, and told Johnnie that he would be well advised to leave well alone.

Kathleen at this juncture emphatically agreed with her.

Johnnie, however, was a determined young man when once he had set his mind on a thing, and pressing further the points he wanted to know about, learnt that gun-running was being done on a big scale. The arms came from an American source and were off-loaded somewhere along the coast so that they could be brought up into the hills for safe keeping until such times they could be shipped to some of the African States by air freight.

"It's all done secretly, of course," Mrs Moore said, "but the right type of scoundrel prepared to kill people he knows nothing about can get a good price in fighting the private wars of the would-be dictators in Africa."

"And the training, I presume, is carried out in the Knockmealdowns?" Johnnie enquired eagerly.

"Most of it, I believe, and certainly the bulk of the arms supplies are hidden up in the hills. . . . Not all of it, you can be sure, in that cottage you found. I have heard that the Mitchelstown caves are a sort of arsenal, but that. . . ." She shrugged her shoulders.

"You doubt it?" Johnnie probed.

Mrs Moore gave him a shrewd look.

"I don't doubt it at all," she answered, "but I feel you had better forget that I mentioned it. It could be the headquarters of the group."

Johnnie was more than satisfied with what he had learnt, but pressed home one final point.

"What are the police doing about it all?" he asked.

Mrs Moore gave him another look, this time less penetrating as if she doubted the wisdom of discussing the matter further.

"There have been occasional raids," she admitted at last. "But nothing else. No arrests. You must know how things are in this country. . . ."

Johnnie nodded. He knew only too well, and felt that he would have to act, for the moment at least, entirely on his own.

But he said nothing of what was in his mind to either Mrs Moore or her daughter, and when later that evening he set off for home, Kathleen accompanied him as far as the bridge at Araglin, promising to call on him at the cottage the following day.

After they had parted, Johnnie half-wished that he had put off Kathleen's visit for a few days. He was anxious to make more investigations in the hills near the lough.

Still, he could do a lot in the morning, and in a few hours he might discover much.

5

The young man whistled a tune as he strode on in the gloom. By the time he came to the track leading to the cottage, the stars were bright in the sky, and the upthrust of the mountain was etched clearly on the horizon.

Suddenly he was aware that Wolf was close against him and walking stiff-legged, his ears pricked and his nostrils widely flared.

"What is it, boy?" Johnnie whispered.

He instinctively put out one hand and grasped the dog by the collar. Ahead, the cottage rose up like a smudge against the rising slope of the mountain. A star fell like a beacon light down the sky. The wind moved amongst the bracken and fern.

Johnnie felt disturbed. Wolf was growling as if he scented danger.

"Too late, mister—the dog is inside—you're coming with us."

The young man felt a need to gain the security of the cottage, and hastened his steps. He was still holding Wolf firmly as he inserted the key into the lock of the door, ignoring the fact that the animal was bristling and obviously wanted to be free. Perhaps he had scented a marauding fox.

When the door swung open, Johnnie pushed the dog inside and made to follow. But the door was brought to a slam in his very face, with Wolf now securely shut inside. At the same moment he was gripped on either arm.

"Too late, mister," said a voice. "The dog is inside, and you come with us."

A burst of savage barking broke the silence that till then had been so profound. Wolf's heavy weight crashed upon the door in fury, the forepaws scratching in vain for freedom.

"He's a killer surely, that feller," said the voice again.
"March!" another voice commanded tersely.

The next instant he was propelled forward. He tried to demand an explanation for such an assault.

Neither of the two men replied, and Johnnie could do nothing but submit.

Back at the cottage, Wolf continued to bark with increasing violence, the sound echoing over the whole mountainside. But the two men beside him appeared not to worry, and continued to push him on, the track now climbing steeply.

His captors began to breathe more heavily, but neither attempted to speak. Johnnie also walked in complete silence, and being the younger man, felt the strain less. Once he glimpsed the twisted shape of a thorn tree black against the stars, and then the wrinkled stretch of water he knew to be the lough he had visited earlier in the day. There was such a feeling of loneliness about the place that he could not repress a shiver of foreboding that suddenly encompassed him. A stone rolled beneath his feet, and the grip on his arm tightened so that he cried out in pain.

Some minutes later he knew he was standing on the road that wound up from the Waterford side of the mountains, and then, at what was known as The Gap that divided the County of Waterford from that of Tipperary, he beheld the black shape of a motor van.

He was hustled towards it, still without a word being uttered, and as silently thrust into it. He then heard the motor start up and guessed it was travelling in the direction of Clogheen in County Tipperary.

It was almost daybreak before the van reached its destination, another mountain slope, this time of limestone. Still in silence, Johnnie was hurried from the van and pushed towards the yawning entrance of a cave.

He suddenly remembered what Mrs Moore had so recently said, and sensed that he had been brought to what were the headquarters of the movement—the Mitchelstown Caves.

Almost at once, however, he found himself being guided along a narrow passage, rich in stalactites, which soon gave way to a large circular chamber, and a voice remarked ironically "Here is the House of Commons, and here you will meet the Prime Minister!"

A laugh accompanied the remark, and then Johnnie saw that there was another man at the far end of the chamber, and he knew him to be the leader of the gang!

6

The sun was a glowing amber as Kathleen Moore took the winding track across the moors to Knockshanhullion. She was pleased—even excited—at the thought of Johnnie waiting for her up in that cottage of his. Would he come down the slopes of the hills to meet her, she wondered. Would he?

It was after Foildarrig that she had her first inkling that something might be wrong. An old peasant woman came by with a hen in her arms and hailed her as she passed.

"Is ut to himself yeer after goin'?" she asked.

"It is," Kathleen answered.

"Ye'd best hurry then. That dog of his hasn't stopped barkin' all night. There he goes again . . . the creature!"

She inclined her head to listen and Kathleen did the same. Wolf's bark came rasping down the mountain slopes, and it was clearly a call of distress.

Kathleen said goodbye and hurried on her way, this time striking up over the open mountain in order to reach the cottage a little sooner. She hoped events had not taken an unexpected turn with Johnnie in serious trouble as a result.

Wolf must have grown weary of barking for no sound reached the young woman as she toiled breathlessly up the track leading to the dwelling. Then as if aware that help was at last coming, the dog let out a burst of barking that made her quicken her steps.

The moment she opened the unlocked door the Alsatian

"That dog of his hasn't stopped barking all night."

greeted her frantically, and then she saw that what she had been dreading had actually happened: Johnnie's bed had not been slept in!

An idea came to her. She let Wolf out and followed close behind him.

"Seek!" she said.

Wolf, however, needed no telling. He went loping over the moor, his nose to the ground and his tail plumed. So rapidly did he move that Kathleen had the utmost difficulty in keeping up with him.

When the dog approached the lough she felt dismay. She was sure that Johnnie had not set off unaccompanied, and she dreaded what now seemed a possibility—that he had been slain and his body thrown into the lough.

But Wolf skirted the shore, swinging around the narrow goat track that thrust up steeply to the Cappoquin–Clogheen road. It was when he came to the point where the van had been parked that he came to a halt. He whined as he cast about in an effort to pick up some further trace of his master. As the dog ran backwards and forwards over the crown of the road, always returning distressfully to the one spot, she looked hard at the road herself as if trying to wrest from it the secret it held.

Then she saw it—a patch of motor oil, and knew at once that the trail had not really ended here, but had taken a more difficult course.

Then like Johnnie, Kathleen recalled her mother's remarks about the Mitchelstown Caves.

She wasted no further time in useless conjecture. She set off for home, bidding Wolf to follow, which he did reluctantly.

There was only one person who could help her now—her mother!

7

Mrs Moore's reactions were prompt, surprising even her own daughter. She telephoned immediately the local inspector of the Guarda Siochana, the police force of the Republic. The inspector, a close friend of Mrs Moore, came himself to Ballysaggart House within ten minutes of the call, and listened intently to what both the elder woman and her daughter had to say.

"I have long expected something like this to happen," he said at last.

"What is being done then?" Mary Moore enquired suspiciously.

"We are not always without resources when it comes to taking action," came the reply. "That gang of arms experts has been under surveillance for some weeks now, and we had a shrewd suspicion that the young Englishman would sooner or later get involved. He lives too near the centre of their activities."

"Then why weren't the men stopped before this? It can be the Englishman is in danger of being killed."

"I already have men out on the hills, and the police at

Mitchelstown are on the move. We have held back because we wanted to catch the brains behind the enterprise, the man with the contacts in the United States."

"Is he in Ireland now?"

"He is indeed . . . arrived this week with the last supply of arms. We just had to be sure before taking action. The Englishman set things in motion a little earlier than we anticipated . . . that's all."

The inspector rose to his feet. "I'm away now to the hills," he said.

"I'm coming too," Kathleen said quickly.

The man looked at her speculatively.

"Can you handle that dog?" he asked, indicating Wolf who had remained at her feet during the entire discussion.

"Yes, why?"

"We might need him to scent out his master's exact whereabouts."

"Oh, he'll do that all right," Kathleen replied at once.

"But Kathleen. . . ." her mother protested.

"It's no good, mother, trying to stop me. I've got to help find Johnnie before it's too late. Wolf will certainly take care of me and help to find Johnnie, too."

In less than an hour, the girl, together with Wolf, were in a police car travelling up over the mountain road to The Gap.

8

Johnnie Dale shivered in the damp darkness of the cave. His legs were numb, the rope binding them cutting his flesh. His arms, secured to his sides, had almost ceased to feel pain. Complete darkness engulfed him and he could hear only the dripping of water through the limestone.

Nobody had come to him; he might have been completely alone in the caves under the mountains . . . maybe left there to die. . . . Only the final words of the leader of the gang sustained him. The fellow had said menacingly: "When we have done what we have to do, you will be our next consideration."

The man had laughed when he finished speaking. His accent had marked him as one of the Irish-Americans, one with a chip on his shoulder, and all the more dangerous because of it.

But the conversation had taken place hours ago. . . . This, Johnnie felt, was the longest night he had ever known. . . . In between fear and dozing from cold and exhaustion, he had tried to think. But the darkness appalled him, pressed down on him, threatened to stifle him. There was not one point of light anywhere . . . nothing but impenetrable darkness, and that slow drip-dripping from the stalactites above his head.

The hours passed slowly, drawn out and never ending. . . .

Then Johnnie Dale was jerked out of his semi-conscious sleep. A blinding light shone in his eyes and the long night was ended.

He was gripped by the collar of his coat and forced to his feet while another man bent down and released the rope about his legs. He would have collapsed but for the grip still on his collar and the wall supporting his back.

He was half-carried through the main cave and gasped for air when he was eventually brought into the open. It was dark and he could just glimpse the moon, lying on its back and sinking westwards. Once more he was thrown into a motor van. He tried to hear what the two men in the driving seat were saying, but only a couple of sentences came to him clearly, uttered with a marked deliberation as if it were intended he should hear them.

"The Commandant says we have to get rid of the fella behind. Sure, it's an informer that one is and there's only one way to settle him for good."

After that, there was a mere mumble of voices, punctuated by the sudden quickening of the car engine as if the vehicle was approaching a steep mountain grade.

Johnnie had no idea of the time, but now a grey light began to filter through the back windows of the van, and he guessed that it was nearing daybreak.

251

He was jerked out of his semi-conscious sleep.

At last the car topped what had been a steep gradient, glided down a slope and stopped. The rear doors were opened and Johnnie was hauled out. He gazed about him stupidly. He had no difficulty whatever in recognizing the mountain on his right. It was Knockshanahullion! They were alongside a stretch of water, dark as ebony even though the day was breaking in violent colours.

"March!" commanded a voice, and Johnnie was prodded over the road verge to where a few feet away the rock beneath the turf fell sharply into deep water.

There was the scent of moist earth in his nostrils, and on his face the cool touch of wind coming in from the west. But the thoughts in his mind were all of the lough: "It's bottomless," somebody had once told him. "It's never been known to give up its dead," another had said.

Beside him, revolver in hand, stood the man in charge of the operation: "This is journey's end for you," he said briefly.

But it was not what the fellow said that stirred Johnnie into life. It was the sight of his companion who was casting around for a huge stone and was even then on his knees tying a rope to it. This, he thought savagely, they would tie to his corpse and sink it. The barbarous implication stung him into madness.

9

The police inspector had calculated well, but he had not reckoned on the burst tyre that lost them many precious minutes in pursuit. Kathleen was frantic with anxiety as they changed a wheel; then back they all crowded into the car.

Almost the very moment they topped The Gap, the police driver sighted their quarry. At a word from his inspector, he shut off his engine, dowsed his lights and coasted downhill in a surprise approach.

Wolf, his ears erect, recognized his master long before the car halted. Without warning he reared up and scrambled through the open window, and bounded swiftly and silently towards the trio by the lough. His approach came at the precise moment Johnnie decided to die gamely. Although his arms were bound, his legs were still free. He would throw himself sideways into the water, risking a shot, and kick out and dive.

Johnnie acted quickly and jumped, and the black waters broke with a resounding splash.

The fellow on his knees got up in alarm, but the other merely took careful aim with his revolver at the struggling figure in the lough.

"If he wants it this way he can have it," he said harshly.

It was the last utterance he was to make for several days, for at that very moment Wolf leapt at his throat and the gun spun from his hand. The police running from the car were only just in time to save him. . . .

The task of hauling Johnnie from the lough was more difficult than had been expected, his bound arms giving them no help and the rock face being at this point six feet high. A policeman, however, took to the water, and towed Johnnie along the lake till they reached the rocky shore-line. There the others helped to pull out both.

10

That afternoon, with the autumn sun going down behind the mountains in a glowing splendour of colour, he heard how the guards at Mitchelstown had surprised both the gang and the leader only a few minutes after he had been taken away in the van.

Information had been flashed to the inspector who guessed that the vehicle was heading for the Knockmealdowns, and when it had been seen passing through Clogheen, its progress was carefully plotted and final arrangements for its intervention made accordingly.

Thus when Johnnie was brought down to Baylough, the inspector and some of his men, anticipating the move, were ready, waiting.

"So you see," Kathleen said, "you were in no real danger."

Johnnie shook his head, thinking of the leader of the gang and the long hours he had spent in the darkness of the cave under the Kilworth Mountains.

"I'm not so sure," he answered slowly. "If it weren't for you coming up to the cottage when you did, nobody would have suspected what had happened."

"Wolf did most of the work," Kathleen replied. "He led me to The Gap where they put you in the van, and from there on, it was mostly guess-work, based on certain knowledge already in the possession of the police."

They both smiled, and Wolf looking at them wondered at the strange ways of folk who seemed to talk far too much instead of taking him out.

As the fellow took aim, Wolf went into action.

The dog walked over to the window, and rearing up on to his hind legs, placed his paws on the sill and stared out. Nothing moved in all the wild panorama of the mountains; and it was very silent with the sun gone and only the afterglow smouldering behind the western hills. . . .

ACKNOWLEDGEMENTS

Editor and Publishers would like to thank the authors, their representatives and other publishers with whom arrangements have been made to include in this collection certain copyright stories: William Macken and Macmillan and Co., Ltd., for "No Medal for Matt" from *God Made Sunday*; Jack Schaefer and Andre Deutsch, Ltd., for "Something Lost" (slightly abridged) from *The Pioneers*; James Aldridge and The Bodley Head, Ltd., for "The Shark Cage" (slightly abridged) from *Gold and Sand*; Dan Knowlton and *Argosy* for "The Rockslide" (originally called "On the Mountain"); Neil M. Gunn and Faber and Faber, Ltd., for "The Boy and the Salmon" (a chapter, slightly abridged, from *Highland River*; A. B. Guthrie and Hutchinson and Co., Ltd., for "Indian Medicine" (originally "Mountain Medicine") from *The Big It and Other Stories*; Kenneth Anderson and George Allen and Unwin, Ltd., for "The Spotted Devil of Gummalapur" from *Nine Man Eaters and One Rogue*; The Executors of H. G. Wells and Ernest Benn, Ltd., for "Jimmy Goggles the God" from *The Short Stories of H. G. Wells*; Jack Finney, Eyre and Spottiswoode, Ltd., and Harold Matson Company, Inc., for "Contents of the Dead Man's Pocket" from *The Clock of Time*; Captain W. E. Johns for "The Case of the Submerged Aircraft" from *Biggles Presses On*; and Edward Lindall and *Argosy* for "Secret Airstrip".

T.665.RA.
© Odhams Books, Ltd., 1965
Phototypeset by Keyspools Limited, Golborne, Lancashire
Printed in Holland